Published by Blue Mendos Publications
In association with Amazon KDP

Published in paperback 2022
Category: Fiction
Copyright Dave Bartram © 2022
Copyright Dean Rinaldi © 2022
ISBN : 9798365918061

Cover design by Jill Rinaldi & Ade Griffiths © 2022

All rights reserved, Copyright under Berne Copyright Convention and Pan American Convention. No part of this book may be reproduced, stored in a retrieval system, or transmitted in any form or by any means, electronic, mechanical, photocopying, recording or otherwise, without prior permission of the author. The author's moral rights have been asserted.

This is a work of fiction. Names, characters, corporations, institutions, organisations, events or locales in this novel are either the product of the author's imagination or, if real, used fictitiously. Any resemblance to actual persons (living or dead) is entirely coincidental.

King of the Teds
Infiltration

by

Dave Bartram

with Dean Rinaldi

Dedication

To lovers of Rock 'n' Roll everywhere.

Acknowledgements

Jill Rinaldi for the excellent book cover design. My friend and ghostwriter Dean Rinaldi.

The book launch team, Facebook group admin and the supporting members.

Chapter 1

The Ledbury Estate, Peckham, South London, 1976

"Here Jerry, knock us up a bacon sandwich, would yer?" Tim Moore said as he poured three mugs of tea.

"Are you having a laugh or what?" Jerry Hudson said as he shovelled three heaped teaspoons of sugar into his mug.

"Nah, I'm starving," Tim said, smiling broadly and rubbing his stomach.

"Then you should have stopped at the café on the way here because I ain't about to start frying up breakfast for you or anyone else," Jerry said as he stirred his tea.

Billy Simpson reached out and took a mug of tea from the kitchen worktop.

"Is this your first job, Billy?" Jerry said as he took a sip from the mug.

Billy shook his head.

"I wasn't too sure about you at first," Tim said, turning to face Billy.

"Archie has never steered us wrong before," Jerry said, placing his mug on the kitchen table. "If Archie says he's alright then that works for me."

"You weren't the first choice for the job Billy," Tim said.

"Archie said it'll be a nice touch and so I was in," Billy said.

"My mate Nick Worsfold should have been with us. I like Nick, he's one of our own," Tim said as he blew over the rim of his steaming hot mug.

"Well we all know what happened to the Playboy, don't we Tim?" Jerry said with a chuckle.

"You would like him Billy, he's a right ladies' man is our Nick," Tim said, leaning back into the kitchen chair. "We all call him the Playboy because he's got birds lined up all over London. After our last blag we were all out celebrating up the West End and Nick has copped hold of this dancer and mate, she was right a right cracker. I'm talking big old bazookas and legs that were as long as the M1 motorway. So, old Nick is smooth talking this sort, what was her name Jerry?"

"Tania," Jerry said.

"That's it, Tania," Tim said.

"Her real name is probably Sandra or Tracey," Jerry said with a chuckle.

"Anyway Nick is spending a bit of cash and he's got this Tania bird right on the firm and come closing time he's gone back to her place and by all accounts this Tania has done a right turn. Well, the sun's come up and Nick isn't hanging around for the exchanging telephone numbers bit and has made a hasty exit out the front door only to find his old woman, Bridget, sitting in his new Granada. Well you can imagine the look on his face when he's seen his wife giving him the evil eye. So, Bridget has wound down the window and asked him what he has to say for himself but Nick is bolloxed. The poor bugger has been caught on the job. She's told him to get in the motor and rather than cause a scene he's just got in and decided to front out the grief, make some apologies and promises to never do it again but she's started giving him king size grief about all that she's done for him, stuck by him when he was banged up in Parkhurst and then she'd got really serious and was asking if he really loved her. Nick was giving it 'of course' and all that, but then she's slammed her foot down on the accelerator and in his new motor taken off. Nick is like, slow down, slow down it's a new motor and as the red traffic lights come into view, she just put two hands on the steering wheel, stopped talking, and screamed up the road and straight through the traffic lights, just missing this milk float. Nick is trying to talk her down with promises of love and change but she's just going hell for leather down this side street, and then she's clipped the kerb, lost control of the motor and it's gone smack straight into this wall. Well, Bridget has shot out of the seat and straight through the windscreen, and ended up slumped over the crumpled bonnet in a pool of blood, but Nick is still inside the motor and he's been hurt. The ambulance has turned up and to cut a long story short, Bridget is in a bad way but Nick had got away with just two broken legs and a fractured arm. The doctor said that the only reason he wasn't in intensive care with Bridget was because he was wearing a seat belt," Tim said before reaching for his tea.

"I suppose his loss is my gain," Billy said as he lit a cigarette.

"So Billy, how many jobs have you done?" Tim said, leaning in towards the table.

"I don't keep count and I never share details. No offence but it's my business," Billy said.

"None taken," Jerry said. "But you best understand that this is our bread and butter. We take shooters to shoot up the security guards and make sure that any 'have a go heroes' will think twice. You best believe that if one of the guards doesn't play nice or it comes on top then we will use the hardware. Make no mistake about that."

Billy smiled.

"Archie said you were a serious team which is probably why he put me forward. Jerry, Tim, I will take anyone out, and I mean anyone that stands between me, the cash and my freedom," Billy said in a harsh, menacing tone.

"Archie never fails to deliver," Jerry said with a smirk.

"We should all go up town afterwards and get hammered," Tim said with a broad grin.

Jerry stood up and turned the volume up on the radio as *'December 1963'* by The Four Seasons began to play on Radio One.

"I love this song," Jerry said.

"Didn't Frankie Valli have some kind of connection to the Mafia?" Tim asked as he stood up and walked over to the kitchen window.

"Maybe, I don't know," Jerry said as he closed his eyes and sang along to the chorus.

"Did you know that Billy?" Tim said as he stared out of the window.

"No mate," Billy said. "This isn't really my kind of music. Now if it was Gene Vincent, Eddie Cochran or Jerry Lee Lewis, you'd have my interest."

"Ah, he's a rock 'n' roller," Tim said with a wry grin.

"Nothing wrong with rock 'n' roll," Jerry said, turning the volume down. "I would say that it's what's influenced all the music we listen to today. Back in the 1950s rock 'n' roll burst onto the scene as the music of fun, enthusiasm and teen energy. In many ways it dawned a new generation. I was just a kiddie but I remember my old mum jigging around the kitchen in her apron to the American imported records that my old man had bought from his mates on the docks.

Jerry, Tim and Nick grew up on the Brandon Council Estate in Kennington, Southwark, South London. The estate consisted of six eighteen storey blocks and were, in 1958, the tallest blocks in London. They were constructed as part of the directive to house one hundred and thirty six people per acre. The lads were friends throughout school and during their teenage years they began to travel out by underground train to the more affluent areas of Chelsea, Kensington and Hammersmith to rob homes of cash and small high value goods which included jewellery and watches. Jerry was the brains of the outfit, while Tim was a brave, loyal friend without fear and Nick went along for the money to spend on chasing women. The lads quickly learnt that the best way to sell their goods was through a man known only as Archie, who bought stolen goods and lived on the estate. As the relationship and trust grew, Jerry discovered that Archie had strong contacts in the police force, the security companies and links with villains across London. He was a powerful middle man with the knowledge to create lucrative opportunities for those with the balls and brains to take a sawn off shotgun. After one successful robbery that netted the trio over one thousand pounds in cash, Jerry put the team forward as armed robbers and offered to do the first job for nothing. He promised that Archie would receive one hundred percent of the haul on the understanding that the team would get future work. It was a risk that worked in their favour as Archie began to put an increasing number of armed robbery work their way, with banks, wage snatches and security vans. The team became known as 'The

Grim Reapers' after a series of shootings during the raids that included a shoot-out with armed police officers that left two officers hospitalised.

The super grass, Bertie Smalls, put Jerry, Tim and Nick in the frame for the robberies and the authorities placed a highly skilled undercover police officer, Billy Simpson, on the Ledbury estate, to infiltrate the gang and bring them down.

"There's a blue transit van outside. It must be Lenny," Tim said as he pulled back the kitchen net curtain to get a better look.

"Good," Jerry said before reaching into the kitchen drawer and throwing the legs of a woman's brown tights to each of the men.

"Are these used?" Tim said, taking a long sniff and bursting out laughing.

"Yeah," Jerry said. "They're your mum's, now stop fucking about and let's go to work. Are you ready for this Billy?"

Billy shrugged his shoulders, grinned and said "Always."

Lenny Harris was a former Gold Roof stock car champion. He was a pioneer of the oval track sport back in the 1950s. The American V8 monster powered cars were powerful, impressive and very fast with racetracks being set up all over the country. Race nights regularly attracted crowds of thirty thousand at Haringey, New Cross, West Ham, Walthamstow, Crayford, Stains and Aldershot. As a Gold Roof champion, Lenny would always start at the back of the starting grid. Contact was allowed if you were unable to pass an opponent. You were permitted to push, bump or hit an opposing car in the rear in order to pass. Lenny was a race master and would exhilarate, thrill and stir the crowd with an exciting spectacle as he charged ruthlessly through the field. Increasingly, there was a rivalry between the promoters with allegations of dodgy dealings. Lenny could see the writing was on the wall and the sport would soon be regulated. One of the promoters made Lenny an offer that would provide a lucrative exit from the sport. He took it and made enough money to set up a garage that specialised in building race engines, parts and full turn-key race cars. Lenny had a second revenue stream. Through Archie, his gateway to the London underworld, Lenny would supply stolen, prepared, getaway cars and to an even smaller handful of known, trusted faces which had included Alfie Kray, he was a freelance getaway driver.

Jerry left the kitchen and returned a few seconds later carrying a black sports bag. The three men left the flat and took the elevator down to the ground floor.

Jerry opened the back doors to the van and Tim and Billy climbed in. He closed it and ran around to the passenger side door.

"How's it going Lenny?" Jerry said slamming the door shut.

"Yeah, alright Jerry," Lenny said as he shifted the gearstick into first gear, checked the side mirror and drove away.

"Did you hear what happened to the Playboy?" Tim said, opening the sports bag and exposing three sawn off shotguns, two handguns and several boxes of ammunition.

"Yeah, I did," Lenny said as he shifted into third gear and cruised through Peckham just below the speed limit.

"I reckon I'm going to have a pop at that Tania bird myself tonight," Tim said with a raucous laugh. "The Playboy reckons she went like a shit house door in a storm!"

"Oi, enough! Get your masks on," Jerry commanded.

Tim reached into the bag and handed Billy a sawn off shooter. Billy cocked the barrel and slid in two cartridges. Tim loaded Jerry's gun and passed it over the seat.

***

On the Wandsworth Road was a parked unmarked police car with officers from the serious crime squad.

"Guv the security van has come into view," a voice on the police radio said.

"Right, listen, this is DCI Wilson. You will move on my word and my word alone. Do you understand?" Detective Chief Inspector Mike Wilson said firmly.

Several officers confirmed on the radio.

Detective Chief Inspector Wilson, a Detective Inspector and a Detective Sergeant watched as the black security van came into view.

"Guv, how will we know our man?" the Detective Sergeant said.

"He'll be wearing a brown leather jacket," DCI Wilson said, putting the radio back onto the car's dashboard.

The black security van stopped outside an office block. Both the security guards walked around to the back of the van. They looked to their left and right before opening the doors. On the opposite side of the road, the blue Transit van started up and raced across the road with both wheels screeching as they tried to grip the tarmac road. A blue mini swerved violently to miss the van and crashed into the bus stop, narrowly missing a young mum with a pram. The Transit came to a screeching halt with Billy, Tim and Jerry leaping out of the van carrying their shotguns.

"What the...?" one guard called out.

Jerry smacked the barrels of his sawn off shotgun into the ribs of the guard. The guard cried out, doubled up and fell to the floor. The second guard held up both his hands and stepped away from the bags of cash.

Tim took his position at the front of the van ready to tackle anyone or anything that interrupted their heist, while Jerry and Billy grabbed the bags of cash and threw them into the back of the Transit. Across the road two builders came out of the house they were working on. The largest of the men wore a hard hat and crossed the road carrying a seven pound sledge hammer.

"What do you think you're playing at?" the builder yelled out as he swung the long handled sledge hammer above his head.

Tim threw the last of the bags into the back of the Transit and turned to face the builder. He lowered the barrel and pulled the trigger.

BANG!

The builder cried out as the pellets hit his leg. He dropped the hammer and fell to one knee. Tim walked towards him. He stopped just a few inches from the builder, looked down on his victim and began to shake his head.

"You fucking idiot" Tim said calmly as he raised the stock of his shotgun and then smashed it into the builder's face.

"Let's go!" Jerry shouted.

Lenny Harris revved the engine of the Transit van as the robbers all climbed back in. When the last door slammed shut, he dropped the clutch and the van lurched forward with both wheels spinning. Lenny quickly slammed the gear shifter down into second gear.

"GO –GO – GO!" Detective Chief Inspector Wilson ordered over the radio. "Target vehicle is a blue Transit van, registration Yankee, Mike, Echo, Eight, Five, Hotel!"

The unmarked green Cortina MK3 screeched away sideways and was quickly joined by two police cars, a blue Rover 3500 V8 and a white Triumph 2000 with an orange stripe.

Lenny looked over to the side windows and spotted the cars racing up behind.

"We have company," Lenny said calmly.

"How the fuck did the old bill get here so quick?" Jerry muttered.

Tim reloaded his sawn off shotgun and then reached into the sports bag and took out a handgun.

"Do you think it was the Playboy that grassed or opened his big mouth?" Tim said as he closed the chamber on the handgun.

"I'll have the other shooter," Billy said, reaching into the bag.

"Says who?" Tim said as he pulled the bag towards him.

"You best listen up," Billy said firmly. "I ain't going down for no one so you best give me the shooter or fucking use it!"

Tim hesitated for a second and then let the sports bag go.

"I hope not, but he has got a gob on him when it comes to the birds," Jerry said as he turned back to see Billy loading the handgun.

Lenny raced towards a set of traffic lights. A bus ahead had slowed, so he slammed the gear shifter down into third gear and planted his foot back down hard on the throttle pedal and then swung the van sharply to the right so he was facing the on-coming traffic. The driver of a Ford Escort came to a screeching halt. Lenny grabbed the gear lever and wrenched it down into second gear and then half mounted the pathway. The Transit van screamed rapidly past the Escort with just an inch to spare between the two vehicles.

The Rover and Triumph both had their lights and sirens on and had almost come to a stop behind the bus. Detective Chief Inspector Wilson grabbed the police radio.

"GO, GO, GO!"

Both police cars backed up and mounted the kerb with the sirens and lights blazing.

"Guv, that must be the driver we've been looking for," the Detective Sergeant said.

"He's good, really good, but we're better!" DCI Wilson said as they too mounted the kerb and drove on part of the pavement on the opposite side of the road.

The Rover police car cleared the traffic and made up the lost ground quickly as the officer thrashed the three and a half litre V8 through the gears. The cars ahead of them slowed down and pulled over and very quickly the Rover was on the tail of the Transit van as it sped through the busy streets of South London.

"DCI Wilson, sir, we're on his tail," a voice said through the police radio.

"Is the road clear and are you safe to take them out?" DCI Wilson said as he leaned forward and placed his left hand on the dashboard. He turned to the driver "Well come on, Sergeant, get a bloody move on!"

"Yes sir," was the reply on the radio.

Lenny checked his driver's side mirror and saw that the Rover police car was attempting to overtake him. Lenny gently lifted his foot off the accelerator and the van slowed down a touch. The Rover police car pulled out and raced alongside the van with the sirens and lights blazing. The officer wound down his window and shouted out 'Stop in the name of the law!"

Lenny dabbed the brakes quickly so that the Rover police car shot past. He then quickly slammed the gear stick into third gear and accelerated while steering slightly to his right. Lenny positioned the Transit so that the bumper was touching the rear bumper of the police car. Without lifting his foot off the accelerator, he shifted the transit into fourth gear. The van pushed the police car to the left. Lenny could see the police officers panicking inside the car as he held his foot down and the police car slowly but very surely lost control of the steering and was veering left. The driver of the police car fought with the steering wheel to no avail. With Lenny gaining momentum, the police car spun wildly to the left while the Transit van surged forward. Lenny looked into the rear view mirror and watched as the police car surged violently to the left and then to the right before crashing into a lamppost.

"Nice one Lenny," Jerry said.

The Triumph police car and the Cortina were closing in fast.

"We're going to stop at the park ahead. Get out, grab the cash and run to the other side. There's a silver Jag waiting," Lenny said as he looked in his rear-view mirror.

Tim and Billy braced themselves in the back of the van as it came to a screeching halt. Tim kicked open the back doors and saw the two long thick black tyre marks. Jerry raced around and grabbed two bags of the cash. He dropped his sawn off and then looked back to see the police were almost upon them.

"Fuck it!" he shouted and ran through the park gate carrying the cash but leaving his shooter behind. Lenny led the men across the park. Tim was huffing and puffing with the years of smoking forty cigarettes a day taking its toll. Billy overtook him and was just a few feet behind Lenny.

The Triumph police car mounted the pavement and crashed through the wooden chain link fence. Both police cars were travelling at speed across the park's green grass in hot pursuit. Lenny was the first out of the gate and bolted across the road to the silver coloured Jag. He quickly opened the boot. Billy was the first to throw his two bags of cash in, Jerry was next, promptly followed by Tim. As Lenny climbed into the driver's side door of the getaway car, the Triumph police car smashed through the wooden fence. The officer hit the brakes with both feet but the car's speed and momentum propelled it across the road, crashing into the side of the villain's getaway car.

Jerry turned to see Lenny slumped over the steering wheel, unconscious. The Green Cortina came to a halt with the three officers, led by DCI Mike Wilson, brandishing handguns.

"Fuck you cozzers!" Tim shouted as he took aim and fired at the officers.

DCI Wilson ducked down and rolled to his right on the tarmac road. He straightened up, took aim and fired. Tim was shaken as the bullet hit his shoulder. He raised the sawn off but before he could shoot DCI Wilson took a head shot and Tim fell to the ground.

"Put your hands up!" DCI Wilson called out.

Billy immediately dropped his gun and put his hands in the air.

"You fucking wanker!" hissed Jerry as he crouched down to pick up Billy's gun.

The Detective Sergeant had the shot and took it. Jerry had been shot in the leg. He got onto his feet but fell against the crumpled getaway car. He let off a shot that passed the officers but shattered the Cortina's windscreen. DCI Wilson was on his feet and with the gun aimed at Jerry, he fired.

BANG....BANG....BANG!

Jerry slumped down on the tarmac in a bloody heap.

One of the uniformed police officers reached inside the getaway car to feel for signs of life from Lenny. He turned to face his DCI and slowly shook his head.

"Billy, you're with me," DCI Wilson said as he holstered his hand gun.

Billy raced over to the parked Cortina and the two officers sped away from the scene.

Chapter 2

Billy Simpson and Detective Chief Inspector Wilson drove back to Scotland Yard. The Detective Inspector had clear instructions about how he wanted the crime scene reported. Members of the fearsome 'Grim Reapers' armed robbery gang were shot dead following a violent wages snatch where a brave member of the public had been shot and injured. The gang's getaway driver had a long history of major crime dating back to the 1960s and was killed while trying to evade capture. One of the robbers managed to escape.

"Good work Billy. Well done!" DCI Wilson said, sitting back in his high back leather chair. "That's another firm of violent armed robbers taken down."

"Thank you sir, it's Bill. I only use Billy when I'm undercover," Bill said as he lit a cigarette and inhaled.

"That's your third successful undercover operation Bill. We make one hell of a team," DCI Wilson said with a broad grin.

"Yes sir," Bill said as he drew heavily on his cigarette.

"When it's just the two of us, you can call me Mike. I've told you that before," DCI Wilson said before standing up and getting a bottle of Jameson whiskey and two glasses from his cabinet.

"Yes sir, I mean thanks Mike," Bill said as he leant forward and flicked the ash from his cigarette into the ashtray.

"I bet you could do with one of these to calm the old nerves?" DCI Wilson said as held up a tumbler of Jameson's whiskey.

"I'm fine, thanks Mike," Bill said as took another draw on his cigarette.

DCI Wilson ignored his comment, poured two large measures and handed Bill the glass.

"To teamwork," DCI Wilson said as they clinked glasses.

"Teamwork Mike," Bill said magnanimously.

The two officers swallowed the whiskey in one.

"Hmm that hit the spot," DCI Wilson said as he looked at his empty glass.

"Cheers, sir. I mean Mike," Bill said before taking one last draw on the cigarette and stubbing it out in the ashtray.

DCI Wilson took both glasses and the bottle of Jameson whiskey, placed them back in the cabinet and then turned slowly to face Bill.

"We have another job."

"Really? I thought I might have some time off Mike. Maybe get out of London for a bit," Bill said with a hint of disappointment.

DCI Wilson smiled and then slowly shook his head.

"We need you Bill."

"Mike I've been undercover for eleven months. I could really do with some time off," Bill said as he put his hands on the desk.

"We all could Bill, but I'm sure you'll agree that we have to take the opportunities when they present themselves. Besides I think you'll enjoy this one," DCI Wilson said with a chuckle.

"We all could, Mike?" Bill said. "What do you mean we all could? With the greatest respect, I don't get to clock off and go home like you lot of desk jockeys in here. I'm out there twenty-four/seven playing the part with real villains, where one wrong word could have you killed."

"And we all appreciate that Bill. This job is back in your neck of the woods... The Milton Road Estate."

"What about it?" Bill said, sitting back in his chair and trying to show his disinterest.

"We had an officer, Detective Sergeant Ray White, down there, and he was cleaning the place up with a series of major arrests. The boys upstairs liked his clean up and he was due to get fast tracked to Detective Inspector and moved up here to Scotland Yard. Unfortunately he was set up with a high class brass. There were pictures, cassette recordings, the lot, and that was it. DS White was off the force and I think his wife left him too. Anyway, I interviewed his partner, Detective Constable Bernard Jacobs and managed to get hold of all DS White's paperwork and notes. You have to believe me Bill, he had some pretty wild theories which, when you think about how he eventually got taken down, actually made some sense," DCI Wilson said. "You lived on the Milton Road Estate didn't you?"

Bill frowned, nodded and sighed deeply.

"I thought so. I took the liberty of checking through your file. I would imagine a great many people on the Estate would remember you, which would give you a distinct advantage for going undercover, wouldn't you agree Bill?" DCI Wilson said, his eyes firmly fixed on Bill's.

"Probably, but I moved away with my family maybe six, seven years ago now," Bill said wearily.

"That's right, your father moved you all to North London. Do you know why?"

"You already know all that Mike. I was a snotty nosed teenager who was going a little off the rails. Now, if you had lived on the Milton Road Estate then you'd know and understand how easy that would be to do," Bill said gruffly.

"That's right, and so your father, very rightly, moved you and the family away and it was only a few years after that that you joined the police force and met me," DCI Wilson said with a broad smile.

"Yeah and one way or another I've been undercover ever since," Bill said bluntly.

"I thought you were perfect for undercover work Bill, and I was right, because you know and understand these people. They like and trust you, which is why you are the best person for this operation. We have stabbings and a missing thug believed to have carried out the stabbing of one Deano Derenzie," DCI Wilson said as he read from the file on his desk.

"I know him," Bill said with a hint of excitement in his voice.

"You knew him Bill. I'm afraid it's past tense now because Mr Derenzie was shot dead outside the Cadillac Club in Streatham a few weeks back. Reading through this," DCI Wilson said holding up a large file of notes, "Suggests that there is a whole lot more going on within that estate than we know about, and DS White believed there to be strong links with Frank Allen."

"*The* Frank Allen" Bill said as he digested his words.

"I think it's time we made a serious dent in the criminal activity that emanates from that estate. I want Deano Derenzie's murderer and I want his accomplice. I also want the Eddy Boyce murder case cleared up. Bill, I want you to get in there knee deep and get right amongst everything that's going on and then slowly but surely we'll pull it all down around their ears. I want an officer of the law inside the notorious Milton Arms pub, and inside the Cadillac Club's criminal infested VIP lounge, and you, Bill, are the man to make all this happen."

"You don't want much then?" Bill said sarcastically.

"If you do this for me, I'll make sure you get my job when I get moved upstairs. Bill, you'll be the youngest Detective Chief Inspector on the force and running your own undercover operations. You'll be set for life," DCI Wilson said as he leaned back in his leather desk chair with his hands behind his head.

"Or dead trying," Bill said with a prickle of fear in his voice. "If we're talking about Frank Allen then there will be serious obstacles, because that man is like Teflon. Nothing sticks, no matter how hard the establishment tries, because he has people, your people Mike, in his pocket. That's some of those upstairs. Judges, lawyers, politicians... That's people with influence and real power. One wrong word from someone around here and I'm brown bread, dead!"

"I never said it would be easy Bill, only that you're the best man for the job. You do want it, don't you?" DCI Wilson said as he pushed the thick brown file full of DS Ray White's notes across the table.

"I'll be Detective Chief Inspector?" Bill said.

DCI Wilson nodded.

"I'll run this operation when you get moved upstairs?" Bill said as he opened the file.

"There's not a man on the force with your background and experience of being undercover," DCI Wilson said. "You have my word."

DCI Wilson stood up and held out his hand. Bill closed the file and slowly rose from the chair and shook DCI Wilson's hand.

"Excellent!" DCI Wilson said as he opened his desk drawer and pulled out a large brown envelope. "We've managed to get you a flat on the estate."

DCI Wilson handed Bill the envelope. "Inside you'll find the keys to your new place, the address, and there's one thousand pounds to get whatever you need to work your way in.

Bill took the envelope.

"Thank you Mike." Bill said.

"I would suggest that we meet off the manor once a month for updates. There's a number for emergencies. If things go wrong then you call that number and we'll come running," DCI Wilson said calmly.

"Well let's hope I never have to use it," Bill said as he slowly walked towards the office door.

"Good luck Bill!" DCI Wilson with a broad grin. "You can do this. I have faith in you."

Chapter 3

"I can't believe he's gone," Kenny said as he leaned his head against the window of the funeral director's black limousine.

"It has hit everyone hard," Ricky said as he patted him on the shoulder.

"They need to pay for this," Lee growled. "The bastards that did this to Deano need to pay!"

"You ain't wrong Lee," Kenny said, sniffing loudly.

"They will, mark my words. Fat Pat and Clifford Tate will suffer for what they did to Deano," Ricky said sharply.

"One minute we're all celebrating Deano and Melanie tying the knot and the next thing that fat bastard has shot Deano with that jug headed bell-end Clifford Tate at the wheel," Lee said as he became increasingly agitated. "You do know everyone will be looking at us now?"

"Little do you know, lads, this was retaliation for murdering Eddy Boyce. Fat Pat was his uncle and the old-school rules demanded some kind of retaliation," Ricky thought. *"You could argue that Eddy Boyce stabbed Deano but then Deano mugged him off in front of his skinhead mates. This will have to be thought through because the eyes of the old bill will be on us."*

"What will happen to the Ted Army now?" Kenny said as he turned towards Ricky,

"Nothing has changed. The alliance remains in place and we'll finish what Deano started," Ricky said firmly.

"There will be some out there looking for Deano's spot. You do know that don't you Ricky?" Kenny said.

Ricky shrugged his shoulders.

"I'll deal with whatever or whoever as and when it happens," Ricky said, grinning nastily.

"Deano had only been in hospital a couple of days after the stabbing and Jock Addie and his Croydon Teds were plotting a takeover. There will be others. You can count on that," Kenny said. "With Deano gone, the King of the Teds crown will be seen as being up for grabs."

"Deano never got to sort out Carly Thompson and the Mile End Teds either. I wouldn't put anything past him. I mean… what kind of guy pulls a blade when you're negotiating an alliance?" Lee said, shaking his head slowly.

"He's on the list too," Ricky said as he turned to look out the window.

"I think this might be the limousine we sat in for Specs' funeral," Lee said.

Kenny grimaced.

"I didn't mean anything by it, Kenny," Lee said.

"Good, because I'm not doing all that again. I've beat myself up more than anyone ever could over Specs taking his life, but I'm done with that now. I've moved on and so others have to as well. If Deano forgave me then that is more than enough for me," Kenny said firmly.

Ricky turned and nodded in complete agreement.

"I didn't mean anything Kenny. We all need to stick together mate, now more than ever," Lee said.

"Has anyone seen Melanie?" Kenny asked.

"Yeah, I did, a few days back. She's broken mate. I did what I could to console her but Deano was the love of her life. Kaz and Donna were with her. They've been good friends," Ricky said.

Kenny chuckled and shook his head slightly.

"I remember when Deano first built up the courage to ask Melanie out. You couldn't believe that Deano the Dog, famed for tearing up two and three lads at a time, is quivering in his brothel creepers when it came to asking Melanie out."

"Yeah, but she was the best looking girl in school though. I mean she looked eighteen when she was fourteen. You know, with all the…" Lee said, raising two cupped hands over his chest.

"Yeah, she was certainly ahead of the game in that department," Kenny said with a chuckle. "I'm not sure who would have paid the price if she'd turned him down."

"Tell you what, I don't think anyone would have had the balls to ask her out if they knew she had turned Deano down," Lee said.

"Those two were made for each other," Kenny said with a wry smile. "Sure, they had their issues but that's just relationships, ain't it? They were happy together. She knew what Deano was all about and never tried to change him. She loved and accepted him for the man he was and you've got to respect her for that."

"It won't be the same without him," Lee said. "You, Ricky, will have big brothel creepers to fill mate."

"Tell me about it," Ricky said, still peering out of the window.

"You'll have everyone in the Milton Road Teds behind you, but this Ted Army alliance is pretty fragile without Deano. Whatever you plan to do, you'll need to do it fast," Kenny said.

The limousine came to a halt behind the hearse carrying Deano's body. Along the side of the glass windows were red flowers woven into a wreath spelling out 'King of the Teds'. Ricky looked around at the hundreds of Teddy Boys that had travelled from all over London. The roads around the cemetery were jam packed with Ford Consuls, Zephyr's, Zodiacs and PA Cresta's.

"Deano would have been made up if he knew he'd get a turn out like this," Kenny said. "There must be five, six hundred Teds here."

"There's more to come," Ricky said. "Ronnie at the Arms has been taking phone calls all week asking about the arrangements."

A familiar face approached Ricky. He reached out and shook his hand.

"My deepest condolences Ricky. Everyone, and I do mean everyone in the Croydon Teds are with you, and right behind you and the Ted Army. You'll not be getting any grief from us," Jock Addie said. "Deano was one of a kind, a man amongst men. He'll be missed but will go down as a legend in Ted history."

"Thanks Jock, when the time is right, I may call on you," Ricky said.

"Anytime," Jock said.

Melanie, Kaz and Donna wore matching black outfits and were talking with Doreen as she smoked a cigarette by the side of the church.

"Ricky, mate, how are you bearing up?"

Ricky turned around to see Everard James, the leader of the Teds up on the St David's Estate.

"I'm fine Everard, and thanks for asking mate. It's been a tough couple of weeks for everyone," Ricky said as they shook hands.

"I can only imagine. Deano was a mate and one hell of a Ted. He was my inspiration as I came through the ranks and it was Deano who encouraged me to create my own Teddy Boy gang. Believe me, Ricky, what I really wanted was to be in with Deano and the Milton Road Teds but that just wasn't going to work. I mean I didn't even live on the estate," Everard said with a sad smile. "Now is not the right time, but there is something that I could with a bit of advice on."

"Sure, Ted Army business?" Ricky said.

"Well, no not exactly, which is why I'd like a private chat at some point," Everard said.

Ricky reached into his inside pocket and pulled out one of his 'London Tyre Co' business cards.

"You can get me at work most days and my home number is written on the back. Give me a call when you're ready," Ricky said.

"Cheers Ricky. We're not the biggest of gangs but you do have our support," Everard said with a reassuring smile.

The congregation moved slowly into the church despite scores of Teddy Boy gangs still arriving by mini-bus, shared cars and taxi cabs.

The service concluded with Ricky, at Melanie's request, being asked to read his eulogy.

"Good morning. For those who do not know me, my name is Ricky Turrell. I stand here before you to pay tribute to Deano Derenzie who was known to almost everyone here as Deano the Dog. Deano was my mentor, my friend and an inspiration.

I remember watching Deano and the Milton Road Teds wander around the estate, hanging around on street corners or plotting up at his special table at the end of the bar in the Milton Arms. The Teds, in their smart drape suits, silk shirts, bootlace ties, drain pipes and brothel creepers were what I aspired to be, but the reality was Deano didn't even know I existed until one fateful day when he broke down in that old PA Cresta of his. I was a mechanic, well, an apprentice anyway, but I managed to get him going and he offered to buy me a pint the next time I was in the Arms. Well, circumstances changed and I managed to scrape enough money together to buy a drape suit from 'Let it Rock' on the Kings Road."

Ricky stopped, took a deep breath and chuckled.

"Actually, the truth was the shop 'Let it Rock' had changed owners and I walked up and down Kings Road at least half a dozen times before entering a shop with four-foot high pink letters spelling out 'SEX'. I was fortunate because they still had old 'Let it Rock' stock out the back. Anyway, I played a couple of Rock 'n' Roll tracks while I dressed back at home and then waltzed into the Milton Arms and asked for that drink Deano promised me. I think it would be fair to say that that was the beginning of our friendship that only grew. Now, to this day, I don't know what Deano did for a job but his love and passion was being a Teddy Boy and with a character and reputation as large as his, like-minded Teddy Boys from all over London gravitated towards him. Deano was just as much at home with the Teds in Battersea as he was with those in Islington, Camden, and Wandsworth."

Ricky stopped to take a sip from a glass of water that had been placed on the pew.

"But being a Ted was not his only passion. Melanie, his fiancé, was an important part of Deano's life. She was his support and the relentless encouragement to drive his ambitions and make them a reality. If they say that behind every great man is a great woman, then for Deano that would be Melanie."

Ricky paused to look around at the congregation and the row upon row of drape wearing Teddy Boys as far his eyes could see.

"With over one thousand Teddy Boys here today, I cannot, sadly, mention, you all by name, but please know that if you wore the drape suit, then you were a trusted friend and you could have called upon Deano anytime during your time of need. His loyalty to the drape and the alliance he created had no boundaries, and it is our collective responsibility to ensure that what he created remains as his legacy to Teddy Boys everywhere. I was told when I first started writing this eulogy that it was important not to place Deano on a pedestal and I should mention some of the flaws in his character but to me Deano the Dog was King of the Teds and a legend."

The congregation began to clap with more and more Teddy Boys standing and clapping their hands for their lost friend.

"As I conclude, I will allow Deano to speak through me once more. He asks me to tell you that life is short and yet it is all we have. So, when you make a mistake, apologise. Dream big and drive those visions to reality with relentless passion. Care for the ones you love, treasure your friendships and finally get to know yourself and do good by yourself."

Ricky stopped and looked around at the congregation. Many of the girls had tears in their eyes or were consoling each other. Kenny had turned away.

"Watch over us Deano, my mentor and my friend," Ricky said evenly as he folded his eulogy paper and placed it in his drape jacket's inside pocket.

Ricky, Kenny, Lee, Terry and Steve were called to the front of the church to carry Deano's coffin out to where he would be laid to rest.

Before the service Ronnie, the landlord, had asked several lads to spread the word that he had laid on a light buffet back at the Milton Arms and all were welcome.

***

Back on the estate, the Milton Arms was packed with locals and Teddy Boys from all over London.

"Ronnie, mate you've laid on a terrific spread, thank you. Let me know what you're owed and I'll sort it," Ricky said.

"No, no. Deano and you lads are my customers and this is the very least I can do for Deano," Ronnie said.

"Thank you," Ricky said, shaking Ronnie's hand. "Hopefully you'll do the same for me one day."

"Hopefully I won't have to," Ronnie said.

"Ricky, do you think anyone would mind if we had a proper drink? You know, to see Deano off in our own way," Jock Addie asked.

"No mate, I'm sure it'll not be a problem," Ricky said as he scanned the room for Melanie.

Melanie was standing with Doreen and a guy he didn't recognise. Ricky walked towards them.

"Melanie, how are you coping?" Ricky said as he checked that her coffee cup was full. "Would you like something stronger?"

Melanie nodded. "A strong gin and tonic would nice, thank you Ricky." Her voice was quivering.

Ricky turned, raised his hand, and motioned the barman over in a friendly manner.

"Doreen, what are you having?" Ricky said, looking down at her empty cup.

"I'll have the same, thank you," Doreen said with smile.

"What about you mate, what are you having?" Ricky said, looking the guy up and down.

"No, thanks. I'm alright," the guy said before taking a final long sip from his coffee cup.

"Ricky, this is Bill, Bill Simpson. He used to live on the estate back in the early days. He was good friends with Deano," Melanie said.

Ricky reached out and shook Bill's hand.

"Good to meet you, Bill," Ricky said before turning to the barman and giving him his order.

"Bill is living back on the estate," Doreen said. "I remember his mum, rest in peace, she was such a sweetie and would always be kind and polite when we spoke, but would never buy anything a bit dodgy."

"Both mum and dad were like that Doreen. They didn't mean anything by it. It was just dad liking to pay his own way," Bill said.

"Yeah, I know that sweetheart," Doreen said. "But you've certainly grown up, and dare I say you're looking pretty good too. Is there a Mrs Simpson?"

"No chance," Bill said. "I'm too young for all that serious stuff."

"So, what brings you back?" Ricky said, looking Bill up and down.

"Circumstances dictated a move and this place, strange as it may seem, always felt like home," Bill said.

"How on earth did you manage to swing a council flat if you're not married?" Ricky said.

"I was thinking the same thing," Melanie said.

"Me too," Doreen said.

"You all know how it works. If you drop a nice size drink in the right person's hands, then you rocket up to the front of the queue," Bill said. "One hundred quid and one week later I've got myself a nice little two bed place."

"I'm not sure that I would pay to live here," Ricky said.

"It's like I said. It's more about feeling like home. Who knows, I might be here a year or a decade but for right now I'm happy to be back, but gutted that Deano is no longer with us. I've got a head full of memories with that fella that would scare the life out of most people," Bill said.

"I remember when he first asked me out," Melanie said. "I didn't think he would ever get around to asking me. He walked me home after school every night for a week and it was on the Friday that he finally asked if I was going to the local dance hall. I said yes and he just grinned that big cheesy Deano grin, and said great, I'll see you there. It was hard to believe sometimes that he could be so violent and brutal in a street fight and yet be so sensitive and caring when we were alone."

"You were lucky to have seen a side to the man none of us ever knew," Ricky said.

"I remember that well," Bill said. "He was absolutely smitten with you."

"More like he was taken by my well-developed fourteen year old tits," Melanie said with a slight girlie giggle.

"Well, I think they might have had something to do with his all things Melanie infatuation in the early days," Bill said.

"I knew it, I bloody well knew it," Melanie said as tears began to well up in her eyes. "I'm going to bloody miss you Deano. You had no bloody right to leave me like this."

Melanie turned to Ricky.

"He cannot get away with what he's done to my Deano, Ricky. You were his friend, he respected you and made you his second in command. This cannot be allowed to slide unpunished," Melanie sobbed as she wiped away the tears.

"It's all in hand, Melanie," Ricky said.

"Do you know who it was?" Bill said.

"Bill, you might have lived here donkeys years ago and been a pal of Deano's back in the day, but mate, this has fuck all to do with you, alright?" Ricky said firmly.

"Ricky, I'm sorry. It's just, well, like I said, this place was my home. Deano, Melanie, Doreen and most of the regulars here were neighbours or friends, so mate, if I over stepped the mark then please accept my sincere apologies," Bill said as held up both his hands.

"That was a bit harsh Ricky," Melanie said.

"Sorry Melanie, but Ted business is strictly private and Bill, you seem like a nice enough bloke but I don't know you from Adam," Ricky said.

"No, no, Melanie, Ricky has a valid point. I'm living here now and I'll be drinking here so maybe, with time, and as a friend of Deano's, we may become mates," Bill said. "Maybe you'll give me the same chance to prove myself that Deano gave you."

"You sly bastard," Ricky thought. *"You're quoting me back my eulogy. I don't know you mate, and right now I'm not sure who I can trust or what's coming next so you, matey, are a pretty low priority!"*

Ricky spotted Terry and Steve standing by the bar.

"Melanie, Doreen, I'll catch you later. Good to meet you Bill," Ricky said as he went over to the bar.

"How's it going Terry, Steve?" Ricky said softly.

"We did the last of the motors yesterday. They're all hid away and ready for shipping," Terry said.

"Nice one. I spoke to Frank briefly on the phone and he has a big export order for us. I'll be seeing him Saturday which is when I'll wedge you out for the last lot of motors. How are you getting on with the other cars?" Ricky said.

"What, the ringers?"

"Yes, keep it down mate," Ricky whispered.

"We've got two of the Granadas and a blue Cortina 2000E, but we're struggling to find a red 2000GT Cortina MK3, but don't worry we're still on it," Terry said.

"I've had six motors put aside for me. They're all Fords and there's no red two door Cortina's this time" Ricky said with a smile.

Ricky turned to see that both Kenny and Lee were talking to Bill.

***

"You're looking well Bill, life must have been good to you mate," Kenny said as he declined the offer of a cigarette from Bill.

"It's been alright Kenny, but as sad as it sounds, I missed this place and thought about it and you lot often," Bill said.

"So what are you up to these days?" Lee said.

"I duck and dive a bit in the motor trade. I buy up motors that need a bit of work and then pass them on. It's a living and gets me by," Bill said.

"Oh, right, then you and Ricky will have something in common," Kenny said.

"What, is he in the motor trade then?" Bill asked as he lit his cigarette, turned and blew the smoke away.

"Ricky is one smart fella, you'll like him," Lee said. "He's got a tyre bay down on the Industrial estate and he's like you, he buys up motors and moves them on. Never short of a few bob is our Ricky," Kenny said.

"I spoke to him earlier. Melanie introduced us and he seemed a bit intense, you know. I'm not sure he took to me," Bill said as he stubbed out half the cigarette in the ash tray. "I've got to knock this smoking lark on the head."

"He's got a lot on his mind with what happened to Deano and, of course, the Ted Army," Lee said. "Once you get to know him, he's alright, you know, and solid, totally reliable."

"He can have a right row too," Kenny said. "He made light work of this mob over in Fulham and I mean it was bloody brutal, no mercy."

"Was that the reason that Deano was, well you know, shot?" Bill said.

"No, that was something else," Lee said. "They will pay for that. Ricky won't let it go. There's too much at stake."

"Nasty business," Bill said, shaking his head. "I couldn't believe it when I heard that Deano got shot. I know that I hadn't seen him in years but some people, you know, they just stay with you and even if you don't see them for years you can just pick straight up where you left off. I always felt that with Deano and now, well, he's gone. I hope the bastards that did it rot in hell."

"They've gone to ground but they will be found. The Ted Army has eyes and ears all over London. They will be found," Lee said confidently.

"Ted Army? What's that all about?" Bill said.

"That was Deano's legacy mate. He brought together almost all of the major Teddy Boy gangs in London under a single banner. The man had a vision and he made it happen. There's not many people on the planet that could pull together an army of over fifteen hundred soldiers and Deano achieved that. It's like Ricky said, Deano was a legend," Kenny said.

"Fifteen hundred soldiers? That's pretty serious," Bill said. "What happened to Mickey Deacon. I haven't seen him in here?"

"Banged up," Lee said abruptly.

"Oh, right. Nothing serious I hope," Bill said.

"Nah, we hit the Bedford Boot Boys where they live, and I mean it was carnage with raging street battles. The ground was littered with battered Skinheads and game locals. The old bill turned up and Mickey has just steamed straight in. He's hit this young copper so hard his legs just buckled and he fell to the ground like he'd just fallen asleep or something. I saw the copper fall and while Mickey was knocking out more old bill, I raced over and picked up the copper's helmet and fucking legged it. It's over there behind the bar," Lee said, puffing out his chest.

"Nice one Lee," Bill said looking over and laughing. "So that's what Mickey got nicked for?"

"Yeah mate, but he wasn't the only one. They gavvered up a few of the Bedford lot too. It was just after that when Deano made Ricky his second in command. To be honest I was a bit pissed at first, you know having been around the Milton Road Teds longer than him, but he stepped up pretty quickly and once again Deano was right with his choice," Lee said.

"He's a good bloke, Bill," Kenny said.

"Is the Cadillac Club one of your regular haunts now?" Bill asked. "I mean with what happened to Deano there, I just wondered..."

"We do get down there but the main reason for that was for the Steve Maxted 'Wild One' show. Mate, he is one hell of a DJ, bloody brilliant! We even talked about venturing down into Kent to see him again," Kenny said.

"I've never seen him. If you lot are going again will you let me know?" Bill said.

"Yeah, of course, Bill. It's good to have you back mate and yeah, it's like you said earlier. There are some people you can just pick straight up with where you left off," Kenny said.

"Yeah, good to have back," Lee said.

"Cheers," Bill said. "If it's at the Cadillac Club, maybe we'll get into the VIP Lounge and live it up a bit."

"Don't raise your hopes mate. The only person I know that drinks in there, other than Doreen, is Ricky," Lee said.

"He must have pulled a few strings to get in there," Bill said.

"I don't know about that, but he knows Frank Allen and that's enough. I mean Frank even ventured in here once to see Ricky but I would never ask. It ain't my business," Lee said.

"That's right Lee, it's not," Kenny said sternly.

"Absolutely," Bill said. "Doreen hasn't changed, she's still a flirt and I bet she's still working the wall with hooky gear."

"You know what Doreen's like" Kenny said in a joking way.

"What about Double Bubble, is he still doing what he does?"

There was a short silence while Kenny and Lee looked at each other.

"Nah, he's gone," Kenny said finally.

"Fucking good riddance," Lee said venomously. "I never liked him."

"No one did," Kenny said, "But he provided a service. He lent money to those who couldn't get it anywhere else."

"What a rip off though. Borrow five quid and pay back ten," Lee said.

"Those are the terms and if a person doesn't like it then don't borrow the money," Kenny said.

"Bloke was a fucking grass!" Lee said.

"A grass? You're kidding me," Bill said. "He didn't seem the type."

"He was marked up with 'GRASS' sliced into the slag's forehead. He'll never work the street corners again. He's done, a spent force," Lee said, struggling to disguise his disdain.

"So, who has taken over?" Bill asked.

"No one yet, why… are you interested?" Kenny said.

"Yeah, I am actually. It's like you said. Someone needs to provide the service and as long as it's fair and reasonable then why not? Do I have to see someone to get their go-ahead or just plot up outside the wall and go to work?" Bill said.

"If I were you, I'd speak with Ricky first," Kenny said. "Just not today, Bill. Give it a couple of days and then I'll drop it casually into a conversation. Leave it with me."

"Sure, cheers Kenny."

***

Bill stayed, drank and caught up with old neighbours and friends until closing time. Ricky had left early which gave him the opportunity to sit with the Milton Road Teds. Ronnie called last orders and Bill wandered back to his flat where he laid back on his bed and put his hands behind his head. He looked up at the ceiling and thought back to his days of growing up on the Milton Road Estate.

The family had moved there from New Cross when the first of the tower blocks had been built and was opened for occupation for the council tenants. Bill learnt quickly that his new home was unlike the road he had lived in previously. The Estate was a place where the kids had to grow up fast, be tough and become streetwise. It was a place where his friend's parents viewed criminality as a way of life. There were families of petty thieves, fraudsters and at the top of the echelon were the armed robbers. The fathers of these friends would carry guns and rob banks, jewellers or security vans for the cash they carried. These were the most respected of all the families on the estate. The lads would huddle together on street corners and delight in hearing about their friends' fathers' daring heists or how the police had kicked in the front door of their home and hauled their father in only to find he was out on bail just a day or two later. These people were a million miles away from his own family. His father was a proud, working class man that grafted on twelve hour shifts to provide the best he could for his family. Bill felt honoured to be one of the few families on the estate that had annual summer holidays down on the south coast. He loved that time away, the clean sea air and mixing with kids who looked up to him and the antics he would share about the Milton Road Estate.

Bill was befriended by Deano Derenzie. He lived in the same block and was a couple of years younger than him. Bill, Deano and a few of the lads on estate would run around, jumping and hiding while playing at cops and robbers. No one ever wanted to be a cop. As the lads got older, Deano encouraged them to toughen up and would wander off the Estate in search of other gangs to fight. During one altercation with several lads, Deano had floored three big lads, all older than him, before the fight even started. From then on Deano became Deano the Dog. Bill recognised that Deano was rapidly becoming a formidable force on the Estate with the toughest and meanest kids around gravitating towards him.

At home Bill had learnt to balance and adapt his life out on the Estate and at home with his parents. A couple of lads invited Bill to join them on a robbery they had planned on a nearby industrial estate. The three lads broke into the back of a parked truck and made away with over a hundred large jars of pickled onions which they stacked up in a stolen car. They took the haul back to the Estate and sold them at the 'wall' outside the community centre at five pence a jar or three jars for ten pence. Every jar was sold within a few hours and the lads shared out the takings equally.

Bill remembered how proud he felt when he first saw that someone had hand painted 'Turn Back or Die' on the Milton Road Estate sign. Increasingly he had become addicted to the street fights, violence and agro associated around Deano the Dog. It was at this time that his father had seen the change in his son, no matter how hard Bill tried to hide his double life. One by one these friends were being arrested and shipped off to Borstal and so Bill's father, wanting to protect his son from friends that would lead him into a life of crime, moved his family away to North London. Bill remembered sitting in the back of the family's Ford Anglia and seeing Deano and a few of the lads standing outside the Milton Arms pub dressed as Teddy Boys. All the lads had loved listening to rock 'n' roll music at Deano's parents' home and wanted desperately to beg, borrow or steal enough money to buy a pair of brothel creeper shoes, drain pipe trousers and a bootlace tie.

Bill settled in North London and in a bid to win favour with his father he applied to join the police force when he left school. His parents were thrilled and proud that their son had turned his back on a life of crime and would instead be out catching criminals and making the street safer for decent law-abiding citizens. Within just a few years as a Bobby on the beat, Bill had come to the attention of a senior police officer, Detective Chief Inspector Mike Wilson and was coaxed into utilising the skills he had honed growing up on the Milton Road Estate to infiltrate some of London's violent criminal gangs.

His father and mother were involved in a car accident that took his mother's life instantly. Bill held his father's hand in the hospital while he fought for breath and clung to life. His last words to Bill were 'I'm very proud of the man you've become son'.

Chapter 4

Ricky drove onto the industrial estate and stopped outside his business, London Tyre Co. It was just after 8.00am and already the tyre bays were full, with two cars waiting to be served. He had spoken with Michelle on the telephone when he got back from the Arms and Deano's funeral. Michelle had wanted to come over and stay but Ricky put her off saying that he had to be up early for work and would appreciate the time and space to come to terms with the loss of his friend. Michelle had seized the opportunity to suggest that maybe it was time to hang up the drape suit and put some distance between him and the Milton Road Teds. She told him that he was now the owner of a successful business and should maybe focus on that rather than hanging around with thugs and potentially getting into trouble. Ricky hadn't answered her, so she had tried a different tack, saying that it was only because she cared that she was suggesting leaving the Teddy Boy scene behind, and that she couldn't bear it if anything like that happened to him. It was a difficult conversation and not the support he had hoped for.

"I'm a Teddy Boy and a businessman. Michelle just doesn't get that," Ricky thought. *"Being a Ted is what and who I am and my business interests provide me with choices to live where I want, drive what I want and dress how I want. The businesses do not define me, they're just a part of who I am. I could never walk away from the buzz and excitement of being a Ted. I'd miss my mates, the music, the agro and all the confrontation. Fuck it, I'd miss the tear ups too. I will step up and run the Milton Road Teds and one way or another I will keep Deano's legacy in place by ensuring that the Ted Army gets through this."*

An almost new bronze coloured Ford Escort MK1 1300E parked up behind Ricky. He looked in his rear-view mirror and watched Doughnut get out of the car. He was wearing a smart pair of black trousers and a white shirt. Ricky had bought the car on hire purchase through the business as part of his promise to Doughnut that he would be promoting him to the position of sales representative. He watched as Doughnut locked the car, walked across the road and came into the office.

Ricky crossed the road and walked through the busy tyre bay.

"Morning Barry," Ricky said as he passed the lad he had poached from his closest competitor and made Branch Manager of London Tyre Co.

"Morning Ricky," Barry said as he handed a socket to one of the new lads removing a wheel from a customer's car.

"It's looking busy," Ricky said.

"Yeah, it's a good mix of trade and retail. Those adverts you placed are really paying off."

Ricky entered the office and called Doughnut over to join him at the desk.

"Doughnut, I couldn't have your business cards printed with 'Doughnut - Sales Representative' so I asked Barry what your real name was," Ricky said, opening his desk and handing Doughnut a box of professional business cards.

"Wow, these look great," Doughnut, said, taking a card from the box.

"How is the car?" Ricky said.

"It's great Ricky. I'm really grateful to you for giving me this opportunity," Doughnut said with a broad smile.

"There are some sales people that drive around all day just drinking tea and making small talk. I must have seen that a hundred times when I was an apprentice. That isn't what I want from you," Ricky said.

"Okay," Doughnut said, pulling his chair in closer to the desk.

"You, Doughnut, are a sales machine, and your primary role is to open trade accounts," Ricky said, taking out a big bundle of trade account application forms from his desk. "I need you to scan through the Yellow Pages and then go out and call on every taxi cab business, transport companies with light vans, and trade businesses that carry out deliveries in vans, and I want you to sign them up.

Ricky handed him a price list.

"I've looked at the costs and what others are doing in the area, and these prices for tyres coupled with free wheel balancing with every purchase, will win you that business, but Doughnut… London Tyre Co is much more than that. We will prioritise our trade customers by taking appointments. Their costly drivers will not be sitting outside waiting. If they have a booking for 2.30pm, then they are the priority. I want everything, Doughnut, retail and trade. Retail customers might buy a set of tyres once in three years, but trade customers with vans and taxis will rapidly wear through those tyres and come back. Now just getting them to complete the form isn't enough. You must then follow up with them, advising that their account is now open and asking if they can book a vehicle in. Oh, one last thing. All trade customers will have their punctures repaired same day. If they drop the tyre in during the morning it will be repaired and ready to collect the same day. Doughnut, you've been fitting tyres for over five years, do you think this will win us business?" Ricky said as he pushed himself back into his chair.

Doughnut put the price list down and began nodding.

"Ricky there isn't anyone out there offering this level of service," Doughnut said excitedly.

"So we have the best quality brand name tyres, a service beyond anything in the tyre trade and prices that leave the competition behind," Ricky said.

"We've got it all," Doughnut said as he punched the air.

"Good, because this is your new account target," Ricky said as he handed Doughnut a sheet which listed the twelve months and the expected number of accounts to be opened each month.

"Can we cope with all this Ricky?" Doughnut asked.

"Between you and I Doughnut, this is the first of many branches. I've already got my eye on the next acquisition. You keep that to yourself and go and get me this business because I know you can do it," Ricky said.

Doughnut beamed.

"Thanks Ricky. If I need any help with anything I'll call in," Doughnut said as he pulled all the paperwork together and reached over for the Yellow Pages phone book.

***

One of the new lads brought Ricky a cup of tea.

"Cheers," Ricky said and then picked up the telephone as it rang.

Ricky: Good morning London Tyre Co. How can I help you?

Connor: By getting a big wad of cash together. It's Connor, mate, and that bit of business has been done. Justin came through just as he said he would.

Ricky: Good news, is he alright?

Connor: Yeah, he's sweet. He went in to have breakfast as planned and we had the full truck of tyres away. There must 300, maybe even 350, tyres on board.

Ricky: When can you get them to me?

Connor: That's why I'm calling. We'll dump the truck later and do a couple of runs in a transit later this afternoon. Is that alright for you?"

Ricky: Sooner the better mate.

Connor: Right see you about 3.00.

Ricky: See you later.

Ricky hung up the phone and turned to who he thought looked like Everard standing by the door to the office. Ricky got up and walked over and opened the door.

"I thought that was you Everard, how are you mate?" Ricky said.

"Not good, to be honest Ricky. I needed a word and you did say to give you a call and so, as I was in the area…" Everard said.

"Yeah, of course. Look, let me grab my car keys. I've got to get over to Mitcham to have a look at some motors. Join me and we can talk in private on the way," Ricky said.

Everard nodded.

Ricky opened the door and shouted to Barry that he would be back in three hours. Everard followed Ricky over to the Rover P5B and got in. Ricky started the engine. *"Under The Moon of Love'* by Showaddywaddy was playing. Ricky quickly turned the volume down.

"Sorry about that, but I do love a bit of Showaddywaddy on the way to work," Ricky said.

"No problem Ricky."

Ricky pushed the gear lever into 'drive' and drove slowly through the Industrial estate and out onto the main road.

"So what's the problem Everard?" Ricky said.

"I've got aggravation with a group of lads," Everard said.

"No problem, we'll sort them," Ricky said.

"Well it's not exactly me that has the problem," Everard said.

"Okay, so spell it out for me," Ricky said.

"It's my younger brother, Alex. He's not a Ted like me and this group of lads have been giving him a hard time because of me being a black Teddy Boy. I mean they gave him a proper hiding about a week ago and every ounce of my being wanted to get down there and smash seven sorts out of them, but I can't ask the lads to back me up because it's not Ted business. I suppose what I'm asking is what would you do Ricky?"

"In the centre consul you'll find a pen and notepad. Jot down the names of these fellas and where they drink and you can leave the rest to me. There will be no come back on you," Ricky said.

"I don't know what to say," Everard said.

"There's nothing to say. We're friends, allies in the Ted Army. Your problem is now my problem and I will take care of it, but you must be patient, okay?" Ricky said.

Ricky and Everard discussed the future of the Ted Army with Everard pledging his loyalty to Ricky no matter what the future held.

There were several nearly new, accident damaged cars that Ricky found of interest and he bought them all. Ricky drove back to the London Tyre Co and dropped Everard off at his 50s Ford Consul MK1. Connor and Sean arrived at 3.00 and the tyres were quickly unloaded and stored away. It took three trips and afterwards Ricky handed Connor a brown envelope. Connor told him that the job they had been scoping in the Medway Towns would be coming off next weekend. They agreed on the same price per unit regardless of make or tyre size and shook hands.

Chapter 5

As Ricky drove through the Estate, he looked sharply to his left as an accident damaged Ford Granada GXL caught his attention. The whole side of the car had been stoved in with some roof damage. Ricky knew instantly that the car would have been an insurance write off, as an accident that bad would have caused chassis damage and the cost to repair the car would be more than it was worth. He pulled over and took a closer look at the car. It was an 'N' registration which meant it could have only been a year or so old. He concluded that if the owner had the registration document then it was a prime motor for ringing.

"Can I help you Ricky?"

Ricky turned to see Bill Simpson.

"Yeah, it's Bill isn't it?" Ricky said as he bent down to look at the severity of the side impact damage.

"Yeah, we have met," Bill said as he leaned against the car.

"What's with the motor?" Ricky said.

"I buy the occasional motor from a mate with a salvage yard, do them up and sell them on. The right motor can make a nice few quid. The wrong one will be a money pit. I've had experience with both," Bill said with a friendly laugh.

"What about this one?" Ricky said as he patted the roof.

"I've not made my mind up yet. The price was right, so I bought it," Bill said.

"You have a mate with a salvage yard. Does he have a lot of motors like these?" Ricky asked.

"Oh, yeah he's a good source," Bill said.

"Do you want to sell it?" Ricky said with a smile.

"Maybe," Bill said.

Ricky reached into his pocket and produced a large wad of folded money and made what he thought was a fair offer. Bill looked down at Ricky's hands as he counted out the cash.

"That's about the same as I paid for it," Bill said. "What about this. I'll sell you the motor and I'll keep passing on motors like this from my contact, at my cost plus a small handling fee in return for your blessing to take over Double Bubble's money lending spot. Sooner or later someone will step up and fill the void, so I'd like it to be me."

Ricky chuckled.

"Mate I don't dictate who does what around the Estate," Ricky said.

Bill held out his hand.

"All I want is your go-ahead. We both know it carries weight around here and you can have this and another one or two a week if you want," Bill said. "Come on Ricky, make a deal with me."

Ricky shook his hand and handed him the cash.

"You do have all the documentation, right?" Ricky said.

"Of course," Bill said as he put the cash in his pocket. "I'll go and dig out the keys and log book. I'll meet you around the Arms for a pint in, say, fifteen minutes?"

"Yeah, alright. Just so you know, I like fast moving Fords, Granadas, Cortinas and the sporty Escorts, you know RS2000s, Mexicos and stuff like that. Nothing more than eighteen months old and must have all the documentation. I have a fair idea of the market rates, so I'll pay that plus fifty quid for each car as a finder's fee. Two cars a week is good and three or four is better. I will take whatever you have and pay you cash straight away. Oh, and no red two door Cortina GTs," Ricky said with a grin.

"Okay, we can do that. What's with the red GTs?"

Ricky shook his head.

"That's a long story," Ricky said.

Bill went off back into his flat while Ricky drove around to the Arms. As he approached, he saw three people, including Lee, standing by some fresh graffiti. In bright red two foot tall lettering it read 'Dead Dogs Don't Bite!'

Ricky got out of the Rover, locked the door, and strode towards the small group.

"Have you seen this?" Lee said through clenched teeth. "Some bastard is having a pop at Deano!"

"They must have done this late last night or during the early hours," Ricky said.

"It's that Clifford Tate," Lee said, pounding his fist into his hand. "I heard a rumour that he was about again but didn't take any notice. I didn't think anyone would be that stupid."

"If it's him then he's sent a message that he's back, and he clearly thinks that with Deano out of the frame he can take liberties," Ricky said.

"This is well out of order Ricky," Lee said.

"It will be sorted," Ricky said as he turned away and entered the pub.

"You want a pint?" Kenny said as he motioned the barman over.

"Cheers mate," Ricky said.

"I take it you've seen what's outside," Kenny said as the barman placed the first pint of Carlsberg on the bar.

Ricky took a sip from the ice cold lager and nodded.

"Just let me know what you want to do and we're all in," Kenny said as he handed a pound note to the barman.

Ricky and Kenny strode down the bar and sat at the usual table. Ricky sat in Deano's seat. Melanie, Kaz and Donna were chatting with Doreen over by the jukebox. Kaz put a coin into the slot and selected a record. *'You See the Trouble With Me'* by Barry White played.

The pub door entered and Bill stormed down the bar.

"Do we know who fucking wrote that outside?" Bill said as he handed Deano an envelope with all the car's documentation inside.

Bill was wide eyed and angry.

"Yeah, we think so," Kenny said.

"I want in," Bill said as he angrily clenched and unclenched his fists.

There were a few a few moments silence. Kenny looked at Ricky.

"He was my mate too," Bill said. "You know that Kenny!"

"It's not my call," said Kenny.

Ricky lifted his glass of lager and took a sip. As he put the glass back down on the table he looked up at Bill.

"Listen, and listen carefully. If you want in with us then be very clear that when we land on their plot you will show no signs of fear. If we're outnumbered you do not run, and if it kicks off then you will punch and kick until some fucker takes you out. If you let us down then you best pack up your gear and move off the Estate quickly, because you will have me to deal with and I will show no mercy to those who let us down. So, Bill Simpson, are you sure that you still want in?"

"Oh yeah I'm in," Bill said vehemently.

"Good," Ricky said, and then handed him a ten-pound note. "Go get a round of drinks in and gin and tonics for the girls."

"He won't let you down," Kenny said once Bill was out of earshot. "I've seen him. It might have been a few years back but he was fearless and could have a tear up."

"He's in," Ricky said. "Do me a favour, would you? Let everyone know that Bill has taken over Double Bubble's slot. Make it known that he has Double Bubble's black book and he is expecting those that owe to make good."

"Right, good move Ricky. Bill is spot on for the job, he's fair but won't take any bullshit. Will he really have Double Bubble's black book?" Kenny said as he reached for his pint.

"No, but no one else knows that, do they?" Ricky said with a wry smile.

"You are good, Mr Turrell, very good," Kenny said.

Bill returned and put the large tray of drinks on the table. He handed Ricky back his ten pound note.

"This one is on me," Bill said.

'Jeans On' by David Dundas had just started to play when Doreen and the girls took up their seats around the table.

"Bill got these drinks in," Ricky said.

Everyone took their drinks and raised their glasses or said 'cheers'.

Kaz had sat next to Bill.

Bill turned so he was partially facing Kaz. He unconsciously gazed at her silky eyelashes and acorn shaped eyes. He took in the shape of her cute little elf like ears, her pert little nose and effervescent-champagne brown eyes and smiled as gazed up at the locks of her chestnut-brown hair and how they curtained over her pretty face. Kaz looked up and spotted the gaze, but Bill quickly turned away and then turned back and smiled. They began to chat and Bill found the opportunity to say something funny yet sexy. Kaz wore a pale blue open collar blouse. The third button had come undone, exposing a glimpse of cleavage. Bill, wide-eyed, ogled for a few seconds and then quickly looked away in an obvious manner. Kaz giggled and buttoned her blouse. As they drank their second drink, Bill complimented her on how well her short mini skirt hugged her hips. He watched intently as she blushed. Kaz took a Rothman's cigarette from her packet and as Bill reached for her lighter their fingers gently grazed. She pulled her hand away and Bill lit the cigarette for her.

Doreen was just telling Ricky how difficult it would be to get him one of the new two-tone steel and yellow gold Rolex Submariner watches. Ricky had seen an advertisement in a magazine while waiting to have his hair cut, and took an instant liking to the watch. He said that he would put five hundred pounds in an envelope and mark it 'Doreen' and would give it to her if and when the opportunity presented itself to have one away. Doreen ended the conversation saying that she would make no promises but would keep his order on her list.

"Oh no, look who has just walked in," Doreen said.

Ricky, Melanie and Donna all looked up.

"Who is she?" Ricky said.

"Kathy the Candle," Doreen said. "You wouldn't know her Ricky. She's a bit before your time. A right nasty piece of work that one."

"I remember her," Melanie said. "Didn't she get banged up?"

Doreen nodded, keeping her eyes fixed on Kathy.

"Yeah she must have just got out of Holloway. She must have done four years for GBH," Doreen said.

"GBH?" Donna said.

"Yeah, she had a young kiddie, sweet little thing she was. She would leave the poor little mite at home without food or electric while she was out here gallivanting about causing trouble. I'm not kidding when I say that she was responsible for more marriage break ups, fights and arguments than everyone on the estate put together. Her next door neighbour, an elderly woman, took a tumble on the concrete steps. She was lying on the floor in pain when Kathy came down the stairs. The woman pleaded for help and do you know what she did?"

"No" Melanie and Donna said together.

"She bent down, opened her handbag, took her purse and then stepped over her," Doreen said.

"No way," Donna said.

"Oh she did, and she's done worse. It was only a question of time before social services were called in to rescue the little kiddie from the daily abuse and neglect. Well, Kathy has just grabbed a small brass candle stick holder and belted the social worker with it. She was knocked spark out. The old bill arrived and she was carted off, and while she was on bail she walked around in here and the Estate carrying that candle stick holder in her handbag. I know of at least four women that she belted with it. That's how she got the name 'Kathy the Candle' and boy did she revel in it. I watched her in here once as she stared a young girl down over some smear campaign that everyone knew Kathy had started. The look of joy in her eyes as she reduced that girl to tears in front of everyone in the pub is something I'll never forget. Kathy the Candle is cruel, vindictive and ruthless. She's a dangerous woman," Doreen said.

"I'll keep out of her way," Donna said.

"Probably best you do. Look at her, she's doing it right now," Doreen said.

"Doing what?" Donna said.

"Look at her standing at the bar and just scoping the pub. That woman has to compete and right now she's looking at good, happy, well liked and married people that are not short of money. She's clocking it all and then she seeks out the weak, blind followers, which she'll keep around her until she gets bored."

The girls watched as Ronnie handed her a large drink and then leaned over the bar and kissed her on the cheek.

"Did you see that?" Donna said. "Are they together?"

"No, she's a paying customer and Ronnie is just being Ronnie," Doreen said.

Kathy the Candle was in her early forties and a little over five foot tall. She had thick mousy blonde hair, fashioned in a 1960s puffy off-centre parting that waved and curled into the left of her face and away from the right. Her deep brown eyes were sunken back with deep, dark, heavy bags under them. Her lips were unusually small with pronounced lines from years of smoking cigarettes.

Kathy spotted the group and walked towards them.

"Hello Doreen," Kathy said, "It's been a while."

"Alright Kathy," Doreen said looking down at her drink.

"Don't fucking look away from me. I'm talking to you!" Kathy yelled.

People in the pub went quiet. Some turned to see what was going on.

Kathy was revelling in the attention, especially when she heard her name 'Kathy the Candle' in whispers.

Doreen slowly looked up at her.

"Hello Kathy, it has been a while," Doreen said sheepishly.

"Are you still hoisting?" Kathy asked bluntly. "Because I need some work to get back on my feet."

"I can't help you," Doreen said meekly.

"Can't or won't?" Kathy said menacingly, taking a step closer to the table.

"Why don't you back off!" Melanie said sharply.

"Oh now isn't that little Melanie. My, you've grown up since the last time I saw you. I heard about Deano the Dog but I wasn't surprised. A flash bloke like that, playing the tough guy, was always going to get taken out by someone sooner or later," Kathy said.

"That's enough," Bill said rising to his feet.

"Oh what do we have here? Are you the new number one, Deano's replacement? I suppose you're shagging his bird too," Kathy said.

Ricky looked up with scowling eyes.

"That would be me," Ricky said in a low but assertive tone. "And to be clear, Kathy the fucking Candle, I'm as happy smashing seven sorts of shit out of a mouthy, toxic, nasty piece of work like you as I am anyone brave enough to cross me or any of my friends. Am I making myself clear?"

The pub went deadly silent. Ricky had slipped his fingers into his brass knuckle duster and even though he deplored the thought of a man hitting a woman, he was struggling to keep his cool after hearing what Doreen had said about the elderly woman, how she had disrespected Melanie and then callously insulted the memory of Deano. Kathy was playing a psychological game and Ricky knew it. He stamped his authority down with words but would, if needed, back it up with violence.

"You must be Ricky Turrell," Kathy said with a chuckle. "Your reputation precedes you. My apologies, I meant no disrespect to you or your friends. I've been away for a while in a place where you forget the civilities that people on the outside are accustomed to."

"Kathy," Ronnie called out. "There's a drink on the bar. Let's catch up."

"Well it's nice to see you all again," Kathy said as she slowly nodded at Ricky. "Doreen, we will need to chat soon, very soon."

Neil entered the bar. He looked down at Ricky and began walking quickly towards him and accidently brushed against Kathy's arm causing her to spill her drink. Kathy instinctively reached for her open handbag.

"I'm sorry about that," Neil said with a genuine smile. "Let me get you another."

"Thank you, young man," Kathy said.

"It's the least I can do," Neil said. "Make it a large one would you please Ronnie? And whatever Ricky and the others are having. Cheers mate"

Neil handed Ronnie a ten pound note and told him to get himself one.

Neil took the tray of drinks to Ricky's table.

"Alright," Neil said. "Ricky can I have a quiet word please mate?"

"Sure," Ricky said as he stood up. "Let's take a walk outside."

The two friends stood by the two foot lettering that insulted the memory of Deano.

"What's up mate?" Ricky said before taking a swig of his drink.

"It's Jackie. She's found out, well I accidently slipped it out that I'm still getting motors for you and she's hit the roof, and I mean she threw a bloody dinner plate at me and everything. I tried mate, I really tried to reason with her. I told her that we go back a long way and the money's good but she was adamant that I had to stop working with you."

"Okay," Ricky said in a very matter of fact manner.

"Okay? Won't this cause you a problem?" Neil asked.

"Would it make any difference Neil?" Ricky said.

"I'm sorry mate." Neil said.

"I have it all sorted Neil. I suppose it's just lucky for me that I didn't take you at your word," Ricky said as he turned smartly and walked back into the pub.

Chapter 6

Ricky watched as the last of the extra fifty tyres that Justin had aboard his delivery truck were rolled away and stacked in the new shelving that Ricky had installed to cope with the increase in tyre stock.

"Do you want a quick cuppa?" Ricky said, nodding towards the office door.

"Yes, please Ricky. I'm parched," Justin said.

Justin followed Ricky into the main office and joined him at his desk. Ricky handed him a wad of money for the stolen tyres.

"Cheers Ricky. Same amount next week?" Justin asked.

"Sure, and more if you have them," Ricky said.

One of the tyre fitters brought them both over a cup of tea in the new mugs Ricky had Doreen get him along with several items for his apartment.

"I deliver out to these partners in Croydon. They've got three tyre bays. They're totally straight. I mean they don't buy nothing, not that I'd say if they did, but Nick, one of the partners, wants to sell. He's had a right falling out with Matt, the other partner, and now Matt is coming in late, not pulling his weight and trust has gone right out the window. Could be something for you," Justin said as blew over the hot tea.

Ricky handed him a pen and paper and asked Justin to write down where the depots were and the telephone number. He asked a number of questions that convinced Ricky that it was a good business but was suffering from the breakdown between the owners.

"I appreciate this Justin. Keep it to yourself mate and there will be a right good drink in it for you if I can pull it off."

"I won't say a word Ricky. Nigel is alright and probably the best person to talk to. Matt can be a funny sod. I don't know what's got into him. A few years back they were flying, the bays were full and they opened the two new branches in just twelve months and then all of a sudden Matt thinks he's too good to talk to the staff or the delivery drivers.

"I'll give him a call," Ricky said.

***

Just before 5.30pm Ricky called 'N&M Tyres' and asked to speak with Nigel.

Nigel: Hello, Nigel speaking how can I help you?

Ricky: Hi Nigel. This is Ricky Turrell over at London Tyre Co.

Nigel: Oh yeah I've heard about you.

Ricky: All good I hope.

Nigel: It sounds like you're doing alright.

Ricky: I am but I'd like to do better. Are you open to some confidential chats about buying your business?

There was a short silence.

Nigel: How serious are you?

Ricky: If we can agree on a number then I'm ready to go when you are.

Nigel: How do you want to move forward?

Ricky: I'm going to drop into the Cadillac Club about sevenish. It's only up the road from where you are. Come up to the VIP Lounge and I'll tell the doorman to expect you. We can have a quiet drink and see if we can work something out.

Nigel: Okay, see you there.

Ricky hung up the phone and helped Barry to close down the depot for the night.

"We had another record day on the punctures, Ricky, and the adverts are paying off with plenty of retail business. The lads only had half an hour for lunch today. We've been staggering lunch breaks to make sure that everything gets done," Barry said.

"Excellent, well done, Barry. We'll go over the final numbers on Monday morning and I'll make sure there's something extra for you and the lads," Ricky said as he pulled on his black leather box jacket.

Ricky drove back to his apartment and took a quick bath with his Brut soap-on-a- rope and then ordered a taxi to take him up to the Cadillac Club. He told Cookie, the doorman, to expect a visitor. He saw that Frank was busy and ordered a malt whiskey from the bar and sat at an empty table close to the door. Within five minutes a man entered the club looking lost. He scanned the room until he caught Ricky smiling and waving him over.

"Ricky Turrell, good to meet you," Nigel said.

"You too Nigel, and thank you for agreeing to meet me at such short notice," Ricky said as he motioned the waitress over.

"What would you like to drink?" Ricky said.

"I'm not sure, what are you drinking?" Nigel said.

"Malt whiskey, you'll like it," Ricky said.

Ricky ordered two large malt whiskeys for them and asked for one to be sent to Frank's table.

The two men talked about the tyre business and Nigel said that while his partner, Matt, owned fifty per-cent of the business, it was him that had driven its success but now he wanted out. He wanted to sell up and move out of London and maybe settle in Worthing or Bognor with his wife. He said that his children had no interest in tyres and his wife was becoming increasingly impatient with the frustration Matt was causing by not pulling his weight. Nigel threw out a number that would make him sell up and move on. Ricky made a counter offer which would be half by a cheque from the business and half in cash to reduce any tax liabilities. Nigel closed the conversation by saying that it was acceptable to him and that he would speak with Matt in the morning and call Ricky at work during the day tomorrow. The two men stood up, Nigel finished the large tumbler of malt whiskey, shook his hand and left.

Frank sat alone. He looked up and spotted Ricky and beckoned him over.

"Hi Frank," Ricky said as he took a seat.

"Hello Ricky, is everything going okay? Are there any problems I should know about?" Frank said as he held up his empty glass.

"No problems Frank," Ricky said.

"Good. I don't like problems just solutions. That shooting has brought about some unwelcome attention," Frank said as he sat back in his chair.

"I lost a good friend," Ricky said.

"Tell me, was it true that he had built some kind of army from Teddy Boys all over London?"

"He had the vision, Frank, but I'd like to think that I played a part in that," Ricky said.

"So are you running the Milton Road Teds now?"

Ricky nodded.

"What about all that army of Teddy Boys?" Frank said.

"Most are still loyal to the Ted Army. I have a few problems to sort out but I will bring it back together," Ricky said.

"Impressive, very impressive. So you will be running this army of over a thousand Teddy Boys?" Frank said as he took a long swig from his tumbler.

"I will," Ricky said firmly.

"These lads, are they from council estates all over the capital then?"

"There's over fifteen hundred and they cover all four corners of London. I might have a few issues with some lads in the Mile End Road but that will be taken care of during the next few months. I have a plan Frank," Ricky said.

"Good, good. Now tell me Ricky do you have a passport?" Frank said.

"I'm ashamed to say that I've never left the country Frank."

"Okay, so can you get one organised? I plan on taking a trip over to Spain during the next few months and I'd like you to come with me. It's business related and I think it's something you'd be interested in," Frank said.

"Yeah, sure, I'll get a photo done and pick up an application form. Do you have a date?" Ricky said.

"You do that and I'll let you know when I'm ready to go. I'll try to give you as much notice as possible," Frank said.

Ricky stayed on for another couple of hours in the VIP Lounge bar. He chatted with Connor and Sean who assured him of a job they were planning which could bring him several hundred tyres. Ricky confirmed his interest and that the unit price they had already agreed stayed the same. On the way back to his apartment Ricky wondered what kind of business would interest Frank in Spain and why it would include him. He discounted stolen cars because the Spanish drove on the left hand side of the road. Once he was back home, he turned his stereo on then selected his album, Trocadero, with its gate folded sleeve, by Showaddywaddy. Once the record's needle dropped and the record began to play, he slipped off his brothel creepers, sprawled back into his arm chair and thought about how he could make the 'N&M Tyres' acquisition work.

Chapter 7

Ricky had overheard a conversation between Kenny and Lee about a fight over on the St David's Estate. When he pushed for details, they could only repeat a story they had heard, which was that it was bad and someone ended up getting stabbed. Ricky immediately thought of Everard James. He left his pint and drove over to the Estate. He parked up and approached the Dog and Dick pub. As he entered he stopped in the doorway, scanned the pub and spotted Everard sitting with half a dozen Teds. Ricky approached the barman.

"Hello mate, I'll have a pint of Carlsberg and send over whatever the lads with Everard are drinking.

"That's Carlsberg all round," the barman said as took down a straight pint glass and began to pour.

Ricky turned to face those inside the pub. It was like most pubs on council estates. It had its die hard regulars, faces, villains, hard men and lads looking to make a name for themselves.

One of the Teds looked over at Ricky and nudged Everard. He looked up and immediately got to his feet and sauntered over to where Ricky was standing. The Teds shook hands. Ricky led him to a table that was away from prying ears.

"I heard some rumours about it kicking off over here. Was that anything to do with 'our' problem?"

Everard shook his head slowly and ran his hand over his face and finally looked Ricky in the eyes.

"Ricky mate, I know I should have been patient just like you said but when they turned up in here giving it all the big one, me and my two brothers went down there to have it out with them. The whole thing got out of hand really quickly. Those boys hated us, and I mean proper hated us for what? Being black? Being a Teddy Boy? There was a huge fight with tables going over and my brothers and I have steamed in and then this one lad, Daryl Carr, was having it with my baby brother, Alex, when he's pulled out this fucking great carving knife and stabbed him in the gut. I did what I could to get to him but that fucker Carr had it on his toes and I'm just holding my baby brother in my arms."

"Bloody hell, Everard, how is Alex?" Ricky asked.

"The ambulance was there in no time along with old bill. Alex is in intensive care. He's on the critical list and none of us have been able to see him. My mum has hit the roof. She hates any kind of the trouble and the old bill have been treating the family like we're the ones responsible. Fucking coppers, bloody racists, the lot of them!"

"What did you tell them?" Ricky said.

"Nothing, nothing at all. I'll take care of him myself," Everard said.

"No mate you can't do that. The gavvers will come down on you in a micro second the minute anything happens to him," Ricky said.

"I can't let him get away with it Ricky. That bastard stabbed my baby brother. He might not make it," Everard said.

"Everard now listen to me, okay, and this time can you please do as I say? Do not go looking for this Daryl Carr. In fact, do nothing that could point the finger at you. It will be dealt with, but this time trust me to take care of it," Ricky said.

"Yeah, sure I will," Everard said.

"That said, if you hear where he is or spot him anywhere then you make me the first call you make, okay?" Ricky said.

"Yeah, will do Ricky," Everard said.

"Good, now get yourself back up to the hospital and stay with your brother," Ricky said before shaking Everard's hand. "I mean it Everard, you leave this with me."

***

Ricky waved over to the Teds before he left the pub. The barman had placed the round of drinks he'd bought them on the table so they raised their glasses.

"This will need sorting and sorting soon," Ricky thought as he drove back to Milton Road Estate.

Back in the Arms, Ricky passed Ronnie the landlord. He was sitting on the opposite side of the bar with Kathy the Candle. Ricky spotted Ronnie remove his hand from hers as he passed by their table. He took his usual seat at the end of the bar with Bill and the Milton Road Teds.

"So, what do you reckon then, Ricky?" Kenny said. "Do you reckon Ronnie is banging Kathy the Candle?"

"That's nasty," Lee said. "Ronnie is far too good for her."

"Got a thing for Ronnie have you Lee? Well mate, I'm proud of you for finally coming out. We have all had our suspicions for some time but it's good that you felt you could finally share it with us," Kenny said with a raucous laugh.

"Bollocks, I was just saying," Lee said.

"Of course you were," Kenny said. "It would explain those late nights helping to clear up after Ronnie's called last orders.

The lads were all laughing.

"So let me get that right Kenny. Are you saying that Ronnie is a homosexual?"

The smile instantly dropped from Kenny's face.

"No, I didn't mean it like that," Kenny said defensively.

"Should I just wander across and tell Ronnie that you think we're a pair of homosexuals?" Lee said as he rose to his feet.

"No, no, don't do that. I was just having a bit of a laugh. You know me, Lee," Kenny said. "But, do you think he's at it with Kathy the Candle?"

"Would it matter?" Bill said.

"Yeah, of course it would," Ricky said. "Kathy is probably the most hated woman on the estate and Ronnie is a face. He's respected and he runs the pub. If she's in with Ronnie then others will have no choice but to afford her respect. It's a clever move on her part."

"Yeah, I can see that," Bill said.

"Plus the ugly birds tend to be the better shags?" Kenny said with a dead pan expression.

"What makes you say that?" Lee said.

"Well it stands to reason doesn't it? Have a think about it. The good looking birds have all the blokes chasing after them so when it comes down to bumping uglies they don't have to work so hard. It's like they think they've done enough just letting you get that far.

Believe me, Lee, I've smashed the granny out of bundles of good-looking birds and the slightly overweight ones or just average looking girls were by far the best and most adventurous between the sheets. It's like all their inhibitions go out the window the minute the bedroom door is closed," Kenny said.

"So, what you're saying, Kenny, is that Kathy the Candle probably goes like a shit house door in the wind," Bill said.

"Hmm, maybe," Kenny said.

Lee looked over at Ronnie and Kathy and shook his head. "That doesn't bear thinking about. She'd probably get a knife out and stab you for finishing up too quick."

"So premature ejaculation is something you know about then Lee?" Kenny said, as he motioned the barman to bring over another round of drinks.

"Bollocks," Lee said.

"I reckon by the end of your life time, Lee, you will have caused tens of thousands of ejaculations," Kenny said. "And all single handed."

"Give it a rest," Lee said.

"I remember when you went to your first premature ejaculation society meeting. It turned out that you came too early," Kenny said as he looked around the table for another round of laughter.

"Kenny you're about as funny as a dose of the clap," Lee said.

The lads around the table were all laughing as Ronnie approached their table.

"Alright Ricky, lads," Ronnie said as he collected a couple of the empty glasses. "I'm organising a Beano down to Margate. It'll be a shame not to make the most of this heatwave. The coach is booked so I'll need to know soon if you're up for it.

"I'm in," Ricky said.

"Me too," Bill said. "Can you reserve a seat for Kaz too?"

"Can you reserve seats for Terry, Steve, Melanie and Donna too, please Ronnie?" Ricky said.

One by all the lads confirmed that were up for a trip down to the Coast

"Kathy will do that now," Ronnie said.

"You and Kathy getting on alright then?" Kenny said.

"Why, what's it got to do with you?" Ronnie said abruptly.

"Nothing mate, I was just making conversation," Kenny said.

"Right lads, does anyone want a drink while I'm here?" Ronnie asked.

Ricky looked past Ronnie as the pub doors opened. It was Terry and Steve Parker.

"Yeah, get a round in for everyone," Ricky said as he stood up, "And a couple of pints for Terry and Steve.

Ricky left the table and caught up with Terry and Steve half way down the bar.

"I have a bit of business, if you're interested," Ricky whispered.

The brothers looked at each other and then back at Ricky.

"There's something that needs taking permanent care of. It's for a mate, one of us, and there's five hundred in it," Ricky said.

"Just let us know where and when," Terry said.

"Sweet," Steve said.

Chapter 8

"I told you I was good for it," Bill said.

Ricky looked at both of the accident damaged cars outside Bill's block of flats. Both were less than two years old and Bill had all the supporting documentation. Ricky was pleased and paid Bill's price, which included a fifty quid finder fee on both cars.

"Nice one Bill. Can you get any more?" Ricky said.

"Yeah, sure. I've put my name against two Cortina's. I'll get myself over there later and pay for them," Bill said.

"How's the money lending going?" Ricky said.

"Yeah, it's alright. There's a nice steady flow of business. I was half expecting that lunatic Kathy the Candle to be wanting a sub. Her not paying would make it difficult with Ronnie and it would send the wrong message to the others who owed me," Bill said.

"It's not for me to say but I would make a violent public example of the next person that doesn't pay as promised. You need to send a very clear message that there will be consequences for anybody, male or female, that tries to swerve payment and if Kathy approaches you then fuck her off by saying that she's not good for it. If she goes running to Ronnie then he'll stump up the cash, not you," Ricky said.

"Yeah, I'll do that. Cheers Ricky. It's still early days so I'm treading a fine line and just finding my feet," Bill said.

"When we hit Clifford Tate and the Bedford Boot Boys you'll have your chance to make a name for yourself. Either that or you'll be in hospital," Ricky said with a chuckle.

"I'm looking forward to it," Bill said through clenched teeth.

"Look mate I can't hang about here all day. I'll have the motors picked up during the next day or so," Ricky said. "Give me a bell when you get the next lot in and I'll be straight down with your money. Remember, mate, I'll take everything that you can get."

"Yes mate, noted. I'll catch you later," Bill said.

Ricky got back into his Rover P5B and drove back to his apartment. He wanted to call Michelle to see if she fancied going out. He picked up the phone and dialled a couple of numbers.

"I know, I'll make out I'm a friend. I'll call myself Duncan or something and make out we were at University together and then when her parents hand the phone over, I'll break cover and ask her out," Ricky thought.

Ricky dialled two more numbers.

"That old man of hers will never fall for it. The minute he hears a bloke's voice it'll be one question after another probably wanting to know where I live, what my parents do for a living and if I have career prospects to even be talking to his daughter," Ricky thought.

Ricky dialled another two numbers.

"Fuck him I'll just front it out and tell him the kind of bollocks he wants to hear," Ricky thought. "It's a risk. I could be putting Michelle and I at risk. Maybe she'll call me. Yeah, why not? The sun is shining and it's a nice day. Maybe she fancies a trip out to the *countryside and a ploughman's lunch in some pretty little country pub that's full of straw chewing locals."*

Ricky put the telephone back on the receiver.

"Sod it!" Ricky thought as he turned on his stereo.

He picked up his 'Step Two' album by Showaddywaddy and took the vinyl record out of its cover. Ricky ran his record cleaning anti-static cloth around the record and placed the 'A' side on the deck. *'Three Steps to Heaven'* began to play as he slouched back into his armchair.

"I'm bored," Ricky thought. *"But I don't fancy a drink at the Arms. What I would like is for Michelle to call me, or better still for her to turn up here in a bright, flimsy, little summer dress and just spend a few hours in the bedroom and then eat naked together with just some cool tunes playing."*

***

Ricky's day dreaming was interrupted by the phone.

Ricky: Hello

Everard: Ricky, it's me, Everard, mate. My brother, Alex, has died. He passed last night while I sat at his bedside reading him his favourite book 'Catcher in the Rye'. He must have read that damn book a dozen times. My mum is beside herself. She's been crying non-stop. Ricky the whole family are just numb, they can't believe that he's gone. Fucking hell mate, I can't believe he's gone and that bastard, Carr, is still walking around.

Ricky: Have you seen him?

Everard: I've not seen him myself but I was told that he's back in his old boozer, The Prince Albert, lording it about like he's the fucking guvnor or something. It's like he's rubbing the death of my brother in my face.

Ricky: I might need you to find yourself a cast iron alibi at short notice, can you do that?

Everard: Yeah, I mean yes mate. I'm sure I can do that.

Ricky: I'll be in touch shortly.

Ricky hung up the phone and called Terry Parker. They arranged to meet at 10.00 outside the Arms. Ricky called Everard back and told him to be with as many family members as possible until gone midnight and then hung up.

Ricky drove over to the Milton Road Estate and arrived outside the Arms just before 10.00. No sooner had he turned off the ignition when a red BMW 2002 stopped behind him. Ricky checked his rear-view mirror; it was Terry and Steve with a car from the list he had given to them a few days earlier. The brothers got out of the stolen car and got into the back seat of Ricky's Rover.

"Thanks for coming at such short notice," Ricky said.

"No problem," Terry said.

"Who's the target?" Steve said.

Ricky handed them a piece of note pad with a name and address on it.

"Daryl Carr," Terry said as he read the note. "We know him."

"Yeah, we went to school with him," Steve said.

"Is that a problem?" Ricky asked.

Both Terry and Steve shook their heads.

"I never liked him," Steve said.

"We've got some tools in the boot. How bad do want this?" Terry said calmly.

"Shut him down for good," Ricky said as he handed over an envelope with five hundred pounds in it.

"Done," Steve said.

***

Terry and Steve watched as Ricky drove away. They got back into the stolen BMW and headed over to the St David's Estate.

"I never liked Daryl," Steve said.

"Me either," Terry said.

"I remember him at junior school swanning around like he was some kind of celebrity. He never liked me and would talk lies about me to some of the other kids. I remember going up to kids at playtime that I thought were my mates and they just ignored me. He'd turned them against me," Steve said.

"Because he was the best at playing football it was always him and that other kid, George Frett, that picked the teams at lunch time. Me and this Asian kid, Hussain, were always the last to be picked and it was because of Daryl. He would take the mickey about how I had run for the ball or missed a shot. I hated him," Terry said.

"He hit me once," Steve said. "He punched me in the face."

"You never told me that," Terry said.

"I was embarrassed because he made me cry," Steve said. "I just went into the boys' toilets and closed the cubicle door. I stayed in there all lunch time."

"He never hit me but he would purposely bump my shoulder when he was giving it the big one strutting down the hallways with his bunch of mates," Terry said.

"Do you remember that girl, Lorraine Brown?" Steve said.

"Yeah, you liked her didn't you?" Terry said.

"I did, I really liked her, and she liked me. When we played kiss chase I would always chase Lorraine and she would always let me catch her. That was until Daryl told her that I was weird and she must be weird if she liked me," Steve said. "We never played kiss chase again. When I walked over to her in the playground she just turned her back on me and started talking to someone else."

"We should have done something about it back then," Terry said.

"I'd forgotten all about it until you said his name," Steve said. "But I'm happy to make him pay for his past deeds."

"Me too," Terry said.

Terry stopped the car opposite the Prince Albert pub. They watched patiently as patrons left the pub and disappeared into the night.

"That's him," Steve said. "Even after all these years I'd recognise that face."

Terry started the car and watched as Daryl waved to his mates and then turned left. He was alone. With the car in first gear Terry eased off the clutch and allowed the car to creep slowly forward. At the corner he indicated and turned left. Daryl Carr was smoking a cigarette and still alone. Terry accelerated and brought the car to a screeching halt in front of him. Steve was out of the car with his cosh. Daryl was startled and before he could move, Steve brought the cosh down hard on the side of his head. Steve was ready to deliver another blow when Terry spoke.

"I've got an idea," Terry said. "Get him in the motor."

Steve reached down and grabbed Daryl by the hair and dragged him over to the car. Terry opened the back door and together they shoved his unconscious body onto the back seat. Steve raced around to the other side. Terry drove away calmly.

"Where are we going?" Steve said.

Daryl began to regain consciousness, making a series of groans.

"We're going back in time," Terry said.

"I don't get it," Steve said.

"Oh. You will," Terry said.

Terry drove out of the estate and down several side roads before stopping outside the Oaks Primary School. Terry got out of the car and opened the back door. Daryl was barely conscious when Terry stuck the barrel of his hand gun into his face.

"Get out of the fucking motor!" Terry said.

"I don't understand," Daryl whimpered.

"You fucking will," Steve said as he grabbed him by the hair and yanked him clean out of the car and onto the pavement.

"Please, please," Daryl pleaded.

"Shut it and get on your feet," Terry said.

Terry and Steve led Daryl through the open school gates and around to the main entrance by the side of the building. There was just a glimmer of light from a lamppost but it was enough for Terry to wedge the crow bar he had hanging off his trouser belt between the door and frame. With one hard pull the old lock gave way and the timber door sprung open.

"Who are you? Why are you doing this to me? Please let me go," Daryl begged.

"Shut it and move," Terry said firmly.

The three men entered the dark building. The light outside showed through some of the classroom doors and they passed through the hallway. Terry stopped outside the boys toilets. With his gun still aimed at Daryl's head he pushed the door gently. It was open. He reached inside and turned the light on. All three of the men squinted as the bright light came on. Steve gave Daryl a hard shove through the door. He lost his balance and fell to the tiled floor.

"Do you remember this place?" Steve said.

"I went to school here," Daryl muttered.

"Yes and so did we," Terry said as he closed the toilet door behind him.

"I don't understand," Daryl said. "Why am I here?"

"You, Daryl Carr, are here to pay for past misdemeanours," Terry said.

"That was years ago, whatever it was, we was just kids. I don't even know who you are," Daryl said.

"You made my brother's and my life here a misery," Terry said.

"Yeah, I remember you. Terry and Steve Parker, wasn't it? Yeah, I remember you guys. We were friends," Daryl said.

"No we were not friends," Steve said. "You insulted me, hit me and turned people I cared about on me!"

"Come on, that was years ago lads, please," Daryl said.

"See that toilet there?" Steve said as he opened the cubicle door. "I spent an entire lunch time in there crying because you had smacked me one. I couldn't go to my friends because you had been spreading rumours that I was weird, remember that do you?"

"No, not really," whimpered Daryl as tears streamed down his face.

"I remember it Daryl, like it was yesterday. I won't forget how Lorraine Brown turned her back on me in the playground after you spread your lies," Steve said. "You need to pay for that."

"Get in the cubicle now!" Terry said, motioning with the gun from Daryl's head to the cubicle.

"Please, I'll do anything, anything you want. Just tell me and I'll do it," Daryl said.

"There is one thing you can do for us," Terry said.

"What's that?" Daryl said. "Anything, absolutely anything you say."

"You can die," Terry said, raising his gun and pointing it at Daryl.

BANG! BANG! BANG!

Terry fired three shots, one after another into Daryl's body before handing the gun to his brother.

"It's payback time Steve," Terry said.

Steve took the gun, stepped into the cubicle and with the gun just inches away from Daryl's chest he opened fire.

BANG! BANG! BANG!

"That should do it," Terry said as Steve handed his brother the hand gun.

As they left the toilet Steve stopped and turned the light off.

Chapter 9

"Do you reckon they'll turn up?" Kenny said.

"With Deano gone they think it's alright to take the piss," Lee said.

"Well they thought wrong," Kenny said.

"Bill, are you sure you want to be here?" Ricky asked.

"Yes mate, I'm in, all the way," Bill said as he clenched and unclenched his fists.

"By the way, you're looking good in the drain pipes and creepers. A drape jacket would have been nice but I'm still impressed," Ricky said with a grin.

"It's for Deano," Bill said.

"That's what all this is for," Ricky said.

"Good let's see how you handle yourself when it kicks off," Ricky thought.

Ricky had got word over to the Bedford Boot Boys that following the graffiti on the pub wall, a straightener was called for. He set out the tear up. Each side would bring just fifteen lads and the meet would be in the truck car park at the back of the Hackbridge trading estate. Ricky chose it because it was around half way between the two opposing council estates and it was out of the way with no interruptions by the old bill. Clifford Tate had returned his agreement to the terms of the meet.

"Right. Before we move on," Ricky said as he turned to the Milton Road Teds, "First and foremost, this is for Deano, they took the piss and need to pay. Secondly, the Bedford Boot Boys are a bunch of no good lying bastards so when you see more than fifteen lads there do not flinch, just keep your eyes on them. We will show no sign of weakness because what we do here will be talked about all over London in hours. Take no prisoners. We're here to hurt them, don't forget it."

There were several grunts and acknowledgements.

Ricky slipped his fingers inside the brass knuckle duster that Deano the Dog had given him at his first tear up. He smiled and kissed the tip of the thick brass tip

"Is everyone tooled up?" Ricky asked. "Good, let's move."

All fifteen of the Milton Road Teds wore their drapes. Ricky had a full drape suit in Royal Blue with pale blue velvet collar, cuffs and pockets. On his feet he wore a pair of black brothel creepers with a large chrome buckle.

***

At the industrial car park Clifford Tate was dressed in blue jeans, Dr Marten Boots and a leather waistcoat that showed off years of working out with weights. He had a cigarette dangling from his mouth and was surrounded by twenty-two fully booted up Skinheads and Boot Boys.

"Right lads, we're going kick seven sorts out of this little lot. We'll send them and their reputation back to the dark ages. The Bedford Boot Boys are number one on this manor and we're going to show them that they're nothing without that dead slag Deano the fucking

Dog," Clifford Tate said as he punched his giant fist into the palm of his hand

Some of the Skinheads carried blades while others held pick axe handles and baseball bats.

***

The Milton Road Teds swaggered slowly through the industrial park. Ricky led the pack and was closely followed by Terry and Steve Parker, Kenny, Lee and Bill. As they turned the corner Ricky caught a glimpse of Clifford Tate and the Bedford Boot Boys.

"I knew that bastard wasn't good for his word. He must have over twenty lads with him," Ricky thought. *"Let's fucking have it!"*

The Milton Road Teds strutted over to the car park and stood in a line behind Ricky. All eyes were firmly fixed on Clifford Tate and the Bedford Boot Boys. Ricky and the lads watched as their adversaries bounced on the spot, shook their heads and raised their arms into the air. The Milton Road Teds were veterans to gang fights. They knew that what they were witnessing was a bunch of unsure lads trying to build up adrenaline and bounce the fear out of their bodies. Only Clifford Tate stood firm. He pointed to Ricky and then with gritted teeth he ran his finger across his neck. Ricky didn't flinch. The Bedford Boot Boys jostled and began to move forward jeering the Teds on and yelling out.

"I'll cut all of you!" one lad yelled as he sliced at the air with a military knife.

Several of Clifford Tate's lads began to sing while punching the air.

"I'll sing you a song, it won't take long… We are the Bedford Boot Boys!"

Ricky raised his arm slowly and then dropped it. The Milton Road Teds yelled and charged towards their enemy as one force. Terry was the first to swing his homemade cosh and send a Skinhead sprawling to the ground yelling out and cradling his bleeding face. With brothel creepers and Doctor Marten boots kicking, the two gangs clashed. Ricky fired out a right hook with his brass knuckleduster, then a second killer uppercut and the Boot Boy was done and lying unconscious. The Teds, in a wild frenzy, booted and kicked at his limp body. A baseball bat missed Ricky's head by inches. The Skinhead, with blazing eyes and gritted teeth swung again and missed. From out of nowhere, Terry smacked the lad face on with the cosh. Blood spurted out of his nose. He dropped the baseball bat and slumped to his knees. Ricky ran forward and kicked the lad in the face so hard that his whole body was shot back to the floor with his knees still bent. Clifford Tate had grabbed one of the Teds by his collar and was systematically punching his face, screaming 'Fucking die Ted!" Ricky grabbed the baseball bat off the ground. He shoved the end straight into the face of one lad before taking a full swing. The skinhead was down. The blood spurted through his fingers as he cupped his nose. Ricky kicked the lad in the face before moving forward to his next victim. A few of the Bedford Boot Boys had lost their bottle. This wasn't going to be an easy fight. The Teds were steaming forward and taking out everything and everyone in their path tooled up or not. Clifford Tate released the unconscious Ted and turned to face Ricky. He smiled, revealing just a handful of teeth that remained after their last clash with the Milton Road Teds and Deano the Dog. Clifford Tate reached around to the back of his jeans and produced a huge Bowie knife that glistened as the sun caught the razor sharp blade. The Teds were steaming forward with fists and boots flying in all directions while an increasing number of rattled and injured Boot Boys turned and had it on their toes.

Bill was striking out, punching and kicking the lads as they fell under the charge of the Milton Road Teds. One Skinhead made a frantic swing and caught the top of his arm with the end of his switchblade. Bill charged forward with relentless punches and kicks until the lad tried to turn and run. He leapt on his back with his arms around the lad's neck and brought him down. Bill pounded several punches into the back of the lad's head before grabbing his ears and smashing his head into the rough concrete surface until the Skinhead stopped moving.

Clifford Tate stood a solid six foot, four inches tall with a forty-six-inch chest and muscular frame. He crouched forward and passed the blade from his left to his right hand while taunting Ricky with jabs. Ricky stepped forward and Clifford made a lunge with the blade. Ricky dropped to the ground and with a mighty swing smacked Clifford across his lower leg. There was a crack of bone and his leg gave way. Ricky was back up on his feet and swung the baseball bat again, hitting Clifford Tate's right arm.

CRACK!

Clifford's arm went limp and he dropped the blade.

Ricky dropped the baseball bat and brought the fist with the brass knuckle duster up to his chest. Clifford's bones were fractured and broken, yet he continued to shout out.

"You're dead, the lot of you. Just like Deano, you're all dead!"

SMACK!

Ricky had fired a nasty, powerful, punch that shattered Clifford's jaw. He continued to mumble as blood poured from his mouth and nose.

"Right, Clifford Tate, if I ever, and I mean ever, have to call on you again, you'll be joining Eddy Boyce and Deano on the other side. Now look me in the fucking eyes and tell me I'm joking. There can be no second chances. We are the Milton Road Teds and we run all of this fucking manor," Ricky said as he stood over the beaten leader of the infamous Bedford Boot Boys.

Clifford Tate was helpless to move, he was defeated and his lads were either severely injured or had turned and run away.

Ricky helped the Ted that Clifford Tate had been beating back onto his feet before leading the victorious Milton Road Teds out of the industrial estate.

"Kenny, Lee," Ricky said. "Put the word out on what happened here. I want anyone who is anyone talking about what we did today."

Chapter 10

Bill had been out with the Milton Road Teds celebrating their victory in the Arms until after 2.30am. The word had got out as Ricky had ordered, and telephone calls streamed into the pub one after another from gangs of Teds from all corners of London, offering congratulations and support for the Ted Army.

After each call Ricky would order another round of drinks for everyone to enjoy. Bill sat back in his chair alongside the Teds and villains from around the estate. He found himself finding feelings that he had long since forgotten. Strangely, he felt at home with these people. They were honest about who and what they were, and he fitted in and was accepted. For the first time in his career as an undercover police officer he felt that he was struggling to impersonate being a criminal while not crossing any lines. He had convinced himself that he would be securing his position further by putting on the Ted gear and going out with Ricky and the others to avenge their friend Deano and the disrespect he had been shown by the graffiti. Bill had wanted to be there, he wanted the violence he had left behind on Milton Road Estate so many years ago. Deano Derenzie was his friend, they were true mates, and had circumstances been different then he would have been standing side by side with Deano in every conflict they had. Deano's friendship had opened up a world he had previously only seen from the outside and he owed him for that. Bill was struggling with the conflicting emotions of being a police officer charged with the duty of bringing down all the people he was befriending. He liked Ricky. Despite the rocky start, he liked and respected him and he knew that slowly but surely, he was winning the trust of one of the most influential men on the estate with direct links to London's Mr Big, Frank Allen.

Melanie, Kaz and Donna were by the jukebox when *'Cum On Feel The Noize'* by Slade began to play. Several of the Teds, mums, dads and neighbours stood up and sang at the top of their voices.

Bill downed a large malt whiskey that Ricky had brought him and found himself thinking about Kaz. At first the connection was to help bring him into the fold quicker but increasingly he found himself developing feelings for her. She was a sweet girl and he found himself looking beyond the fact that day in and day she was out in London with Melanie and Donna stealing thousands of pounds of goods from department stores for their matriarch, Doreen. He found himself understanding that just because of their background, they wanted more than a job working in a shop, child minding or getting married to some lad on the estate and entering into a life of living on benefits. Kaz and the others were just doing whatever they could to improve their lot and he was struggling to remove that thought and see them as nothing more than criminals.

Bill shook his head and beckoned the barman over. He ordered two large malt whiskeys. One for him and the other for Ricky. He began to think about why he had agreed to become an undercover police officer. He knew that DCI Mike Wilson was playing him and leveraging his ability to integrate with villains for his own ends. However, the promotion was the end game, Bill told himself. It won't be me out on the front line but as the malt whiskey went down, he found himself staring over at Kaz. She caught his gaze and smiled. This is real, he told himself. I have no one. No mum, no dad, no wife, children or siblings. All I have is my career and it's empty and this, this is real, he told himself. I want Kaz in my life, I want to come home to a life partner that loves me. I want to walk into the

Arms and feel respect, friendship and loyalty from people who would stand by your side when the going gets tough.

Bill put the glass back down the table and scanned the pub. No, he told himself. I am a police officer and it's my job to take all you lot down and put you behind bars.

***

The following day Bill met with DCI Mike Wilson at a café in Stockwell.

"Hello Bill, you're looking the part," DCI Wilson said as he looked Bill up and down.

"Yeah, it's working for me," Bill said confidently. "Cup of tea, sir?"

"Yes please, and a sausage sandwich with brown sauce," DCI Wilson said as he pulled out a chair and sat down.

Bill looked up and called out for two sausage sandwiches and two teas.

"I've been reading some of the reports. You appear to be making progress," DCI Wilson said.

"It's going well sir, and I'm in now," Bill said.

"Exactly how do you mean in?"

"I'm accepted, I know the faces and they know me. I'm trusted and looked upon as one of their own," Bill said.

"Good work Bill, good work. How long do you think it will be before we can start chipping away with arrests?" DCI Wilson asked.

"Not for a while yet, sir. They had one rat named Double Bubble, and they found him out and he paid dearly. This operation has huge scope, sir and goes way beyond what we're guessing at. We could be looking at murder, violence, robberies, theft on a grand scale and all that's before we even get to Frank Allen. This will be a long operation but will deliver the kind of results that will push us both up the ladder sir," Bill said.

"You undercover boys do worry me sometimes," DCI Wilson said.

"How is that?" Bill asked.

"When officers go undercover for long periods, they can either start cutting corners in the hope of an early conviction that end up damaging the force's reputation, or they begin to struggle with the balance of playing the part of a criminal and becoming one," DCI Wilson said.

"I'm not like other officers, sir," Bill said. "I'm here to do a job and I'll do that to the best of my ability."

"I know that, Bill, which is why I wanted you on this case. This is not just me, but those upstairs. They want it all broken down and the criminal element put away for a long time. They will want Frank Allen. He's been playing the game for long enough and it's time for him to do a spell inside," DCI Wilson said.

"Thank you, sir, I understand," Bill said.

"In a complex operation like this I needed a proven, relentless officer with a flexible outlook. A man of integrity with the ability to think on his feet and adapt quickly and you, Bill, are the best man for the job," DCI Wilson said. "So, please, don't go making any mistakes. We want them, Bill, and we want them bang to rights with no wriggle room."

"I understand," Bill said.

"Good man," DCI Wilson said as he patted Bill on the shoulder.

"Now, where's that sandwich?" DCI Wilson said as he looked over at the cook and held his hands open.

Chapter 11

Nigel, one of the N&M Tyres partners had called Ricky and invited him down to visit the business. Ricky was excited and looking forward to the meeting. He had been using the library to learn more about business strategy and the acquisition process. Ricky felt confident and ready to deliver the next part of his strategic plan.

Ricky took a taxi over to N& M Tyres main depot. He didn't feel that either the Rover P5B or the Zodiac were appropriate for the meeting. He wanted the partners to be focused on his words and not second guessing his choice of cars. He was pleased to see that all four bays were busy with several cars waiting to be served. Nick bounded out to meet Ricky and shook his hand firmly.

"Thank you for coming along Ricky. It's good to see you." Nigel said.

"I'm pleased to be here, Nigel, and I'm hoping that we can work a deal that leaves everybody happy," Ricky said.

"I'll show you around before we meet with Matt upstairs," Nigel said.

"Great," Ricky said.

Nigel led Ricky through to a large room with three tyre changing machines, two wheel balancing machines and two sets of vehicle tracking alignment gauges. By the side of the oldest tyre changing machine was a stack of wheels and tyres and a young lad dressed in jeans and a T-shirt repairing punctures.

"I try to get all the punctures done the same day providing they're in before mid-day," Nigel said proudly. "I think it's important that we provide the service."

Ricky nodded.

Nigel led him through to another area that had been racked out for tyre stock.

"You seem low on stock," Ricky said.

"Cash flow, Ricky. I set a cash figure for stock in all three depots and aim to turn over what we have quickly and then drive suppliers to provide us the replacement service," Nigel said.

"Do they do that?" Ricky asked.

"I'd like to say yes but the truth is it's only most of the time," Nigel said.

"I appreciate your honesty," Ricky said. "Mine will take upwards of a week so I have to have the stock or risk losing sales."

"I'm sure that we lose sales too, so yes, we would definitely benefit from more stock," Nigel said.

"Is there anything else you'd like see out here?" Nigel asked as he led Ricky towards the staircase.

"What about the lads. How long have they been with you and do you trust them?"

"Two of my lads have been with us since the beginning. Neither are what you'd call management material but they graft. They're both in early, will readily miss lunch breaks if we're busy and stay late to finish up the day's punctures if required. The other lads are what I'd call plodders. They do the job, they're not impolite, but then you wouldn't remember them either. It's a fair wage for a fair day's work," Nigel said.

"What about the other depots? Ricky asked.

"We have two good managers, both from the Nationals. We had to pay them a little more but its peace of mind that the job is getting done. Both are turning over fitters though," Nigel said.

"What is the problem, money?"

"Probably," Nigel said. "Both the depots have local independents that pay more than us but I suspect that you already knew that."

Ricky nodded.

"Let's go upstairs and meet with Matt," Nigel said before turning to a young lad on the telephone and asking him bring up three mugs of coffee.

"Nigel opened a white painted six panel timber door and showed Ricky into a plush office with an expensive L-shaped desk with an executive chair. Ricky stepped onto the thick pile carpet. Over by the window looking out onto the forecourt was a medium build, balding man with thick rimmed black glasses. He wore a black pin stripe suit, white shirt and a royal blue tie. Ricky looked down at his highly polished black leather shoes.

"This fella hasn't fitted a tyre in years," Ricky thought.

"You must be Matt," Ricky said.

The two men shook hands.

"Take a seat Ricky," Matt said. "Nick tells me that you're genuinely interested in buying our business.

"Providing we can get to a place where we're both happy, then yes I am," Ricky said.

"Interesting," Matt said as leaned back on his chair.

There was a knock on the door and a young lad brought in three mugs of coffee on a tray. He left them on the corner of the desk and promptly left.

"Can you tell me why you're selling, or considering selling the business?" Ricky said.

"In truth," Nigel said. "I think it's about time that Matt and I went our separate ways. We've built a good business that provides a decent life style but I want to do other things."

"Would that be in the tyre industry, Nigel?

"No Ricky. I want to try my hand at property developing. I don't mean new builds, just run-down homes that need a new kitchen, bathroom and stuff like that. Buy, refurbish and sell on in three months. Well, that's the plan," Nigel said.

"Are there any lawsuits pending?" Ricky asked.

"No," Matt said firmly.

"Have you tried to sell before?" Ricky said.

"Yes," Nigel said. "We were approached by a National with what I thought was a fair offer."

"I didn't think the offer was fair," Matt said.

"Do you have a copy of your most recent business plan and maybe some of the older versions?" Ricky said.

"We have not performed to plan during the last couple of years," Nigel said.

"Are you profitable?" Ricky asked.

"Just about," Matt said.

"Why do you think that you haven't achieved what you planned?" Ricky asked.

"I think we've lost market share because Matt and I are too busy bickering when we should be focusing on the business," Nigel said.

"That's a fair comment," Matt said.

"We're probably not buying as well as we should be too, which is impacting our gross margin," Nigel said.

"So, your cashflow is so tight that you're losing sales by not having the stock sitting on the shelf," Ricky thought.

"Are you involved in anything other than tyres?" Ricky asked.

"We trialled offering an exhaust fitting service but the complexity was too much and rather than being an additional revenue stream it impacted the cashflow to a point where it was affecting the tyre business," Nigel said.

"So, you're out of exhausts?" Ricky said.

"We still have about ten thousand pounds worth of exhaust stock," Matt said.

"Is it written off or still listed as an asset?" Ricky asked.

"It's still on the books," Matt said.

"Would it be fair to say that you're under price pressure from your competitors?" Ricky said.

"We've already said that we probably don't buy cheap enough," Matt said.

"Have you analysed what your competitors offer? Things like tyre brands, services, prices etc," Ricky said.

"Yes," Matt said.

"No not recently," Nigel said. "I would like to take time out to really analyse our competition like we did when we first started out, but I'm very busy with day to day management."

"What would happen if you stepped away Nigel?" Ricky said. "Do you have someone to manage the day to day business?"

"Right now it's just me," Nigel said.

"Matt, what role do you perform?" Ricky asked.

"I'm a business owner and I oversee everything," Matt said.

Ricky spotted Nigel rolling his eyes and slowly shaking his head.

"Okay, look, the tyre business isn't exactly complex so I've seen enough to know that you're borderline profitable, have insufficient stock so you're losing sales and are struggling to retain staff. But with all that said I am interested in buying your business at the price and terms that Nigel and I have already discussed. I will make a cash payment to you both and write a cheque for the balance. I do have just one condition," Ricky said.

"What is that?" Nigel said.

"That you stay with the business and work alongside me for at least twelve months. I will continue to pay your current salary plus give a five figure bonus if together we deliver the plan. I will provide you with a good manager to manage the day to day so that you can work on delivering the strategic objectives," Ricky said.

"I'm happy with that," Nigel said with a broad smile. "I think we'll work well together."

"Yeah, but I'm not," Matt said bluntly. "I'm not even sure if I want to sell to you."

"Matt, we talked about this," Nigel said.

"Yeah and I said that I would listen with no promises," Matt said.

"What is it that you want, Matt?" Ricky said as he leaned across the table and stared into Matt's eyes.

"I want another fifty grand in cash," Matt said as he stood up.

Ricky chuckled.

"Your entire business isn't worth fifty thousand pounds as it is today," Ricky said.

"Well if you can't afford to buy us, then there's not a lot more to say," Matt said as walked over to the window and turned his back on Ricky and Nigel.

"Ricky, I am so sorry," Nigel said.

"I'm disappointed by your lack of professionalism Matt, and you, Nigel, are in no way responsible for the dead weight you've found yourself lumbered with," Ricky said as he got out of the chair.

Matt continued to stand with his back to Ricky and Nigel.

"I'll show you out," Nigel said.

Ricky followed Nigel out of the office and back down to the tyre bays.

"I don't know what to say," Nigel said.

"It's not your fault Nigel. I'm not going to give up just yet. If I can persuade Matt to see commercial sense will you stay with the business and help to turn this back around with me?" Ricky said.

"There is so much more out there, Ricky, and I know that you can see it. If Matt had been carrying his weight, we would have been an eight or ten tyre depot business by now," Nigel said.

"Do you have a home address for Matt?" Ricky said.

"Sure," Nigel said as he took a pen from his inside pocket and jotted the address down on a business compliment slip.

"I'll be in touch," Ricky said.

"You're a lazy good for nothing waste of space," Ricky thought. *"You will sell me this business, Matt, one way or another."*

***

Ricky knew that London Tyre Co was in good hands with Barry managing the day to day business so he had the taxi driver drop him off at the café opposite Millwall Motor Auctions on the way back. The café had just a few motor traders drinking tea and talking shop. Ricky ordered an all-day breakfast with eggs, bacon, sausages, beans and tomatoes to save him cooking later, and then took a note pad and pen from out of his pocket and began to make notes.

"Right, time for Ted Army business," Ricky thought.

On the left-hand side of the page Ricky wrote down the names of all the Teddy Boy gangs across London with an estimated number of members. Once he had done that, he graded each one with an A, B or C. The letter 'A' denoted that the gang were fully on-board with the Ted Army alliance. The letter 'B' indicated that it was still in the balance and that there was more work to be done. The letter 'C' meant that the gangs had no alliance vision and that they were dinosaurs. When he finished the table, he put the pen down.

"Well I know what I've got to do," Ricky thought. *"Bank all the A's and then bring on the B's and as for the dinosaurs… make them extinct!"*

Chapter 12

"This is a nice car, Bill," Kaz said looking over the blue Granada GXL.

"Cheers, I've only had it a few days. I wanted something special to take you out in," Bill said with a cheesy grin.

"Well, thank you," Kaz said.

Bill opened the passenger side door and held it open for Kaz to get inside. He raced around to the driver door.

"So, Bill, where are you taking me?"

"Now, that would be telling," Bill said.

"Right, so it's a surprise," Kaz said.

"I just thought it would nice for you and I to be alone and just enjoy a day out away from the Milton Road Estate, the Arms and in truth, everyone we know," Bill said as he started the engine and shifted the gear lever into drive.

"That is very thoughtful," Kaz said.

Bill pushed a cassette into the player and *'We Do It'* by R & J Stone played. He drove across South London and then out into Sussex where he picked up the A22. He followed the country lanes until the A275 turn off into East Grinstead. Bill slowly approached the Blue Bell Railway at Sheffield Park Station. He parked in the car park and then opened the passenger side door for Kaz.

"What's this?" Kaz said.

"It's still a surprise," Bill said with a smile.

Bill locked the car door, took Kaz by the hand and led her into the train station.

"Wow this is like the setting from one of those television period dramas," Kaz said. "Are we going on a train?"

Suddenly there was a chuffing noise in the distance and the whistle from a steam train. Kaz turned excitedly as the steam train came into view. The smoke streamed out from the train's chimney.

"What a beautiful train," Kaz said as the train came to a standstill.

Bill took two tickets from his pocket and approached a guard.

"Yes sir, the dining carriage is just there," the guard said pointing to a middle carriage.

"Dining?" Kaz said.

Bill opened the carriage door and held Kaz's hand as she boarded the train. They were immediately met by a waitress who showed them to their table.

"I've never done anything like this before," Kaz said.

"Nor have I Kaz, which is why I booked it. It was an experience that I wanted to share for the first time with you," Bill said.

The smart, period dressed waiter brought over a bottle of red wine which Bill had pre-ordered. He took out a cork screw and removed the cork before pouring its contents into their crystal cut glasses and then handed them both a menu. Bill thanked him and looked down at the menu.

"This is wonderful," Kaz said.

"We have three courses and plenty of time," Bill said.

"What are you having?" Kaz asked.

"Hmm," Bill muttered as he read through the menu. "I think I'll have the Carrot and Coriander soup followed by the braised lamb, vegetables and colcannon potatoes and then to crown it all, the lemon meringue tart."

"That sounds perfect, I'll have the same," Kaz said.

Bill gave the order to the waiter and then asked for the photographer to take their pictures.

"I haven't got a mirror," Kaz said as she rifled through her handbag.

"You look amazing just as you are," Bill said.

Kaz closed the bag and smiled. The photographer took several pictures of them together holding their glasses and posing in front of the train's pull-down window. Bill gave the photographer an address to send the pictures to and paid him. The food arrived and was served piping hot. They chinked glasses and enjoyed their meal. As the waiter took the plates away, Bill ordered two coffees.

"Thank you, Bill," Kaz said. "This has been a truly amazing date."

"You're very welcome Kaz. It's nice to be back in the area and amongst friends," Bill said.

"It must seem a little strange having been away for so long. Lots of changes," Kaz said.

"You're right Kaz and I can see how Deano became friends with Ricky, and after his performance with Clifford Tate's it's easy see why he's now running things," Bill said.

"I can still remember that first time Ricky walked into the Arms wearing a full on drape suit. He looked damn good," Kaz chuckled, "Even Melanie commented on it which was unheard of. You know, what with her only having eyes for Deano. He strutted right up to Deano and Mickey Deacon started giving it his usual mouth but Ricky just shut him down and I think we all saw straight away that Ricky fitted in with us and Deano liked him. He's come a long way since then."

"I bet Mickey Deacon didn't like that?" Bill said.

"No, there was always something between them, but Ricky just kept on proving himself over and over and then Mickey went and hit some coppers during a brawl over on the Bedford Estate and got sent away. I suppose that paved the way for Ricky then, as he quickly stepped into becoming Deano's right hand man," Kaz said.

"He seems to have done well for himself in business too," Bill said.

"Oh yeah, he's a smart fella for sure. How many guys of his age do you know that own their own business?" Kaz said and then lowered her voice. "Rumour has it that he uses the business to launder cash from motors. I mean, none of us know and no one would ask, but that's what most people think. I say good on him and whatever he's doing with Frank Allen."

"You think he's working with Frank Allen?" Bill said.

"No one knows for sure, but we've seen him in the Cadillac Club's VIP lounge and the pair of them do look kind of cosy chatting away with their large malt whiskeys. Yeah, he's doing something," Kaz said.

"There's a lot more to Ricky than just running the Milton Road Teds then," Bill said.

"Yeah, why all the questions about Ricky?" Kaz said.

"A lot has changed since I lived here Kaz, and I'm just trying to get a feel for who is who and what is what. You know what it's like," Bill said.

"Yeah, I suppose so," Kaz said.

"What about you Kaz? How do you see your future?" Bill said with a smile.

"Well, I think I've recently met someone a bit special, but what I don't want is a one-night stand kind of thing. I'm emotionally ready for something bigger and more substantial in my life. I want a man, a good-looking man with standing that can take care of himself. I want that special someone to fall for me as I've fallen for him. He must treat me with respect and as an equal and in return I'll shower him with love, kindness and loyalty," Kaz said with a glint in her eye.

"Do I know this man?" Bill said.

"What can I say? Yes, you have a lot in common," Kaz said with a giggle.

"I like you Kaz, I like you a lot and I would like for us to go out together," Bill said.

"I would like that too," Kaz beamed.

"I have to be honest Kaz. I've not really been one for long term relationships but then I've never met anyone quite like you. So you may have to be a little patient with me," Bill said.

"I can be patient for the right man," Kaz said. "I want to share my life with someone, to live in our own home and create a life together. Who knows, maybe even get married and have children one day. I don't mean now, because there is still so much that I need to do."

"I could do that," Bill said. "I mean, I could do that with you Kaz, but how does that fit with you working with Doreen?"

"It's a job that pays well and I'm saving to buy a home and a lifestyle. I will not always work with Doreen, it's a means to an end. In time I'll do what Ricky did and buy a legitimate business that has the ability to support a couple at first and then a family. Maybe that's a business that you and I could work together in," Kaz said as she shrugged her shoulders and smiled.

"I would love to work with you in a business," Bill said. "I think we'd make a great team."

"I do too," Kaz said.

"How will Doreen take that?" Bill asked.

"She'll get over it. I'm sure she's probably grooming my replacement as we speak. Besides she has Jackie, her star performer," Kaz said.

"Jackie?" Bill asked.

"Yeah, it was Jackie that brought me, Donna and Melanie into shoplifting and I can still remember getting orders, nicking the first thing, and then getting handed over three hundred and eighty pounds on my first week. It looked like a fortune until I saw her hand Jackie a pile of money that must have been at least a thousand pounds. With what she's pulling in and Neil with his motors, they're raking it in," Kaz said. "Funny though because I would never have put Jackie and Neil together but it seems to work."

"So Neil is in the motor game too," Bill said.

"Yeah, he was or still is working with Ricky on bits and pieces," Kaz said.

"Anyway enough about that lot," Bill said. "I'd like for us to become official, you know, an item. We're Bill and Kaz and exclusive to each other. How do you feel about that?"

Kaz beamed.

"I would like that Bill," Kaz said as she leaned across the table and kissed him gently on the lips.

Chapter 13

Ricky had ordered a taxi cab to pick Michelle up at the end of her parents' road and then take them up to Soho. They wandered around looking at neon signs promoting striptease books and magazines. They passed the Keyhole club where two young ladies wearing white stockings, heels and sexy nurse's uniforms stood outside beckoning passers-by in. Ricky took Michelle by the hand and crossed the road passing by the Sex Office Classic Moulin cinema. Ricky squeezed her hand and the couple gathered pace until Ricky led them into Great Windmill Street and stopped outside Miranda's Cocktail Bar & Steakhouse.

"Oh, this is really nice," Michelle said stopping to look at the signage and peer through the plain glass window.

"I wanted to go somewhere special," Ricky said.

"Do you think they'll have a table?" Michelle said, looking a little concerned.

"I hope so, because I booked it two days ago," Ricky said with a broad grin.

Ricky opened the door for Michelle to enter. A waitress immediately approached.

"Good evening Sir, Madame. Do you have a reservation?" the waitress said.

"Yes we have," Ricky said. "It's under the name Ricky Turrell."

"Welcome to Miranda's Cocktail Bar and Steakhouse. My name is Wendy and I'll be your waitress this evening. Would you like a drink at our bar or would you like to be shown to your table?"

"The table, please," Michelle said as she looked over at the busy bar area.

Wendy showed them to their table and suggested their house special 'Miranda' cocktail which she described as being similar to the popular Pina Colada cocktail but with an unexpected twist. Ricky and Michelle both agreed to try one.

"This is lovely, thank you Ricky," Michelle said as she looked around the inside of the steakhouse.

"I wanted somewhere to celebrate and someone special to celebrate with," Ricky said.

Wendy placed their drinks on the table.

"Cheers," Ricky said.

"Cheers," Michelle said with a broad smile. "What are we celebrating Ricky?"

"Well, London Tyre Co is exceeding all my plans and projections and an opportunity to buy a competitor presented itself. Their tyre business is profitable, just, and will benefit from a refit and re-branding to London Tyre Co. I spoke to my bank manager, presented him with a business plan, a profit and loss forecast and they were happy to advance me the money I needed at very competitive rates. When this deal closes, I'll be the proud owner of four strategically placed tyre depots, and Michelle, this is just the start. I have big, ambitious plans. Within five years I'll have twenty plus freehold tyre depots around London. I will give the multi-nationals a run for their money," Ricky said.

"Well done, I'm really proud of you. Are they all yours now?" Michelle said.

"Not quite but I'm confident that I'll get the call tomorrow to say that they've accepted my offer," Ricky said.

"Isn't this a little presumptuous? I wouldn't want it jinxed for you," Michelle said.

"No, not at all," Ricky said shaking his head and grinning. "I'm confident that both the partners will see sense and want to close the deal tomorrow."

"Well here's to you," Michelle said, raising her glass.

Wendy came back to the table with menus and recommended a house special which featured prawns, steak and sauté potatoes. Ricky had asked if she could recommend a good wine. Wendy suggested a bottle of Shiraz. She explained that it was a little more expensive but was worth the few extra pounds. They had both decided against a dessert despite it looking very tempting. Ricky ordered a large malt whiskey for himself and Michelle asked for another 'Miranda' Cocktail.

Suddenly there were several large bangs on the glass window. Everyone in the bar and steakhouse looked down to see several Teddy Boys prancing around outside having fun. One lad stood in front of the window and combed back his hair. Another took the cigarette from his mouth and slowly dogged it out against the window. Finally the smallest of the lads turned his back to the restaurant. He wriggled his hips back and forth and slowly tugged at his trousers and underwear until his backside was on show. The lad flipped his drape jacket up exposing his full butt and then he pushed himself up against the window. There were cries of disgust and horror from all over but no one stood up to confront them. Ricky had to bite his lip in an effort to stop himself from laughing. Finally the Teddy Boys moved.

"Bloody hooligans," Michelle said.

"Just a bunch of lads having fun," Ricky said. "They're harmless."

"So you think that kind of behaviour is acceptable?" Michelle said in a confrontational tone.

"I didn't say that," Ricky said.

"They're Teddy Boys, like you, aren't they?" Michelle said.

"Not quite like me," Ricky said with a smirk, "but yeah, they're Teds."

"You're an enigma Ricky Turrell. On the one hand you book exclusive restaurants, drink fine wine and talk about ambitious business plans and yet you sit here in an outfit that most people would associate with a hooligan or outlandish, yobbish, behaviour."

"You didn't see me like that when we first met," Ricky said.

"But things change Ricky, as we get older and become more mature. You're a successful businessman now. Don't you think it's time to just hang up that drape suit and maybe wear a smart tailored suit from Saville Row or something?"

"I'm not sure that I see things the same way as you Michelle. Why do I have to be one thing or another? Why do I have to fit into some kind of box to suit other people's perceptions? I wear a drape because I'm a Teddy Boy. I love the music, culture and all things

Teddy Boy, but it doesn't define me, just like being a business owner doesn't. I'm a small part of all these things and I need them all to feel complete," Ricky said with a frown.

Michelle rolled her eyes.

"You know that I'll never be able to take you home again to reconcile with my father while you insist on wearing that outfit. He will not take you or what you're doing in business seriously. Don't you think that I want to take you home and proudly show you off and prove what he thought about you wrong?"

"Michelle I like you, in fact I like you a great deal but I'm not going to change who I am just so that your father can give me some kind of approval," Ricky said sternly.

"So you don't care that you insisting on being a Teddy Boy is putting a strain on me and our relationship?" Michelle said.

"Are you saying that me being happy and comfortable with who and what I am is making you unhappy?" Ricky said.

"I didn't say that!" Michelle said harshly as she digested his words.

"It sounded like it to me, Michelle. I want us to be a couple and I'd like to build on where we are, but at no point will I compromise who I am to fit in with someone else's view of normal. That is not going to happen and I would like now to park up this conversation and not spoil a perfectly good evening," Ricky said as he beckoned Wendy over and ordered another malt whiskey.

The couple left shortly after. Ricky had suggested that they take a wander down Carnaby Street before heading back home, but Michelle was adamant that she needed to get back for an early start in the morning. Ricky asked if she would be staying over at his apartment and said that he would organise a taxi in the morning to take her home, but she declined saying that she had a bit of a headache. The taxi dropped her at the end of her road."

"I hope that it all goes as you expect tomorrow Ricky," Michelle said and then kissed him on the cheek and closed the taxi door.

***

It was 3.00am and Terry and Steve Parker had driven over to the address that Ricky had given them. They parked the stolen Jaguar XJ6 destined for Africa a few doors down. Terry handed his brother a black ski mask and a small axe. Steve tucked the handle in his belt and got out of the car. Terry picked up his own small axe and got out of the car. They avoided walking under the street light and carefully opened the gate and walked up the garden path. Terry took out a bank card and ran it between the door and the door frame. The door opened. Terry and Steve entered the house gingerly and pulled the ski masks over their heads. They looked at each other, nodded, and with the axes held firmly in their hands they proceeded to walk up the stairs. Terry led the way. He quietly opened the first door only to find the bed was empty. The second door was the bathroom. The third door was slightly ajar. Terry entered the room and looked down on the sleeping man. He sat himself gently down onto the side of the bed while Steve turned on the bedside lamp. The sleeping man shuffled around a little and began to snort and snore. Steve pointed to an open adult girlie magazine with Mary Millington spread across the centre pages that had been left on the opposite side of the bed. With the axe firmly held in his right hand Terry began to gently shake the man's shoulder. He increased the firmness of each shake until the man groaned and tried to turn over. Terry took a firm grip of his upper arm and shook hard until the man turned back and slowly opened his eyes.

"Hello Matt," Steve said, gently patting the back of the axe's blade into the palm of his hand.

The man sat bolt upright and pushed himself back against his padded headboard.

"What's going on?" Matt stuttered while rubbing his tired eyes.

"Nice magazine," Steve said.

"Take it," Matt whimpered. "Take anything you want, just don't hurt me."

Terry lifted his axe and placed the blade gently against Matt's cheek.

"Matt, unfortunately you have upset a friend of ours and believe me, this friend does not like to be upset," Terry said calmly.

"I don't know what I've done!" Matt pleaded as he tried to push himself further back into the headboard.

"You were made a very fair offer for your business," Terry said.

"Is this Ricky? The bastard has no right to tell me what to do," Matt said, becoming a little more assertive.

"You, Matt, don't get to ask any fucking questions," Steve said as he gripped his axe tighter and took a step forward.

"Okay, okay I'm sorry," Matt said as he looked up at the two masked men wielding axes.

"Let me cut this bastard," Steve said.

"No, no please don't hurt me," Matt pleaded.

"Nick, my friend here, is aching to use his new axe and I am so very tempted to just let him go to work on you because I don't like difficult people either and you just ooze being one difficult, awkward, bastard," Terry said.

"I'm not, please, what do you want?" Matt pleaded.

"Listen to me Matt, and listen very carefully," Terry said, stroking Matt's cheek with the blade. "Tomorrow you will go into work and agree to sell your share of the company. If you do not do exactly as I say then we will be back. It might not be tomorrow, the day after, next week, next month or even next year, but come back we will and there will be no reasonable conversation, just a lot of hacking, cutting and chopping. Am I making myself clear?"

Matt nodded.

"Answer the man!" Terry yelled as he lurched forward with a thrust of his axe that stopped just a few inches from his forehead.

"Yes, yes I understand. I will sell the company," Matt muttered through the tears that were now streaming down his frightened face.

"If you tell anybody, that's the police, your business partner or even a trusted family member about our visit tonight, then you know what will happen. We do not give second chances Matt, remember that when you start to feel brave after we've left," Terry said.

"I won't say anything to anyone, ever," Matt whimpered.

"Good," Terry said.

"Yeah good," Steve said. "If you don't mind, I'll be taking that magazine. Good looking sort that Mary Millington."

Both Steve and Terry stood up. They looked down at Matt's cowering body and gently nodded their axes before leaving the bedroom and the house. Matt, in a state of shock, remained in the same position for over an hour with his eyes fixed firmly on the bedroom door.

Terry called Ricky at his home at 7.00am and simply said that the negotiations were successful.

Chapter 14

Ronnie the landlord placed a tray of lagers on the table.

"Cheers, Ronnie," Ricky said as he handed Ronnie a five pound note.

"What time did they say they'd be here?" Bill asked.

"Anytime soon," Ricky said.

"Did they say what it was about?" Kenny said.

"No, not really. They only said that they needed help with a group of lads in North London. The Temple Drive Teds were amongst the first to sign up with Deano and the Ted Army which is why they reached out to us," Ricky said.

"How many Teds do they have?" Bill asked as he reached for his pint.

"About twenty or so," Ricky said.

"So, they're a decent sized mob," Bill said.

"They're pretty handy lads from what I remember Deano saying," Kenny said.

"Interesting," Steve said.

'Aria' by Acker Bilk was playing on the jukebox when the door opened and the two Temple Drive Teds from Islington entered the pub. Ricky looked up and waved them over. As they approached the table Ricky stood up.

"I'm Ricky Turrell."

"Good to finally meet you Ricky. I'm Tyler and this my second in command Johnny. We were sorry to hear what happened to Deano. He was well liked and respected, not just by us but by real Teds all over London. The alliance and the Ted Army was something we immediately bought into. Not just for us, but we shared Deano's vision of a single Army of Teds when necessary. From what we hear you're still very much an advocate of the Ted Army which is why we're here," Tyler said.

"Take a seat, lads," Ricky said. "What would you like to drink?"

Ricky had Lee go to the bar and bring back two pints of lager. He then went around the table introducing Kenny, Bill, Lee, Steve and Terry Parker as his trusted inner circle.

"What's your problem?" Kenny asked.

"Straight to the point, well that suits me," Tyler said. "Today this is a local problem, but it's a problem that could affect us all in the future. I've got twenty three Teds and each and every one of them will stand up and have a row if and when required. We don't run and we don't interfere with others unless they mess with us. We were all aware of a growing group of Skinheads in Chamberlain House. About a year ago a guy called Eric 'the Hammer' Baron returned from Northern Ireland after a few years in the army. He's a hard bastard but smart. They call him the Hammer because he carries a claw hammer and has been known to use it. He pretty much took the Skinheads from just lounging about on street corners to becoming focused with direction and a hierarchy. The Hammer is about as racist as you can get and he's actively involved with the National Front. He's been out recruiting lads as young as thirteen and bringing them into the local community centre where they are being trained to fight and force fed right-wing ideology. The Hammer expanded his reach out to the North Side Boot Boys and the Borough Bovver Boys. Initially they were allies but its more than that now as the orders are flowing directly from him. He's becoming a bit of an icon and has even taken some Punks into his ranks. He's not the biggest of lads but you'll recognise him immediately because he has a swastika tattoo on his neck. You have to believe me when I say he's forging a fighting force beyond just another street gang. The Hammer is building what he's calling the 'White Boy Nation'. This is something that could rival the Ted Army in time," Tyler said.

"What kind of numbers do they have today?" Ricky said.

"I would say two hundred if not two hundred and fifty lads," Tyler said.

"That's serious numbers," Lee said.

"They'll bleed just like everyone else," Terry said.

"Have they had any run-ins with old bill?" Bill said.

"The Hammer has lads out robbing shops, burgling off the manor and bringing back the cash to fund his vision. The old bill have driven past, taken a look in, but with crime at an all-time low they're pretty much being ignored," Tyler said before taking a long sip of his drink.

"I'm not sure why you're bringing the problem to us," Lee said.

"It's like I said, we don't interfere with who does what in the area as long as they leave us alone. We have our pub, just like you guys, and we have our music, and a landlord that was a Teddy Boy himself back in the day, so he's sweet with late night lock ins and running a tab for when the lads are a bit skint. Anyway, the Hammer and several of his lads have turned up and told the landlord to turf us out because he wants the pub for his lads. None of us were about to take that sitting down, so we decided to front them up at the community centre. We heard that the Hammer would be there so we got tooled up and decided to hit him and any right-wing Skinhead that stood in our way. Well, word must have got back to him because when we came charging through the doors there must have been a fucking hundred if not a hundred and fifty Skinheads waiting for us. We were outnumbered five, if not six, to one. Now I'll have a row with the best of them but we were never going to win against that lot," Tyler said.

"What happened?" Kenny asked.

"I didn't want my lads getting hurt, so I fronted up the Hammer and challenged him to a one on one straightener with the victor getting the pub," Tyler said.

"Fair play," Terry said.

"He wasn't having none of it. We were told in no uncertain terms to fuck off somewhere else or suffer the consequences. Then, and would you believe this, he broke into some kind of sales pitch and tried, with success I should add, to recruit some of our lads into his ranks."

"Cheeky bastard," Kenny said.

"Smart, very smart," Ricky said. "Are you sure about this 'White Boy Nation'?"

"Yeah, he's taken to having leaflets dropped around the area about non-whites being responsible for crimes and job losses and that it was time to rise up and that young white patriots should seek out the 'White Boy Nation.'

"This is a bigger problem than I initially thought," Ricky said. "That doesn't mean that it can't be handled, only it'll take more time, numbers and planning."

"Are you with us then?" Tyler said.

Ricky looked around the table and then back to Tyler.

"This is exactly the kind of problem that Deano foresaw, and why he set about creating the Ted Army. We're in, but it won't be a quick fix," Ricky said as he shook his head. "Like I said this will take time, numbers and planning. In the meantime you'll need to manage things at a local level."

"Thank you," Tyler said as he shook the hands of all those around the table.

"What's the next step?" Tyler said.

"You can leave this problem with me now and I'll keep you posted. So, not a word to anyone, okay?" Ricky said as he handed Lee a ten pound note. "Can you sort some drinks mate?"

Chapter 15

Ricky and Nigel met at a sandwich shop close to the business solicitor's office. Ricky ordered two coffees.

"I don't know what you said to Matt, Ricky, but he was in early and keen to get the business sale underway. The last time I saw him that enthusiastic was when we opened our second branch. This is like a huge weight being lifted off my shoulders. I'm pleased to see the back of Matt, have some cash to start my property investment business, and work with you," Nigel said.

"Maybe he just took some time to really think it through," Ricky said.

"Well whatever it was, it's done now. In a couple of hours, you'll be the proud new owner of N&M tyres," Nigel said.

"It won't be retaining the name, Nigel. The business will be re-branded as London Tyre Co. I want the same uniform branding across all three depots right down to the overalls the lads will be wearing," Ricky said. "There is another thing."

"What you don't want or need me now?" Nigel said.

"Far from it," Ricky said with a broad grin. "I want to appoint you as Managing Director while you oversee the transition. I have a manager lined up and ready to step in and it's then that I want you to drive all the strategic changes. It'll involve working closely with me and we will get it done."

"Managing Director?" Nigel said. "But what role will you take?"

"I'll be the CEO, Chief Executive Officer. While you're driving our business plans I'll be looking for acquisitions, building supplier relationships and networking the industry. This is just the beginning, Nigel. You can stay on for the twelve months as we've agreed, or you can choose to stay and help me build a substantial business right across London," Ricky said.

"I didn't see that coming," Nigel said. "Look, let's get this deal and the rebranding complete then we can have another conversation."

"It's your choice Nigel. There's no pressure," Ricky said before looking down at his watch. "Shall we go and get this deal over the line?"

Nigel nodded.

The deal was signed and sealed dead on 5.00pm. Nigel returned to N&M tyres with two large envelopes full of cash for him and Matt, plus a cheque for each of them. Ricky was now the proud owner of four tyre depots and decided that he would call in to the Arms for a celebratory drink. On the way back to Milton Road Estate, he spotted a nearly new Jaguar XJC Coupe finished in Indigo Blue with white wall tyres in the window of an upmarket car showroom.

"Damn that motor looks the business," Ricky thought." Maybe it's time to get rid of the Rover, maybe even the Mustang V8 powered MK2 Zodiac. It's been in the garage for months now and I've just not had the time or inclination to take her out and tear up some tarmac. That Jaguar with the V12 engine just sits so low on its beefed-up suspension. The colour and the lines of the pillarless coupes are absolutely beautiful."

Ricky resisted the temptation to take a closer look. His funds had been depleted and he needed the cash he had for rebranding the branches and increasing the much needed tyre stock in all three branches.

"It's not for today but I will have one," Ricky thought.

***

The Arms was buzzing with people lined up along the bar two deep and most of the tables were taken. Ricky looked over at the jukebox where Melanie, Kaz and Donna were chatting together and feeding the machine coins. *'Dancing Queen'* by Abba was playing with Kaz and Donna jigging back and forth as they looked down at the playlist.

Ronnie looked over at Ricky and raised his glass.

"Malt whiskey is it Ricky, or a Carlsberg?" Ronnie said.

"I'll have a pint when you're ready Ronnie," Ricky said, "And whatever the others are drinking including the girls."

Ronnie nodded and pulled down a pint glass.

Everyone was in. Bill, Kenny, Lee, Steve, Terry and a couple of the other lads. The pub was buzzing. News of the violence that had occurred up on Bedford Estate was common knowledge around the estate. Ricky's reputation had been well and truly reinforced as leader of the Milton Road Teds and a senior figure on the estate. Ricky had been impressed with how Bill had handled himself. He was fearless and led part of the charge. Any doubts about the validity of Bill arriving back on the estate were quickly diminished when he led part of the bloody violent charge on the Bedford Boot Boys.

Ricky took up his seat at the end of the bar as one of Ronnie's new barmen brought over a tray of drinks.

"You're new?" Ricky said.

"Er, yes," the barman said.

"I'm Ricky Turrell, what's your name?" Ricky said.

"I know who you are Ricky. Everybody on the Estate does. I'm Rod. I lived in the same block as you when you were at home with your mum and dad. Your mum, Caroline, used to give me sweets when I was playing outside with the other kids," Rod said.

"Well it's good to meet you Rod. I'm trying to remember you but I'm struggling," Ricky said.

"I was just a kid but I remember the first time I saw you in your drape suit. I remember thinking back then that I would be a Ted when I grew up. That probably sounds pretty silly now," Rod said.

"Not at all," Ricky said. "I felt the same way when I first clapped eyes on Deano the Dog and this lot. Would you do me a favour Rod?"

"Sure, anything," Rod said.

"Would you take these drinks over to the girls by the jukebox?" Ricky said, pointing towards Melanie, Kaz and Donna.

"Yeah, of course," Rod said.

"Ricky put a ten-pound note on the tray. "Get yourself one Rod."

"Cheers Ricky," Rod said.

"Oi, Rod, get a move on, I've got thirsty customers that need serving!" Ronnie called out.

"Two minutes Ronnie," Rod called back as he raced over to the girls.

"You To Me Are Everything' by The Real Thing was playing as the girls joined them at the table. Kaz was beaming as she sat by Bill. Ricky spotted her squeeze his hand below the table. Bill suddenly looked very serious when Pip Foster strode through the pub's doors.

***

Pip Foster was born in Lambeth and moved down to the Milton Road Estate with his wife, Irene, when it was first built. Pip was a thief and a career criminal. He had only held one job after leaving school which was working in a meat factory alongside Buster Edwards. It wasn't too long before cuts of meat were disappearing and being sold around the area. Buster moved on to working alongside Bruce Reynolds, doing armed robberies and then the Great Train Robbery. Pip never progressed beyond petty theft but after the Great Train Robbery he made out to everyone that would listen that he and Buster were tight. He served several short sentences for burglary and breaking into warehouses, but never made the big time. In the Foster household it was either feast or famine. When business wasn't so good it would have been Double Bubble, the money lender, that would see him through to the next score. With Double Bubble out of the way Pip had borrowed money from Bill.

"Ricky, that bastard owes me money," Bill whispered. "I lent him a hundred quid three weeks ago and he's been avoiding me."

"What do you want to do about it?" Ricky said.

"Front him up," Bill said.

"Well don't look at me. It's your business," Ricky said.

Bill got up, pushed his way passed Kenny and Lee and strutted over to Pip who was now standing at the bar having a conversation with Rod the new barman.

SMACK!

Bill threw a right hander that sent Pip sprawling back against the bar.

Rod, wide-eyed, jumped back from the counter.

SMACK!

The second punch put Pip on his back.

People around the pub stopped talking with all heads facing the confrontation. The only sound to be heard was the chart hit, *'Mississippi'* by Pussycat.

"You owe me!" Bill shrieked as he bent down and grabbed Pip by the scruff of his neck.

"You've no idea who you're messing with," Pip muttered.

SMACK! SMACK!

Pip's head rocked back and forth with the ferocity of each punch.

"I don't care if you're a reincarnation of Jack fucking Dempsey. You owe me!" Bill said forcefully.

"Alright, alright," Pip said as he tried to hold his right hand up. "I've got about a hundred quid in my pocket.

Bill let him go and forced his hand into Pip's pocket and pulled out a wad of cash. With his knee firmly placed on Pip's chest he counted out the money.

"There's two hundred and thirty quid here and you still owe me," Bill said.

"Oh, come on Bill that's all I've got to my name," Pip pleaded. "Look, I've got this nice little tickle on next week. It should be good for a grand if not more. Let me have a hundred back and I'll double it next week."

Bill peeled off three ten pound notes.

"Here's thirty quid to put food on the table and you still owe me. Don't try and avoid me again, Pip, or next time I will hurt you," Bill said as he threw the money at Pip and got back on his feet.

"Sure, sure," Pip said. "I'll find you Bill."

People in the pub began to continue with their conversations. As Bill turned and walked back to Ricky he was motioned over to the bar by Ronnie.

"Bill, a quiet word in your shell like. If you want to start making an example of people in my bar then, out of respect, you speak to me first. Ricky might give you the go-ahead as top dog on the Estate but this is my bar and some of that money in Pip's pocket was coming my way. I don't want you to forget that," Ronnie said.

"Understood," Bill said. "My apologies Ronnie, can I get you and the staff a drink?"

"Yeah, we'll have large brandies," Ronnie said.

Bill returned to the table and sat next to Kaz.

"Sorry about that," Bill whispered to Kaz.

"If he didn't pay then he had it coming," Kaz said.

"Well sorted," Kenny said.

"Isn't Pip best mates with Buster Edwards and the Great Train Robbers or something?" Lee said.

"So what?" Bill said.

Kathy the Candle had been sitting at the bar chatting to Ronnie between him serving customers. Her head turned sharply as her gaze followed Doreen across the pub. Doreen began to chatting to Melanie. Kathy fidgeted on her stool and then got up and walked over to the jukebox. She reached down and pulled the plug out. The music came to an abrupt halt. Melanie, Doreen and the girls turned to see what had happened to their selection of music. Kathy put the plug back into the wall and the lights on the jukebox came back on but the back log of paid for songs were lost. Kathy placed a coin into the machine and made a selection. She turned and faced Doreen. *'Double Barrel'* by Dave and Ansell Collins began to play.

"Is that bitch having a pop at us or what?" Kenny said. "That's a Skinhead song."

"It was also a record that was in the charts before she got banged up for GBH," Lee said.

"Yeah, right I suppose so."

"Kathy the Candle is playing a psychological game here," Ricky thought. *"She's letting Doreen know that she wants in on the shoplifting. Clever move, it's a warning."*

Chapter 16

Ricky had reserved a conference suite at the Aerodrome Hotel on the Purley Way. He had invited management and staff from both N&M Tyres and London Tyre Co to meet with him at 6.30pm. Ricky had decided not to wear a drape suit and selected a pair of black trousers and a light blue shirt from Marks & Spencer. The taxi arrived on time and had Ricky at his destination with time to spare. The receptionist greeted him and told him that people had already arrived. Ricky felt a little nervous and yet was excited to be talking to his new, extended team. He took a deep breath and entered the conference suite.

As he entered all eyes were on him. He smiled, disguising any nervousness he had, and walked straight over to greet Nigel Chambers, the former partner of N&M Tyres. The two men walked up onto the small stage area and looked out on the mix of thirty-three managers, telesales staff and tyre fitters. The chatter subsided and Ricky stepped forward.

"For those who don't know me, my name is Ricky Turrell. I'm the owner of London Tyre Co and have just completed the acquisition of N&M Tyres. This, for those in London Tyres, is Nigel Chambers, who will be the Managing Director of the new combined business. Now I know that there will be those in the room that have worked with the Nationals who will be concerned about their roles and possible redundancies. Let me be very clear," Ricky said as he turned to face each and every person in the room. "There will no job losses. Far from it; this is step one of a much bigger plan. Acquiring existing companies in an industry allows the business to build on the strengths and capture synergies and most importantly grow market share quickly and leverage an advantage over our joint competitors. Both businesses have a good mix of trade and retail business and there is tremendous scope to build further on that. Nigel will be overseeing the rebranding of N&M tyres to a uniform London Tyre Co. Each location will have the same livery, overalls, trading practices and the same terms and conditions. As the business grows, let me make this very clear to every person in the room. You have the opportunity to grow with this new business. You might be fitting tyres today and then managing your own depot as we grow. I do not care about bits of paper that you were given at school. What Nigel and I are looking for is a work ethic, the ability to deliver to all our customers quality branded tyres with an unrivalled service and at prices that keep bringing those customers back. The driving ethos is Quality, Service and Price and those who consistently deliver that to all our customers will be rewarded financially and with career advancement. Unlike the Nationals, you are more than a number on an accountant's spread sheet. Does anyone have any questions?"

Doughnut's hand shot up. "Ricky, will you still be with the business?"

"Absolutely, I will be working on strategic objectives that will reduce prices, increase our market share, and profits and I'll be out hunting for more businesses to acquire. Nigel is a very experienced business manager and has my every confidence that he will bring the combined businesses together to our agreed timetable.

"Hello Ricky, I'm Phil Green, Manager of South Croydon. Will we able to increase our stock of tyres?"

"That's a good question Phil, thank you," Ricky. "Nigel and I will be reviewing stock levels at each location to ensure that future sales are not lost. In the meantime, I would encourage you to call managers from other depots and that includes London Tyre Co when your fast-moving stocks run low.

"I have two Nationals close to me and I know that we could run circles around them if I could bring on experienced fitters and market ourselves better," Phil Green said.

"Barry is my Manager at London Tyre Co, maybe he could answer that for you," Ricky said.

Barry stood up and cleared his throat.

"I'm Barry and I manage London Tyre Co. Previously I was an assistant manager with a National that had made countless empty promises about promotion. I met with Ricky and he appointed me as manager immediately. I brought with me two of the best fitters in the industry, in my opinion. They will both make excellent managers one day. Ricky created a marketing plan that increased both the bread and butter trade sales and the very profitable retail business. We are as busy on a Monday as we are on a Friday now. Ricky has introduced something he calls key performance indicators and we measure the business performance by it. I'm proud to say that as a team we have beaten everyone and continue to grow. I would suggest, Phil that you make notes, create a plan for South Croydon and meet with Ricky and Nigel, and if the numbers stack up then you will get the support you need to beat your competitors."

"Thank you, Barry," Phil said. "I look forward to working with you and presenting my plan to both Ricky and Nigel."

"Ricky," Doughnut called. "Will I continue to be out on the road generating trade business?"

Ricky smiled.

"I told you that I would have something else for you. Nigel's new role leaves the position of Branch Manager open. As promised, it's yours if you'd prefer that to being a sales representative," Ricky said.

Doughnut was beaming.

"I would very much like that," Doughnut said with the broadest of smiles.

"Good, then please make an appointment to meet with Nigel. So," Ricky said as he addressed everybody in the room. "That leaves an opportunity for a trade sales representative. Can potential applicants please contact Nigel Chambers. Nigel, would you like to say a few words?"

"Yes, I would, Thank you Ricky. I enjoyed building N&M Tyres to a successful business with three depots. As we were, it was never going to be the kind of size that we should have been, but now with Ricky and bringing N&M tyres into London Tyre Co, I'm excited about the future and creating opportunities for those that work hard and deserve them. I'm looking forward to working with all of you," Nigel said.

Ricky looked down at his watch and then addressed the team

"If you would like to follow us down to the bar, we can celebrate our merger until we're called in for dinner," Ricky said.

The team all got up from their chairs and began talking. Ricky watched as Phil strolled straight over to Barry and shook his hand.

"Excellent," Ricky thought. *"That's exactly the kind of synergy that I had in mind. I want these lads working together to not just beat the Nationals but massacre them. In our little corner of London I want our competition losing sales and their good people to us. That's the disillusioned management and fitters."*

Chapter 17

Ricky reached into his wardrobe and took out his pale blue drape suit with the royal blue velvet collar, cuffs and pocket tops. He slid it over his white silk shirt and adjusted his bootlace tie with the crossed Colt hand guns. He stepped back and looked at his reflection in the mirror.

"Yeah, not bad Ricky," Ricky thought. *"A Beano down to Margate is a welcome break in the action. You deserve this, a few drinks with your mates, sun, sea and sand. It'll be fun. Bloody gutted that Michelle couldn't make it. We seem to be drifting apart and I know it's probably as much my fault as hers. Anyway, it's a Beano, so liven yourself up! Upwards and onwards."*

Ricky dabbed a touch of Brylcreem onto his fingers and ran it through his hair. With his steel comb he combed it back off his face.

"This bit of grief with the right-wing Skinheads in North London is a right result and couldn't have come at a better time," Ricky thought. *"It's exactly what I need to bring the Ted Army together against a common enemy. We're going to give this lot a right proper seeing to. I need to lead these boys to a victory that will have every Ted in London talking."*

Ricky heard a car toot its horn outside so he went to the bedroom window and saw it was the taxi he'd booked the night before. Ricky pulled back the net curtain and waved then grabbed a bundle of notes and his brass knuckleduster from his bedside drawer.

"You never know," Ricky thought.

Ricky sat on the corner of the bed and slipped on his blue suede brothel creepers and then checked his reflection for the last time.

He bounded down the stairs, pulled the door open and ran over to the waiting taxi.

"Hello mate," Ricky said as he climbed into the taxi. "Can you take me to the Milton Arms?"

"Is that on the Milton Road Estate?" the driver asked as he pulled away.

"You've got it," Ricky said, sitting back in the seat and putting his seat belt on.

"You're starting early aren't you?" the driver said as looked over and smiled.

"Nah, Ronnie the landlord has organised a Beano to Margate," Ricky said.

"Well you've certainly got the weather for it. They were saying on the television last night that this heat wave is here to stay for some time yet," the driver said. "My old woman has been going on at me about a long weekend away on the South Coast or a week down in Cornwall. I told her in the taxi game you just don't know how it's going to go, so while it's busy I've got to keep at it. The bills don't stop rolling in, month in and month out," the driver said.

"It'll be a shame to waste this great weather though, mate. Maybe meet her half way with a long weekend down in Brighton or something," Ricky said.

"Maybe, what game are you in?" the driver said.

"Tyres. I'm in the tyre game. Here," Ricky said reaching into his inside pocket and handing the driver a business card. "I'm Ricky Turrell. If you have a puncture or need new tyres you come down and see me and I'll look after you. I have deals with loads of taxi drivers."

"Cheers," the driver said as he looked down at the card. "We can go through a set of tyres in a year. I'm Tony"

"Like I said, Tony, if you just ask for me or Barry, my manager, you will be looked after."

As the taxi approached the Milton Arms, Ricky could see the Coach parked up outside and people milling around. The driver stopped behind the coach. Ricky pulled out a wad of notes from his pocket and handed the driver a fiver. The driver reached down to the centre console to give Ricky his change.

"Keep the change mate. Get your wife a bunch of flowers or something," Ricky said as he got out of the car.

Ricky stopped and looked at the crowd of people outside the pub. He immediately saw Lee, Kenny, Terry and Steve all dressed in their Ted gear, and Donna, Melanie, and Bill talking to Kaz. Ronnie was running around organising things with Kathy the Candle traipsing around behind him.

"Looking good Ricky," Lee said, stepping back and admiring the drape suit.

"Not looking too bad yourself, Lee," Ricky said.

Kenny had Doreen and several ladies from the estate around him. Ricky and Lee could hear him holding court.

"See now most of you don't know this, but I've actually been training as a magician for some time," Kenny said as he took a short bow.

"Leave it out," Doreen said with a chuckle.

"No, really Doreen. Now, would I kid a kidder?"

All the ladies laughed.

"So who has a handkerchief?" Kenny said as he scoured the small crowd around him.

"There you go," Kathy the Candle said as she joined the group.

"Thank you, Kathy, or do I call you Candle?" Kenny said, raising his eyebrows.

The crowd of ladies chuckled when they saw that Kathy was smiling.

Kenny held up the handkerchief for everyone to see and then folded it in half and then in half again.

"I think he's going to turn it into a white dove," Doreen said, making the ladies laugh again.

Kenny held up the folded handkerchief and folded it one last time before holding up his right closed hand. Then slowly he began to push the handkerchief through the tight space between his clamped fingers.

"You'll never get a dove out of there," one the ladies said, which kept them all laughing.

Kenny pushed the last of handkerchief between his tightly clamped fingers. He held his hand up for everyone to see and then slowly circled a finger over it before bringing his hand up to his face and then... he opened his hand and blew his nose into the handkerchief.

"Ta da!" Kenny said, presenting Kathy the snot stained handkerchief with both outstretched hands.

Several of the ladies burst out laughing whilst other screwed up their faces and turned away.

"Why you dirty..." Kathy yelled as she made a playful swing at him with her handbag.

Kenny quickly dived out of the way and was still beaming from the practical joke. He put his thumb on his nose and wriggled his fingers at her.

"Kenny seems to be back on form," Ricky said.

"Yeah, he sacked Denise a couple of days ago and has moved in with me. He's well out of it and to be honest it's good to see the old Kenny back, even if he does get on your tits sometimes," Lee said.

"What about the kiddie?" Ricky said as he watched Kenny joking around with the ladies.

"He's going to pay his way but he's not doing the whole under the thumb 'you'll do what I say' bit. Within just a few hours it was like watching this huge weight lift off him. I suppose some blokes just aren't cut out for the whole living together or marriage game," Lee said.

"What about you, Lee?" Ricky said, turning back and facing him.

"What do you mean?" Lee said.

"You've not been yourself for a while. It hasn't gone unnoticed mate and I was just waiting for the right time to ask the question," Ricky said.

Lee took a deep breath and then looked around and lowered his voice.

"I've put a girl in the family way," Lee said, closing his eyes and shaking his head slowly.

"Oh, shit. Are you sure?" Ricky said.

"Yeah, I'm sure. I spoke to Melanie, Kaz and Donna about it the night Deano was killed at the Cadillac Club. Kaz and Donna went around to see her to make sure, you know," Lee said.

"How do you feel about it?" Ricky said.

"Mate it was a one-night stand. I was out at a party and this bird is coming on to me so I just did the deed in the bathroom. It wasn't even that good because people were bashing the bloody door down wanting to use the toilet," Lee said. "I didn't see her again and to be honest I didn't give her a second thought until she's come knocking on the door telling me that she's up the duff with a bun in the oven."

"What are you going to do?" Ricky said.

"We're talking. And look, if I am the dad, of course I'll pay my way, but I can't go getting married like my old man did to mum when she got up the duff with me. He's a miserable bastard and I don't want to end up like him or how Kenny has been. The bird, Trish, is saying things like she loves me and how she thinks we would be great parents. Ricky, that's not for me. If I marry someone it has to be because we truly love each other. Not because I was stupid enough not to wear something on a one-night stand," Lee said as he put his hands in his pockets.

"Do you think that might change when the baby comes along?" Ricky said.

"That's the thing mate. I just don't know. I'm not even sure if I'm ready to be a dad yet. I still like stupid stuff and hanging around with you lot, getting into scrapes and having a bloody good time. I just can't see me trading all that for sleepless nights with some bird that I don't really know," Lee said.

"You have time, mate so don't go making any rash decisions," Ricky said.

"I won't. Please keep this to yourself. I'm just not ready to be answering questions to all and sundry," Lee said.

"Not a word, Lee," Ricky said. "Anyway, park all that up today and have some fun mate. We're on a Beano!"

"Alright, alright, can I have you rowdy lot's attention," Ronnie called out as he waved his arms above his head.

Everyone fell silent.

"Right, firstly thank you to everyone who signed up to the first of our annual Beano's to the coast. As you know we're travelling down to Margate on the South Coast. It's now just after seven and the coach driver tells me that it'll take three and a half hours with a thirty minute stop at the Motorway services. You all know Kathy," Ronnie said pointing to Kathy who was holding a clipboard. "I've asked her to keep a written record of everyone here because we don't want to go leaving anyone behind. If you find yourself lost while we're there, just ask a taxi driver to take you to the 'Jolly Dog' pub next door to Dreamland. One of us will be there all day and ideally, we'd like to be back on the road and heading home by 8.30pm.

"Any chance of a nightcap when we get back?" Bill called.

"Of course," Ronnie said, "That's when the party starts!"

Several of the locals cheered and began to board the coach

"Alright Ricky," Kenny said as he passed him with his arm around Donna's shoulders.

"Yes mate, catch you later," Ricky said.

"Ricky mate, how are you?" Bill said, holding out his hand.

Ricky shook it.

"Ricky, alright," Kaz said as she passed them. "I'll save you a place next to me Bill."

Melanie and Donna held back a few people from getting on until Kaz caught them up. Melanie looked and waved to Ricky.

"So are you and Kaz an item now?" Ricky said.

"Yeah, we've been keeping it low key for a while but yeah, she's fun and a great laugh to be around," Bill said.

"Yeah, Kaz is a sweetheart Bill. I'm pleased for you," Ricky said.

One by one everybody boarded the coach with Kathy placing a tick by each of their names. Ricky went to the back of the coach and sat by Terry and Steve. The group were spread out but the air was filled with loud, excitable, chatter. The coach door closed and Kathy sat next to Ronnie. Just as the driver began to pull away, Doreen stood up and shouted 'Stop!" The driver hit the brakes hard, sending everyone lurching forward. Ricky looked out of the side window where he saw Neil, red faced, and panting as he tried to catch up with the coach. The door opened and Neil climbed on board. Everyone cheered as Neil took several bows. He waved at Ricky and then sat down next to Doreen.

Within half an hour the coach was on the Motorway and Ricky was looking out of the window at the large open fields.

"Here Ricky, do you think Ronnie is at it with Kathy?" Terry said.

"I never thought about it," Ricky said.

"It's just nasty. I can't imagine anyone wanting to slip her a length," Terry said.

"I would have thought Ronnie was too cool to be sorting that," Steve said.

"She's probably just trying to hang around with someone. I mean she's not the most popular person on the estate," Ricky said.

"Tell you what Bruv," Terry said. "I wouldn't shag her with yours!"

Ronnie stood up and started handing out tins of Carlsberg lager.

"Pass them back, that's it Kenny, keep passing them back. Don't worry, you won't get left out," Ronnie said with a laugh.

Ricky cracked open his tin of lager and began to take large gulps from the chilled can. There was a crackle from the speaker above the seat and then *'Silly Love Songs'* by Wings began to play. Ricky watched as Kenny gulped down his can and then immediately opened a second. He got up and staggered down the coach and had a word with Ronnie.

"It's good to see Kenny back to being his old self," Ricky thought.

"The speaker crackled again, then cleared as *'Runaround Sue'* by Dion and the Belmonts began to play. Kenny picked up the microphone by the driver and started singing along at the top of his voice. With the alcohol flowing and the girls passing around bottles of Blue Nun and Black Tower wine, almost everyone began to join in with the sing-a-long. Kenny was thrusting his hips back and forth, waving his arms and belting out the lyrics like he was a young Elvis Presley playing to a sold-out venue in Wembley.

Ricky sang along too. He looked over at Bill and Kaz who were both happily singing. Bill was taking sips from his can while Kaz drank wine from the open bottle. Ricky was impressed with how Bill had made light work of Pip the thief who hadn't paid what was owed, and how quick he was to stand alongside him and the Milton Road Teds over the graffiti disrespecting Deano on the pub wall. Ricky was beginning to see why Deano had befriended him and how they had become good friends. He had decided to cut him slack and being away on the Beano was an opportunity for them to become better acquainted.

The coach driver started to slow down and drove into the Motorway service station. He parked up and Ronnie picked up the microphone.

"This is a thirty-minute stop so get yourself some breakfast and if don't have any, pick up some suntan lotion as it's looking like another scorcher!" Ronnie said.

The coach doors opened and everyone began to file out and make their way into the service station. The queue for breakfast moved quickly with a great number of people complaining about the cost and the size of the portion. Kenny joined Ricky and Lee. His plate was piled up with four eggs, four sausages, two slices of bacon, two half cut grilled tomatoes and a portion of dodgy looking bubble and squeak. He told the lads that he was starving and doubled up to help soak up all the beer he planned on drinking. The lads laughed as he enthusiastically shovelled down the food. Both Ricky and Lee left their bubble and squeak, so Kenny reached over and scraped their leftovers onto his own plate. With ten minutes to spare they made their way back to the coach.

"The last time we went to Margate was with Deano back in 1974 to see Bill Haley and his Comets. Do you remember that, Kenny?"

"Yeah, that was a right good crack. All mobbed up to see one of the originals. I don't think you were about then Ricky," Kenny said, rubbing his stomach.

"Nah, that was just a bit before my time or I would have been there," Ricky said.

"Bloody hell, my guts are playing up," Kenny said.

"I'm not surprised with what you've just put away," Ricky said as they filed onto the coach.

"Lager," Kenny called out reaching down to the box on Ronnie's seat. "I need more lager!"

The coach set back off again in good time with *'Don't Go Breaking My Heart'* by Elton John and Kiki Dee playing. The coach turned off the A2 dual carriageway into Canterbury and followed the ring road until it picked up the A28 which would lead straight through to Margate on the coast. Ricky had noticed that Kenny had stood up to rub his stomach as if in some pain and then sat back down. He did this several times. Finally, as the coach crossed over the railway crossing, Kenny stood up in the aisle with his hands on his hips and with one eye closed and gritted teeth, he let rip.

PPPPPPPPFFFFFFFFFRRRRRRRRTTTTTTTT!!!!!!!

The bus fell silent with just *'Jungle Rock'* by Frank Hazel playing softly.

BBBBBBBBLLLLLLLOOOOOOORRRRPPPPP!!!!

BBBBBBAAAAAAAARRRRRRRRPPPPPPPP!!!!!!

PPPPPPPLLLLLLLLOOOOOOOOORRRRRRRPPPPTTTTT!!!!

"What the fuck is that?" Kathy yelled.

BBBBBAAAAAARRRRRRRPPPPPP!!!!!

"Pee-Yew!" Doreen said, fanning her face frantically.

PPPPPPHHHHHHHAAAAAARRRRRRTTTTTT!!!!!

"That is fucking ripe! Quick, cover your nose Kaz," Bill said, fanning the air around him wildly.

BBBBBLLLLLOOOOOOORRRRPPPPTTTTT!!!!!

The deep bubbly notes and sheer lengths had all those seated around Kenny recoiling back into their seats. Some were fanning their faces while others held their breath. It was then that the putrid, pungent stench of his raunchy fart took hold.

"Has someone shit themselves?" one elderly woman from the front of the coach called.

Donna stood up. She was red faced from holding her breath.

"URRGHH! I feel sick," Donna said before gagging twice.

"Who has just died?" another passenger called out.

BBBBBBLLLLLOOOOOPPPP!!!!!

"Alright Kenny, enough is enough," Ronnie said, screwing up his face in disgust.

"Yeah sorry about that," Kenny said calmly. "Just the one more."

PPPPPPPLLLLLLLAAAAAARRRRRPPPPPP!!!!!!

"Yeah, that should do it," Kenny said with a broad grin. "No, no wait a minute. One last blast!"

PPPPLLLLLAAAAAAAARRRRRRPPPPPPTTTTTT!!!!!!

"That is well out of order!" Bill yelled, as he held Kaz's face tight into his shirt.

The toxic cloud soon covered the entire coach with everyone yelling out, fanning their faces desperately, and gagging and heaving. The coach driver pulled over to the side of the road, opened the door and raced out into the fresh air. The passengers quickly followed, passing comments to Kenny as they passed his seat.

"Yeah, I'm sorry about that but what can a bloke do?" Kenny said, shrugging his shoulders innocently and grinning.

As Ricky stepped off the coach, he saw that the driver had slumped to his knees and was gagging furiously.

"Are you alright mate?" Ricky asked, patting him on the back.

The driver looked up with blood shot eyes and a silver streak of dribble between his lower lip and chin.

"I thought her indoors was bad but that was bloody horrendous!" the driver muttered.

Ricky turned to see that the elderly lady who had first called out was sitting on a bench seat at the bus stop. She was bent forward with her head in her hands. A couple of her friends rubbed her back sympathetically.

Within fifteen minutes the pungent stench passed and the coach was making up lost time. As they passed through Westgate-on-Sea, Melanie jumped up and shouted "I can see the sea!" Everyone looked to their left as the calm, beautiful, blue sea came into view.

"Hoorah!" Kaz shouted and people began to clap enthusiastically.

The coach followed the A28 road into the heart of Margate where the driver parked up opposite the Jolly Dog pub by Dreamland.

Dreamland was an amusement park and entertainment centre based on the traditional funfair. It had been in operation since the late 1800s, and was famous for its wooden rollercoaster named the 'Scenic Railway', and the 'Astraglide, Cyclone', and '20,000 Leagues Under the Sea' rides.

Ricky stepped off the coach, closed his eyes and inhaled deeply. The smell of the sea was almost potent while its salty aroma felt inviting, pleasant and comforting, like the smell of freshly baked bread.

After almost four hours on the coach, Ricky felt relaxed, comfortable and ready to have fun. He looked out towards the beach where parents sat on deck chairs, dads read newspapers while the children ran around in their swimwear laughing and playing in the sand with buckets and spades while others kicked their beach balls, built sandcastles or explored the rock pools. His eyes were drawn to an older man in blue shorts and an open neck shirt. He was wearing a 'Kiss Me Quick' hat and was helping children onto a donkey that he was walking back and forth along the beach. The sign read that it was 25p per ride. Ricky looked up as several seagulls passed overhead squawking. The sun baked down on his face. He was beginning to regret bringing the drape jacket. To his left he saw mothers handing their children bottles of Coke and packets of crisps. There were children were waiting patiently by a large trampoline. The sign read that they could jump for ten minutes for just 10p.

"What's it to be then," Lee said before taking a deep breath of the clean sea air. "Is it the amusement arcade or straight in the pub?"

"I fancy a flutter," Ricky said.

"Yeah me too," Kenny said.

"Sounds good to me too," Bill said. "Are you coming Kaz?"

"No, I'm going to have a look around the shops with Doreen, Donna and Melanie," Kaz said.

"Are you working?" Bill asked.

Kaz nodded, winked and then skipped over to her sister.

"I'm with you boys, if that's alright," Neil said.

The lads entered the amusement arcade to the sound of *'Tequila'* by The Champs.

"Now that is more like it," Kenny said reaching into his pocket and pulling out a wad of notes, "Proper Rock 'n' Roll."

Terry and Steve played on the pool table, while Neil sat by a coin operated slot machine with a £1 jackpot. Kenny found an F1 car racing machine. He popped in the coin and gripped the steering wheel. The light came on with an image of a Formula 1 race car which he had to manoeuvre past other racers and get to the winning line without crashing. Ricky and Bill changed up their money and played pinball machines side by side.

"You're alright Bill," Ricky said. "I wasn't sure at first but, yeah, I can see how you and Deano would have been mates."

"Cheers Ricky," Bill said. "You ain't so bad yourself."

"It's good to see you wearing the Teddy Boy gear," Ricky said as he shook the machine to get the ball bearing to bounce against a bell to win him points.

"Mate, I've always loved the music. We would all go to Deano's place back in the day and just play Rock 'n' Roll and talk about what it must have been like being a Ted back in the 1950s. I feel like I'm back at home, you know, and this would have been me had I never moved. Not that I had any say in it. I was just a kid," Bill said as he frantically pressed the levers to keep the ball from falling through the slot and ending his game.

Ricky and Bill spoke for over an hour as they continued to feed the machines with coins and talk about Deano, Rock 'n' Roll and being a Ted. Neil had spent almost five pounds chasing the one-pound jackpot while Kenny had moved on to a gaming machine where the player dropped two pence pieces through a metal slide in the hope of landing them squarely between moving, coloured, lines. The prizes were two, four, six, eight and ten pence.

"I don't know about you lot but I'm off to Dreamland. I've heard a lot about the rollercoaster," Ricky said as he placed the last of the coins he had changed up into his pocket.

All the lads followed him and they met up with the girls by the 'Scenic Railway' rollercoaster. The line moved quickly and it wasn't long before they were climbing into carriages and having the bar that held the rider in place, pulled down over their lap. Ricky sat by Melanie in the third row of the front carriage. Kenny and Lee were at the front and were already holding their hands high in the air and yelling despite the ride still waiting for the final passengers to board. Directly in front of him were Bill and Kaz.

"They go well together, don't you think?" Melanie said.

"Yeah, Bill is a good bloke and Kaz, well you know that she's a sweetie," Ricky whispered.

"I'm pleased for Kaz. She's not been too lucky on the guy front," Melanie said.

Melanie leant closer to Ricky's ear and whispered.

"I always thought that it would be you and Kaz that would finally get together."

Ricky shook his head.

"She's a mate, you know. That's all," Ricky said.

"Anyway, you'd be too late now, it looks like they've really got it bad," Melanie said, nodding towards Bill and Kaz as they kissed.

The rollercoaster chugged a couple of times and then slowly began to move forward. Ricky could sense the buzz of excitement from the passengers. Slowly the ride began to gather speed towards what seemed like a vertical incline.

"You know this ride is over fifty years old," Melanie giggled.

"Oh cheers for that," Ricky said as he tightened his grip on the safety bar.

Ricky could feel himself being hypnotised by the clinking and clunking of the gears as the carriage slowly climbed up the incline. He glanced over the side to see the ride slowly but surely leaving the ground behind. He eased his grip, wriggled his fingers and then gripped the bar again, the excitement and fear building as the carriage climbed ever closer to the top. Ricky could see the summit through the gaps between Bill and Kaz. Kenny and Lee were still yelling at the top of their voices with both hands high in the air. The ride began to slow down as it reached the peak of the summit. All the chattering, yelling and jeering silenced as a rumble ricocheted through the entire length of the ride. After a couple of seconds pause, the carriage edged forward and very quickly gathered pace. Ricky could feel the wind whizzing past his face. It felt the same as when he was a child and would lean out of the rear window of his dad's car when they went off on their annual holidays to the southern coastline. The ear piercing shrills and screams from all those around him, including Melanie, only served to accelerate the adrenaline rush through his body as the carriage shook and darted sharply at each of the twists, turns and loops. On the second downhill, Ricky became consumed by all the excitement and the rapid sling shot which rocketed the carriage towards the ground. The ride finally came to a halt and everyone got out of their carriages, but Ricky felt like his body was still flying around the track. Slowly the adrenaline wore off and he had an overwhelming desire to do the ride again.

"That was brilliant!" Melanie said, looking at her watch. "It might be time to get a drink now. Are you coming?"

"I think I'm just about ready for an ice-cold Carlsberg," Ricky said as he took off his drape jacket and slung it over his shoulder, holding it with his left hand.

Ricky pushed open the door to the Jolly Dog and led everyone into the bar. They were instantly met with a cheer and raised glasses.

"This could the Milton Arms on a Friday night," Ricky thought.

"What can I get you?" the barman asked as he dried a pint jug.

Ricky took a quick look around him.

"I'll get a double round in to save queuing up," Ricky thought.

"I'll have ten pints of lager and six gin and tonics please mate," Ricky said.

"Coming right up," the barman said, reaching up for the straight pint glasses.

Ricky turned to see Doreen come out of the ladies toilets. She was walking towards Neil so he turned back to the barman.

"Make that eight gin and tonics and make them doubles," Ricky said.

The barman, with the help of a waitress, began to line the pints up on the bar along with the drinks for the ladies.

"Cheers Ricky," Bill said with the others quickly saying the same.

Melanie engaged Ricky in light conversation which had them both laughing and then suddenly, in the middle of the playful banter, they found themselves just looking at each other. Ricky broke the silence with the offer to replace her empty glass with a second one he'd already bought sitting on the bar. As he handed her the double gin and tonic he felt her hand accidentally brush against his.

"Is this what I think it is?" Ricky thought. *"Don't be silly, it can't be."*

Ricky sensed a thinly veiled sexual attraction. It wasn't enough for anyone else to notice, but something was telling him that Melanie was being a little overly friendly.

"She's had one too many," Ricky thought. *"That's easily done in this heat."*

Ricky looked over Melanie's shoulder and saw a group of seven Teddy Boys by the jukebox. One of them had just put on *'Johnny B. Goode'* by Chuck Berry. They were talking amongst themselves and then looking over at Ricky and the Milton Road Teds. A tall, well-built lad in a grey pinstripe drape jacket with black drain pipe trousers, bright green socks and black suede brothel creepers with the single chrome buckle straightened himself and started to walk towards them.

"Terry, Steve, Kenny, Lee sharpen yourselves up pronto!" Ricky hissed.

Melanie stepped to one side as the lads approached them.

"You must be the Milton Road Teds," the Ted said as he stopped directly in front of Ricky.

Ricky had casually placed his right hand inside his right trouser pocket and slipped his fingers through his brass knuckleduster.

"That's right. Who wants to know?" Ricky said firmly as his lads gathered around him.

"Mate we don't want any trouble. We heard what happened to Deano, Deano the Dog, King of the Teds and we just wanted to pay our respects and offer our condolences. Deano was well thought of in Essex. Sorry, I'm Arran Morgan and these are the Five Links Teddy Boys from Basildon."

Ricky pulled his hand out of his pocket with the knuckle duster still firmly in his fist.

"I won't be needing this then," Ricky said as he slipped his fingers out and placed it back in his pocket.

Ricky reached over and shook Arran's hand.

"It's good to meet you mate. I'm Ricky, Ricky Turrell."

"We know who you are," Arran said with a loud exaggerated laugh. "We heard about what you did to that geezer Clem Attlee and that Skinhead bloke, Clifford Tate. Very nice, very nice indeed. People were talking about that all over Essex for ages. Deano and the Milton Road Teds are legends mate. We heard a sniff about something Deano was putting together in London, the Ted Army. Is it still on, because you've got plenty who would want in and we know just about everyone?"

Ricky and Arran introduced the gangs to each other and then Ricky bought everyone a drink. The lads chatted enthusiastically about their exploits as Teddy Boys. As Arran drank his third pint, he held court with a story.

"You lot will love this. There's a bus load of us Teds from Basildon, Pitsea, Billericay and South Benfleet. There must have been about fifty of us traveling up to Copperfields in Bolton to see Showaddywaddy. It was a cracking gig. Everyone was having a really good time except for this bunch of locals. They were all Teds, but were pretty pissed off with the way the band was going. Anyway, there's this one geezer, looked like a farmer's scarecrow in a drape suit that hadn't seen an iron in a year. Well, as the band were coming off stage this geezer has fronted up Dave Bartram and started giving it to him about how the band with number one singles and albums had turned their backs on the real Teds. He was going on about them being on the front cover of some magazine or something. Hold on, Jackie, that was it. Well Dave is trying to be polite with the fella and believe me, us Essex lot would have stepped in had it got nasty. Well this twat has only gone and thrown a punch and the next thing you know Dave Bartram and the boys in the band were down there and swinging those guitars about. They were given a proper good hiding by Showaddywaddy. Fair play. They went through the roof in my estimation after that," Arran said and then took a long swig from his pint.

"Cracking bunch of lads," Ricky said. "It's good to hear they don't take no shit from idiots."

Ronnie stood up.

"Alright, Milton Road lot, the coach will be leaving in ten minutes so drink up," Ronnie called out and then sat down beside Kathy the Candle.

"It's been good meeting you Ricky, and you lads, keep up the good work," Arran said. "If you are ever in Basildon and fancy a drink, you'll find us at The Crown. We're in there Thursdays through to Saturdays most weeks."

As Ricky shook his hand he spotted Neil and Doreen kissing in the corner by the pool table. They hadn't seen that Melanie, Kaz and Karen were pointing at them as they came out of the ladies' toilets.

Kathy the Candle stood by the door of the coach with her pen and clipboard, systematically ticking everyone back on the coach. The coach trip back took a little over three hours. It stopped outside the Milton Arms and all the day trippers, without exception, stopped for a drink. Ronnie had left instructions for a full buffet to be laid out for his valued customers. Ricky and Bill chatted over several malt whiskeys deep into the early hours.

Chapter 18

Ricky pulled up and parked outside his block of apartments. He carried a small paper carrier bag of Chinese food in his right hand. As he climbed the flight of stairs he spotted Melanie standing outside his front door. She was carrying a large black bin bag.

"Hello Melanie, this is a surprise. Is everything alright? Not been black bagged have you?" Ricky chuckled.

Melanie smiled.

"No, the only person that's likely to get black bagged is your mate Neil after what he got up too with Doreen on the beano to Margate," Melanie said.

Ricky opened the front door and let them both in.

"I'm interrupting your dinner," Melanie said, looking down at the paper carrier bag.

"Not at all," Ricky said. "I always get enough for two if you'd like to join me."

"Are you sure?" Melanie said as she placed the black plastic bin liner down on the kitchen floor and looked around. "This is a lovely place."

"I'll show you about in a while. Yeah, look, I always get far too much and it either ends up in the bin or the fridge for the following day. I've got special fried rice, sweet and sour chicken balls, special fried ribs and prawn crackers. Like I said, I've got plenty if you'd like to join me," Ricky said as he took two dinner plates out of the cupboard and placed them on the kitchen worktop.

"That would be nice, thank you," Melanie said with a smile that showed off her dazzling angel-white teeth.

Ricky spooned out equal shares and then carried both plates through to the lounge where he put them on the dining table. He invited her to remove her coat and take a seat. He hung Melanie's coat up in the hallway and then returned to the kitchen to fetch knives and forks.

Ricky sat down at the table.

"Thank you," Melanie said.

"It's good to see you," Ricky said. "I'm not trying to come across all posh or anything, but I quite enjoy a glass of wine with my food these days. Would you like a glass? It's a nice Chardonnay and it's been in the fridge all day so it's nice and chilled."

"That's funny, because Kaz, Donna and I have all taken up having a glass of wine when we get together."

"Excellent," Ricky said as he got up from the table and went back into the kitchen. He returned a few minutes later carrying two full wine glasses.

"Thank you, Ricky," Melanie said. "Now eat up before your dinner gets cold."

Ricky smiled and cut into a battered chicken ball and then dipped it into the sweet and sour sauce.

"Are you still in the flat?" Ricky said.

"Yeah, I have thought about leaving and maybe getting my own place, like you have. It's not like I can't afford it. I've got more than enough money put aside for a deposit on a place," Melanie said.

"That's good Melanie. Listen, if you need some help with a bent mortgage then just give me a call. It'll cost you about five hundred quid and you'll need to put down at least twenty per-cent deposit, but the guy I use is shit hot and he'll get it sorted in just a few weeks. I've been looking at houses in Carshalton Beeches," Ricky said.

"I'm not quite ready yet but I will take you up on that Ricky," Melanie said as she expertly removed the meat from her spare ribs with her knife and fork.

"I have to say I'm impressed Melanie. I always use my fingers when eating spare ribs," Ricky said.

"And so you should. It's cool and manly. Deano would always just strip out every piece of meat off the bone and then threaten to throw it, saying that he was Henry the Eighth," Melanie said with a chuckle.

"I could imagine that," Ricky said, raising his glass and taking a sip.

Melanie placed her knife and fork neatly on her plate and took a sip from her glass.

"Hmm, this is nice," Melanie said.

"Yeah, I thought so too. I made a point of buying several different types of wine and giving them a try. I've never been a lover of that Black Tower or Blue Nun wine and as for that Mateus Rose, it's horrible. I've tried them all, but there are far nicer wines out there," Ricky said.

"Who would have thought it, eh? Ricky Turrell, drinking wine," Melanie said. "I don't mind the Black Tower which is, incidentally, what Kaz and Donna always bring around when they visit, but I'm not a lover of the Blue Nun. It's a little too bitter for me."

Ricky popped the last of the battered chicken balls into his mouth and put his knife and fork together in the middle of his plate. He picked up the glass and drank the last of the chilled white wine.

"I'm sorry, Ricky, but I can't eat anymore," Melanie said before placing her cutlery on the plate and taking a deep breath.

"No problem. It's like I said, I always get too much. As soon as I look at the menu, I just get carried away. I will have another glass of wine. Can I refill your glass?"

Melanie smiled.

"Do you know what, yes, why not?" Melanie said.

Ricky took the plates out to the kitchen, ran them under the hot water and then put them into the washing up bowl with a squirt of washing up liquid.

"I've got to ask," Ricky said as he carried the two wine glasses and put them on the coffee table.

Melanie had left the table and was sitting down on the armchair next to the stereo system.

"Ask away..." Melanie said as she flicked through a few of his vinyl records.

"What's with the black bag?"

"Do you know what, I nearly forgot about that," Melanie said. "That's for you."

"For me?" Ricky said, looking a little confused.

"Yeah, go ahead and take a look," Melanie said.

Ricky went back to the kitchen and brought the black bag into the lounge. He placed it on the floor by the settee, opened it and reached in. He pulled out two of Deano's drape suits and his handmade pair of brothel creepers with the knuckledusters sewn on as eyelets for the laces.

"These are Deano's," Ricky said.

"They're yours now Ricky. I know that Deano would want you to have them. I've hung onto his black drape jacket with 'Deano the Dog' hand stitched in gold thread. I'm not ready to let that go yet," Melanie said as she took a sip from the wine glass.

"I don't know what to say," Ricky said, holding up the coveted brothel creepers. "I always liked these and even asked where Deano got them made but he would never tell me. Thank you, Melanie. I'm really touched that you thought to give me Deano's things. It means a lot to me."

"I know how he felt about you Ricky. He would speak about you at home sometimes and it was clear that he valued your loyalty and friendship. This will probably sound a little crazy but after Deano was first taken from us I could still feel him around me. He would visit me in my dreams and it was just so vivid that I didn't want to wake up. On one occasion we were talking in my dream and Deano was surrounded by this light that was making me squint but when I woke up I just felt at ease, almost at peace with everything. Other times when I feel lost, hopeless, and at my lowest, a record that had meaning to us both would play on the radio and I just felt like it was because of him. That somehow he sensed how I was feeling and made it happen in the kind of way that only Deano could do."

"It doesn't sound crazy to me at all Melanie. Not a day has passed where I haven't thought about my friend and the legacy that he left behind," Ricky said.

Melanie beamed. Ricky found himself noticing her flawless bronzed complexion.

"Do you ever feel him around you?" Melanie said.

"Between you and me, yeah I have. Not in a while but there were times when I'd be alone here in the flat making my notes and I'd feel him around me. It's hard to describe, but if I were to close my eyes then it was like Deano was sitting right next to me," Ricky said.

"I know exactly what you mean. I would be sitting in the bedroom putting on my make-up and out of nowhere I would feel a gentle touch on my back, just as he would do when he was here. There were nights when I'd wake up and the bed still felt like Deano was sleeping beside me. I could smell the Brut aftershave he liked to wear. There was nothing scary about it at all it felt just incredibly comforting," Melanie said.

"That's the last of the wine Melanie, would you like something else?" Ricky said, standing up and walking over to the drink's cabinet. "I've got gin?"

"Gin and tonic would be nice, thank you," Melanie said.

Melanie continued to talk while Ricky made her a drink and poured a large malt whiskey for himself.

"I can remember the first day that I went back shoplifting for Doreen. Bless her heart, she didn't put any pressure on me even though I know she had stacks of orders with people wanting stuff. As always Jackie made up the shortfall. I remember walking into the shop and my head was still a little clouded with thoughts of Deano and I wasn't paying as much attention to what was going on around me as I should have been, and then as clear as a bell I heard Deano tell me to get focused and get on with the job at hand and that he didn't want me getting caught because of him. Ricky, I swear to you, I heard his voice like I am yours," Melanie said.

Ricky handed Melanie her large gin and tonic.

"Thank you," Melanie said.

Ricky watched and smiled as she placed her berry–red lips on the rim of the tumbler.

"Have you heard him Ricky?"

"I've not heard his voice like you've described, Melanie, but there are times, especially when it concerns Ted business, when I could hear this inner voice telling me what I must do," Ricky said.

"I would find myself talking out loud to him sometimes while I was doing the washing up or alone in the bath. There were occasions when I didn't even realise I was doing it. It was like Deano was just answering me like he always did," Melanie said.

"It must have been nice, feeling that he was there," Ricky said.

"I was walking through the town a few months back, I'd been out hoisting, when I had this ringing, or more like a buzzing sensation in my ear. It wasn't loud or uncomfortable and it just felt like Deano was walking beside me," Melanie said.

"I've heard my mum talking about that with her friends. She was saying that it was a past loved one just letting you know that they are present," Ricky said.

"I've told Kaz and Donna about some of this stuff because they're my best friends and I've known them just about all my life. Donna said that she had been told that sometimes the spirits will leave a message, something real that you can pick up and that instantly you know that it must have been them," Melanie said.

"Has anything like that happened?" Ricky asked, reaching out for Melanie's empty glass and refilling them both at his drink's cabinet.

"No, in the beginning all these things felt so strong but then they gradually faded away. Donna said that I should ask for a sign but nothing happened. I looked, Ricky, believe me I did search for that sign, but nothing," Melanie said.

"My mum said the picture she had of my granddad would keep falling off the wall. I remember as a kiddie I'd jump out of my skin when it happened but my mum would just pass it off, saying that it was her dad just letting her know that he was okay and still there," Ricky said.

"That was nice of him," Melanie said.

They both took a sip of their drinks.

"I've been just staring into the dark from my bed, almost willing Deano to appear like a ghost or something but the feeling just isn't there. I think maybe, just maybe he has passed on to the other side where he's already recruiting a gang of Teddy Boys," Melanie said while she shook her head slowly and let out a quiet laugh.

"If he is there, Melanie, then he's probably already recruited the best of the best and is out making a name for himself," Ricky said.

"I'd like to believe that Ricky, I really would," Melanie said. "What would you think if I were to maybe go out with someone? Not now, but in the future. I'm still in love with Deano and I'll never forget him. He will always be with me in my heart but I'm beginning to think that life would be worthless and devoid of meaning without something resembling love in my life."

Ricky took a sip from his drink and put it on the coffee table.

"Melanie I am no expert in affairs of the heart, I'm really not, but life without some kind of romance would be unbearable and you, Melanie, are far too young to think about a life of solitude. Life without feeling and desire is just unthinkable. We all need love, care and affection in our lives and your needs are no different. Besides, I'm pretty damn sure that Deano wouldn't want his, attractive, twenty something girlfriend grieving for him at the expense of her happiness for the rest of her life," Ricky said.

"Thank you, Ricky, I needed to hear that," Melanie said as she leaned forward and put her hand on his knee.

Ricky felt an electrical shiver ricochet through his body.

"Shit, is Melanie coming on to me?" Ricky thought.

"I was listening to a record on the radio as we were coming back from work. It was *'Forever and Ever'*, by Slik, and the words summed up exactly how I felt about Deano when he was alive and by my side. I just wished that I had told him more often how much I loved him," Melanie said.

"He knew Melanie, I'm sure he did. Not a lot got past Deano," Ricky said.

"What about you Ricky? How's your love life? It didn't escape any of our notice that Michelle didn't come on the Beano to Margate," Melanie said.

"It's like I said, Melanie, I'm no expert in these things. I thought Michelle and I had something special. It certainly felt like it. I thought that she understood who and what I am, just like you did Deano, but she's becoming increasingly distant with either working late at her dad's business or she's too tired to come out. I did slip around to her home once, I just had this nagging suspicion that she wasn't being completely truthful, but I saw her pass in front of the window before the curtains were closed. Now that probably sounds a bit creepy," Ricky said.

"No, if I thought something was up then I'd check it out too. Just about every one of us would," Melanie said.

"I think it's hanging by a thread, and if I'm brutally honest I no longer have that special feeling when I see her. It's like I'm waiting for her to bring up how I should give up being a Teddy Boy, wear an off the peg suit and join the Freemasons like her dad."

"Does she?" Melanie said, while still perched on the edge of her armchair.

"Every single time! It's like she wants to mould me into this mini version of her dad. Not that he likes me, in fact he bloody hates me. The first time we met all he saw was a Teddy Boy off the Milton Road Estate and within a few seconds he'd concluded that I wasn't good enough for his daughter and made it abundantly clear," Ricky said.

"But you've met and made up with him since, haven't you?" Melanie asked.

Ricky found himself looking at Melanie's arched shaped eyebrows and thinking how symmetrical they were. Melanie caught his gaze and smiled.

"No, he doesn't know that she's been seeing me. It's a secret because, well, because she doesn't want to upset her dad. I did try to touch on it a couple of times and she said that she would, when the time was right, tell him that we are an item," Ricky said.

"She's a fool if she lets you go Ricky. You're a good looking, nice guy, that has done something with his life and not just sat back and accepted what fate has thrust upon us. That's why I went shoplifting with Jackie. I saw that she had made something of herself and I was prepared to take the risk to make a better life for me. I don't want the paltry existence my parents have and I'm sure you didn't either, which is why you continually push yourself to do more. Some people would just see you, me, Kaz, Donna, Jackie and Doreen as nothing more than criminals and they would be wrong. Some people can use their parents or family to get ahead or the blessing of a good education while others like us, Ricky, use what skills we have to get ahead and if Michelle can't see or appreciate that because of her privileged background then it'll be her loss," Melanie said as she leaned forward and kissed Ricky on the cheek.

She paused for a second and then kissed him again. Her arm reached out around his shoulders as she gently kissed his face and finally their lips locked in a passionate embrace. Ricky had lost all control. He was eagerly kissing her and then pulled her body onto his. He turned her ever so slightly, and Melanie slumped backwards onto the settee while Ricky hungrily kissed her neck and ran his hands over her firm body. Melanie grappled with his trouser button. He was excited and lost all inhibitions as he reached around and unclipped her bra. As Melanie unzipped his trousers he felt a sudden jolt and pulled away.

"Melanie, I'm not sure we should be doing this," Ricky whispered as he looked down on her unbuttoned blouse that was exposing a glorious hint of cleavage.

"We both need this Ricky," Melanie whispered back as she sat up, placed both her arms around his neck and kissed him passionately.

The couple tore at each other's clothing with a passion charged energy. Like repelling magnets Ricky and Melanie's intimacy was more intense with every touch, stroke and movement desperately taking them both to new heights of sensation in delirious proportions. Melanie was like a love potion from the forbidden fruit after weeks of famine. Their passionate love making did crescendo beyond all limits and after the ultimate orgasmic release, their passion didn't dissolve into a calm sweet pool of divinity. They wanted each other again and again until the early hours.

"Are you okay?" Ricky asked, handing Melanie the Harrods dressing gown Doreen had stolen for him a few weeks before.

"I'm more than okay. What about you?" Melanie whispered.

"I feel a slight tinge of guilt," Ricky said as he lay back on the bed beside her.

"Don't feel bad Ricky. What we did was console each other in a physical, intimate way that only a best friend and girlfriend could do. I feel no shame or regret. I feel alive and ready for the next stage of my life and you've helped me do that. You have helped me to understand that I must move on and find love," Melanie said as she turned to face him. "Don't worry Ricky, I don't have any expectations and this will not happen again but what I do need from you are just two things,"

Melanie smiled and stroked the side of Ricky's face.

"Firstly, being around the Milton Road Teds, drinking at the Arms and being part of the inner circle has always been very important to me and Deano made sure that happened. I was never left out. I was always given the choice to attend something or not and that is something that I would like to continue. I don't want to be left on the side lines or lose my place in the whole scheme of things. Will you promise to make that happen for me?" Melanie said softly.

Ricky nodded.

"Yes, of course I will," Ricky said.

"Thank you," Melanie said, her tone and expression becoming serious.

"The second thing I want you to do is a little more demanding and I need you to consider it before simply agreeing and then not doing it. I couldn't bear that," Melanie said.

"Okay, what is it?"

"The bastard, Fat Pat, who shot and killed your friend and my fiancé has to die and I want you to do it Ricky. Not just for me, but for you, the Milton Road Teds and the Ted Army. He has to die. Can you, and will you do that, Ricky Turrell?" she whispered.

"Fat Pat was always going to die for what he did to Deano. I promise you Melanie, that when that fat bastard finally shows his ugly mug, he will be taken care of," Ricky said firmly.

"When it's done, I'd like you to phone me at home, anytime day or night, and just say the words 'Melanie it's been sorted' and it'll never be spoken about again. It will always be our little secret."

"Fat Pat will have a slow, painful exit from this world. I swear that on my life," Ricky said.

Melanie kissed him gently on the lips. Are you able to drop me back at my flat at about 6.00am? I've got an early start with Doreen and the girls and what happened here tonight is the business of no one but us," Melanie said as she removed the dressing gown.

Chapter 19

It was just after 8.30pm and Ricky was still at the office at London Tyre Co. He had been checking through the business plan to ensure that the rebranding and launching of the new tyre depots was going to plan. He then moved onto Ted Business. Ricky had been around and personally visited most of the leaders that he'd called together for tomorrow's big day. Mack, from the Mile End Teds, had phoned and said as much as they all wanted to be there, Carly, the leader, had decided to boycott the alliance. Ricky assured him that all was in hand and to be patient. Once he was satisfied that he had gone over the plan step by step with all who would be involved, he called it a day and headed back to his flat in Carshalton. Ricky was buzzing, he felt like a general pulling together his battle plans. It would be a big day that had the potential to make or break his plans for the Ted Army. Losing wasn't an option.

At home Ricky had poured himself a small malt whiskey and began to thumb through his album collection. He stopped at the cover that read: Juke Box Jive – 40 All Time Rock 'n' Roll Greats! Ricky took the vinyl out of its sleeve and placed it on the record deck before sitting back in his chair. As he took a sip from his drink, *'Summertime Blues'* by Eddie Cochran began to play. He allowed his mind to wander back to Melanie's visit. It had all been so unexpected for him, and yet he felt no guilt. Deano was gone and both Ricky and Melanie were in a blur of mixed emotions. There was pain, fear, shock and denial that they had both kept stored away. Ricky couldn't show any weakness for fear that he wouldn't take over the Milton Road Teds and lose credibility with those who had signed up to the alliance. But when he was alone, he would think of his friend and missed his friendship. It had been Deano the

Dog that had opened a whole new life for him. He owed Deano. Ricky thought about Melanie and how she must have struggled with the immediate aftermath of Deano's death. He concluded that she must have only had the two choices. Either give up and surrender to what had happened to Deano and just disappear from her life on the front line with the Teds, The Milton Arms and her friends, or instead choose to fight the stark reality of life without Deano.

Ricky thought how alone Melanie must have felt, afraid, hurt and even angry, waking up every day in the flat they shared without her larger than life future husband. For many, what they had done would have been wrong, but locked in each other's arms, they had somehow found a reminder that they were both alive and human. They were both grieving in their own way and had discovered that they didn't need to just get over it. Ricky had made a promise to make Fat Pat pay for what he done and he had every intention of seeing that through for him, Melanie, the Milton Road Teds and The Ted Army.

Ricky had been up early and was dressed and out the door. He had a plan to follow.

***

"Is everyone here?" Ricky said, looking around at the twenty plus Teds from the Milton Road Estate.

"Yes mate," Bill said.

"There's no room for passengers today," Lee said.

"What the fuck are you doing here then?" Kenny said with a chuckle.

"Don't you start," Lee said.

"Oh Lee's getting all shirty now. Let's hope he can keep it up for when things get a bit serious," Kenny said.

"I can hold my own just fine," Lee said wearily.

"I had heard that about you Lee," Kenny said as he jerked his half-closed hand back and forth.

"Alright, that'll do," Ricky said as the underground train pulled into Morden station.

Ricky stepped back and watched as the Teds clambered onto the train in their brothel creeper shoes, drain pipe trousers and drape jackets. He was proud to see his lads. Ricky understood that each and every one of them, including Lee, instinctively knew that if they were going to get involved in gang violence then there can be no fear or worry about getting hurt or badly beaten up. Their mind set was that their mates and fellow Teds were standing firm by their side, shoulder to shoulder. They had won before the first punch was thrown.

"What's the plan Ricky?" Bill asked as he held onto the leather hand strap that hung from the train's ceiling.

"All we need to do is arrive as one," Ricky said before looking down to check the time on his watch.

"There has to be more though, isn't there, and where's Terry and Steve?" Bill said.

"Do you trust me Bill?" Ricky said quietly.

"With my life," Bill said.

"Good. Just stick to your part of the plan mate," Ricky said.

As the train pulled into each station along the Northern Line, travellers would look into the carriage of Teddy Boys and then move on.

Ricky looked over at the five large brown canvas sports bags that had been piled on the floor by the door.

"You would be proud of this Deano," Ricky thought as he slipped his hand inside his trouser pocket and felt for his solid brass knuckleduster. *"Mate you were born to mix it up and put wannabe hard bastards flat on their backs."*

As the train came to a halt at London Bridge, several Boot Boys dressed in drain pipe jeans, Doctor Marten Boots and short sleeved shirts passed by the carriage. As they gawped through the window, the Teds returned their stare while Ricky eyeballed the lad who appeared to be their leader. Ricky knew there wasn't time for confrontation but he also knew that street fighting is a mind game too. Had they shown the slightest sign of weakness then there would have been trouble. The Boot Boys moved on, with Ricky maintaining his glare until they were out of sight.

The train rolled on to Old Street and then finally came to a stop at Angel in Islington. The Teds left the train. Ricky looked back to see if the Boot Boys were following. The train left the station with a couple of the lads giving a 'wankers' sign as it left the station.

"All big and brave now the train's moving," Ricky thought. *"It's alright lads. Your cards are marked."*

The Milton Road Teds rode the giant escalator up to the station entrance. As they passed through the barriers, members of the public stepped away or looked in another direction. Ricky saw Tyler standing alone by the main road. As Ricky walked towards him, he could see that Tyler was fingering the top button of his shirt. He looked uncomfortable. Ricky held out his hand and the two gang leaders shook hands. Ricky leant forward and whispered.

"You're looking worried, pull yourself together mate," Ricky said with a smile.

"Sorry mate, I've had a few youngsters out spotting for us, and mate, they have a fucking army," Tyler whispered.

"Good," Ricky said as his body tensed and his eyes flared. "Because we've come for a proper full on brawl. Are your lads still game?"

Tyler nodded.

"Did you do as I said?" Ricky said.

"Yeah, I let it slip to a few people that you and the Milton Road Teds were coming up today just like you said to," Tyler said.

"Did you say anything else?" Ricky said.

"No mate, not a word," Tyler said as he peered over Ricky's shoulder at the five Teds that were carrying large canvas sports bags.

"What numbers have you got?" Ricky asked while he straightened the gold plated bootlace tie that Melanie had given him.

"Twenty of my twenty-three lads are game and up for it," Tyler said.

"What happened to the other three?" Ricky said.

"The long and the short of it is when push came to shove, they bottled it," Tyler said, looking distinctly uncomfortable.

"If they're not up for it then it's better that they're not here. That said though, Tyler, I don't ever want to have them around me or the Ted Army in the future," Ricky said.

"No mate, they'll be fucked off after the no show today," Tyler said.

Ricky nodded.

"Right, lead the way mate," Ricky said.

Tyler walked side by side with Ricky with the Teds following behind. Heads were turning from all around as they walked down the roads and streets. Finally they stopped at the 'Green Man' pub. As Ricky passed through the doors he saw the Temple Drive Teds sat together around several tables. Johnny, the Temple Drive Teds' second in command, stood up and cheered. The other lads quickly followed suit as Bill, Kenny, Lee and the lads shook their hands or patted them on the shoulder.

"This is Charlie Mason," Tyler said as he introduced Ricky. "This is his pub."

"Good to meet you," Ricky said as he cast his eyes over Charlie's dark grey pinstripe drape jacket and black drain pipe trousers.

"Once a Ted..." Charlie said.

"Always a Ted..." Ricky said as he shook Charlie warmly by the hand.

"It's good to meet you Ricky," Charlie said. "I've been a Ted both man and boy, and I still remember getting my first drape suit back in 1952. The upmarket tailors had created suits based on the Edwardian fashion but when they didn't catch on they ended up being sold on the markets in South East London. I'll never forget the first time I saw that suit. I just knew that it was a bit of me. It didn't take long before there were loads of us just hanging about looking good, smoking fags and listening to Frankie Laine and Johnny Ray. I was originally from Lewisham but moved down to Croydon when I was in my teens. I had a mate, Christopher Craig, who shot a copper back in 1953. The copper died and we all thought that he'd get hung for it but being sixteen he was deemed too young. However his mate, Derek, was eighteen. Nice fella, but wasn't the full shilling and he did get hung. It was a nasty business."

"I was talking with a cabbie that had been at the Astoria cinema in the Old Kent Road when it all kicked off during the 'Blackboard Jungle' movie," Ricky said.

"Me and my mates were there too," Charlie said. "I have to tell you though, it had nothing to do with the movie. It was because Bill Haley and the Comets played during the opening and closing credits of the movie. Ricky, it went ballistic. I don't think I've felt that alive since."

Ricky looked down at his watch.

"I don't mean to cut you short Charlie, but we have to get ourselves over to Chamberlain Housing Estate," Ricky said.

"I'm coming with you," Charlie said as he put some coins into a handkerchief and then wound it around his wrist as a make-shift knuckle duster

Charlie was in his late forties, but Ricky could see that he still kept himself in good shape

"It's not necessary Charlie," Ricky said.

"That racist bastard who calls himself the 'Hammer' wants to take over my pub, throw out my customers and throw some kind of birthday party here for Adolf Hitler next year, so yes, Ricky I'm in. It's been a while, but I'm still capable," Charlie said as he pounded his fist into his open palm.

"Good for you Charlie," Ricky said as he then turned to the pub full of battle-ready Teddy Boys. "Right can I have your attention! As Teddy Boys we stick together. We stand by our brothers of the drape and together as one we take on the enemies of our allies. When we rock up on Chamberlain Housing Estate I want you all to stand firm and show no sign of fear no matter how outnumbered we may be. We are Teds and each and every one of you here is worth two if not three right-wing Skinheads. No one, and I do mean no one, no matter how buzzed up you are, is to make a move until I give the order. Right, the Ted Army is on the move."

Ricky and Tyler led the Teddy Boys out through the pub's door and then up the street. Bill and Kenny were walking directly behind Ricky.

"I can't believe that Terry and Steve Parker are no-shows," Kenny muttered. "I would have thought they'd be bang on for this."

"Ricky has it all in hand," Bill said, just loud enough for Ricky to hear.

The lads passed by the first block of flats and into the square behind where they were met by a sea of Skinheads, Boot Boys and Punk Rockers.

"Fuck me," Kenny whispered. "There must be at least two hundred of them, if not more."

"So what," Bill hissed.

Ricky stopped the Teds. The five lads carrying the large canvas sports bags quickly undid them and began to hand out baseball bats, bicycle chains and pick axe handles. The Teds quickly spread out in a line with the Milton Road Teds all carrying weapons.

Ricky could make out one short stocky lad with what looked like a swastika tattoo on his neck. He had positioned himself a couple of rows back from the front line and was surrounded by heavily tattooed skinheads.

"Yeah, I've clocked you Eric 'the fucking hammer' Baron," Ricky thought.

Ricky stepped forward. He had just under fifty Teddy Boys standing solid behind him whilst the Hammer was surrounded by over two hundred lads carrying planks of wood, metal bars and knives in the middle of the square. The White Boy Nation lads began to jeer and shout, while behind them Terry Parker stood alongside the leaders of Teddy Boy gangs from Streatham, Tooting, Clapham Common and Battersea. The lads spread two deep covering one end of the square to other. Over one hundred and fifty hardcore Teddy Boys.

The White Boy Nation carried on jeering, oblivious that Steve Parker and the leaders of Teddy Boys gangs from New Cross, Peckham, Woolwich, Wembley and Fulham filed out to the right of the square, while Jock Addie led out his Croydon Teds alongside the leaders of Ted gangs from Mitcham, Addington and Sutton. Ricky had called Arran Morgan the leader of the Five Link Teds from Basildon. He had brought down another fifty plus game lads from Pitsea, Billericay, Brentwood and South End.

Ricky had secretly brought together over five hundred teddy Boys.

"TED ARMY!" Ricky yelled.

TED ARMY...! TED ARMY...! TED ARMY!

Ricky could see the look of horror as the White Boy Nation lads began to look around and see that they were surrounded on all four sides. The noise from the Teds became louder and louder.

TED ARMY...! TED ARMY...! TED ARMY!

The sound became deafening, with over five hundred Teds yelling out.

TED ARMY...! TED ARMY...! TED ARMY!

Terry Parker raised his right hand and dropped it. Hundreds of second hand steel nuts and bolts rained over the White Boy Nation. Three inch heavy gauge bolts connected with arms, legs and heads. Shrieks of pain could be heard as several bolts hit lads in the face and head. A second wave of heavy steel nuts and bolts rained down hard again. Ricky could see the lads at the back cowering on the concrete, covering their faces and heads when the steel bolts made contact. Steve Parker raised his hand while all the Teds behind gripped their bolts and took aim. As his hand dropped hundreds more bolts flew across the square with an increasing number of lads taking to the ground to protect themselves. As Steve ordered the second wave, Jock Addie and Arran Morgan both dropped their hands and hundreds of heavy steel bolts now smashed down on the right-wing Boot Boys. The White Boy Nation's lads were screaming as the steel bolts cracked bones, tore skin and broke teeth. Ricky could see that several of the larger lads had moved in to protect Eric 'The Hammer' Baron. After the final bolt was launched by Arran Morgan's Essex Teddy Boys, Ricky led the charge.

TED ARMY...! TED ARMY...! TED ARMY!

From all four sides the Ted Army raced in wielding their weapons of violence.

With his knuckleduster firmly held within his fist, Ricky faced a Skinhead with blood streaming from his forehead. The lad threw a wild punch which missed by a mile. Ricky sent a left jab which had the lad turn and face him. He was wide open. Ricky launched a head shot. There was a crack and the Skinhead's knees buckled and then he fell against the skinhead who was fighting to his right. Bill stormed forward. He took out one lad with a punch in the stomach followed by a rapid crack on the temple from his baseball bat. Bill barged past the lad and steamed straight in to the next lad who had been waving a seven inch Bowie knife ferociously. The lad had caught the arm of a passing Ted but was instantly disarmed as Bill's baseball bat thundered down onto his arm. The Skinhead screeched as his arm fell limp and the knife dropped to the concrete. A second swipe from Bill and the Skinhead's eyes closed as he fell to the ground. Ricky was in the thick of it throwing left and right hooks. He took several punches to the face but the adrenaline was racing so hard through his body that he felt no pain. Another right hook with the knuckleduster and now Ricky had his sights on Eric 'The Hammer' Baron.

Stopping momentarily, Ricky could see the Teddy boys beating down the right-wing Boot Boys. Kenny was steaming in with fists flying, while Lee took pot shots at lads with his pick axe handle. A huge Skinhead wearing a white skin tight vest top stepped away from 'The Hammer' and bounded, with gritted teeth, towards Ricky. There was no time to be intimidated by the man's size and physique. He blocked everything from his mind. This was just another obstacle to get him to where he wanted to be. The monstrous sized Skinhead threw a punch. Ricky moved his body and sidestepped the punch while bringing both his arms up to protect his jaw. The second punch whistled past his head with a ferocity that could have put a telephone box on its side. Ricky threw a left hook which caught his cheek, he sent a second in in the hope that the monster would open up but he didn't. A right hander landed. It was a big punch that took Ricky off guard. The monster was coming in for a second. Ricky couldn't move his arms quickly enough. Terry Parker raced past Ricky, launched himself into the air, and with his right hand firmly gripped around his metal cosh he made a swipe. Blood began to gush from the monster's head as he sagged down onto one knee. Terry took a second swipe before soldiering on for his next victim. Ricky began to blink his eyes rapidly as if he was coming out of a deep sleep. As his senses returned, he got angry. He was livid. Ricky wanted revenge and he wanted blood. A Boot Boy yelled and ran towards Ricky with hate in his eyes. Ricky stood still, brought his arms in tight and then, as the screaming lad was almost upon him, he fired a left hook, a left jab and then a brutal right uppercut that sent the lad sprawling to the ground. Ricky looked over towards 'The Hammer'. He still had three big lads standing around him. They only threw punches when a Ted got too close. Everard had fought his way towards the centre alongside Tyler. Both armed with bicycle chains, they swung with savage ferocity bringing down White Boy Nation lads. Everard saw an opening and made a swing with the bicycle chain. He caught one of the Hammer's minders on the side of the face. With his arm outstretched he tried make a swing for the Hammer but he was too slow. The Hammer lunged forward and smacked Everard clean on the forehead with his claw hammer. Ricky strode towards the Hammer, hitting and punching anything and everything that stood in his way. He wanted blood, but not just the blood of any right-wing foot soldier, Ricky wanted the blood of the General. Another of the Hammer's minders stepped out towards Ricky. He was another monster of a man covered in right-wing tattoos and had the physique of a man who worked out daily. There could not be a second mistake. Ricky rocketed a powerful right hook, a left uppercut and second right uppercut that hit with such force that it must have rattled his brain. The huge man's eyes glazed over as his legs gave way. He slumped forward before collapsing clumsily in a heap. Ricky's giant adversary was out cold and unconscious on the concrete. He looked up at Eric 'The Hammer' Baron. Ricky could see the fear in his eyes as all the power and hate he had built was falling under the mighty Ted Army.

This was Ricky's opportunity to cement his position as King of the Teds. The battle was being won but the opponents' General was still standing with his hand firmly fixed around a claw hammer. Ricky had learnt to control his fear and when necessary stand his ground and trade strategic punches. The Hammer was watching his empire crumble around him at the hands of a smarter, better man. His iconic status would be lost unless he could kill or, at the very least, maim Ricky. Ricky sensed his fear, his desperation. The Hammer lost all his composure and began to thrash his arms around wildly. Ricky moved to his left and then right to avoid the claw hammer. The Hammer was fierce and as hard as nails, but he had overstretched himself. When Ricky saw an opening he was fired up and ready. He bulldozed through with a series of hard fast jabs. This was a no nonsense mix of boxing and street fighting. The right hook left the Hammer with a look of utter astonishment and disbelief. Again the Hammer swung the claw hammer with unrestrained violence. He wanted Ricky dead. He needed Ricky to die violently and bloody by his hands if he was to have any future with the White Boy Nation. Ricky sent a right hook that shook him right down to the bone. He could see the blood pour from his face and like a volcano he sent a pile-driver. There was a sickening crunch of broken bone as the Hammer's nose collapsed flat onto his face. The claw hammer had been dropped while the Hammer was swaying like a Saturday night drunk. He tried desperately to stay on his feet, to stay in control and to remain conscious, but Ricky shot a final, devastating, blow. It was all over. The Hammer sagged like a blood-stained rag doll. Ricky stood over the leader of the up and coming White Boy Nation.

Ricky's ribs began to ache with every breath. He'd taken a couple of smacks in the chest from a weapon and had been so high on the adrenaline rush that he failed to notice them. Looking down on the beaten general of a violent street gang with a fearsome reputation for bloody savage violence, he felt a wave of euphoria. Ricky was on top of the world. He was King of the Teds.

"TED ARMY!" Ricky yelled at the top of his voice.

TED ARMY…! TED ARMY…! TED ARMY!

All the Teds shouted out together.

TED ARMY…! TED ARMY…! TED ARMY!

The last few remaining White Boy Nation lads stopped their fighting and held their arms up in submission. They were beaten, their leader was beaten, and the Ted Army were victorious.

"Ricky, you alright?" Bill asked.

"Yes mate. You did good mate, you did real good!" Ricky said.

"What about the old bill?" Bill asked. "Shouldn't we all be having it on our toes before they turn up?"

"We'll be alright for a while. I had some lads phone the local police station and report a series of robberies, scuffles and things on the other side of Islington," Ricky said.

"Smart, very smart," Bill said. "So tell me, Mr Ricky Turrell, what's it like to be King of the Teds?"

The Teds broke off into separate groups and headed away in different directions just as Ricky had planned with the leaders of all the gangs. Charlie had pleaded to the Milton Road Teds to come back to the 'Green Man' for a drinking session but the plan was set and Ricky promised that they would return.

***

Ricky and the Milton Road Teds were back inside the underground station as the flashing blue lights and sirens passed by. The Northern Line had the Teds back to Morden within forty minutes. With a combination of cars, vans and taxis the Teds were back inside the Milton Arms where a slew of witnesses would swear that was where they had all been all afternoon. Ricky had suggested to the leaders of all the other Ted gangs to arrange their own cast iron alibis. In the evening Ricky called out to find out if there were any serious injuries. Everard had taken a nasty knock on the head with the claw hammer but was well enough to be out with his mates celebrating the victory. A couple of the Essex Teds had been cut, but nothing too serious. The talk about the battle of Chamberlain House against the White Boy Nation was, as Ricky had planned, being spoken about in every corner of London and beyond. It was a coup unlike anything that Deano the Dog had achieved before. Deano was respected and readily accepted as having the fastest and most deadly fists in all London, but the new King of the Teds was strategic. He was a thinker with the ability to unite the Teds under a single banner and bring down entire armies.

Chapter 20

Ricky looked up when he heard the front door bell ringing. He'd been sitting back in his arm chair with a pen and paper, making notes and listening to *'Heartbreak Hotel'* by Elvis Presley from the Arcade's 40 Greatest Hits double album. He got up and turned the volume down before opening the front door.

"Bill," Ricky said looking over his shoulder and glancing from left to right.

"Hello mate," Bill said.

"What are you doing here?" Ricky asked.

Bill held up a new, unopened, bottle of malt whiskey.

"I thought I'd share this with a mate, unless you're busy?" Bill said.

"No, no, come in mate. You just threw me a bit, that's all," Ricky said.

Ricky led Bill through to the lounge and fetched two large crystal cut glasses.

"Very nice," Bill said as Ricky put them on the coffee table.

Bill cracked open the bottle.

"How do like it?" Bill said holding the bottle over the glass.

"Straight, large and without ice," Ricky said.

"A man after my own heart," Bill said.

Ricky looked down at his watch before picking up the glass.

"It's a bit early for me really but, yeah why not?" Ricky said as they chinked glasses.

"I wanted to talk to you about Kaz," Bill said.

"Sure, fire away," Ricky said.

"Well you know that we've been seeing each other for a while?" Bill said.

"Yeah, I couldn't be more pleased for you both," Ricky said.

"Well I was thinking about asking her to move in with me or maybe even getting ourselves a place off the Estate. What do you think?" Bill said as he took a long sip from his glass.

"Kaz is lovely girl, go for it. Do what you makes you happy," Ricky said.

"I've been out with plenty of birds, you know, but never wanted anything longer term. In all honesty I've never been the kind of guy that's wanted commitments, but the more time I spend with Kaz the more I think I'd like something more permanent. If she doesn't stay over then when I wake up in the morning I kind of miss her being around. Do you know what I mean?" Bill said.

"If you had asked me a few months back then I would have said absolutely, but not so much now," Ricky said.

"Is everything alright between you and Michelle?" Bill said.

"Your guess is as good as mine. It feels like she fell for this Teddy Boy who is nothing like the kind of lad she'd been going out with before, and then at every opportunity tries to get me to change but I just ain't doing it," Ricky said firmly.

"I did think that something might be up when she didn't come on the Beano down to Margate. I know that Kaz, Melanie and Donna all wondered why she wasn't there," Bill said.

"I did ask her mate, but half expected her to come up with a reason why she couldn't make it, so when she finally said that she couldn't I wasn't surprised," Ricky said.

"I had a mate of mine, cracking fella, the real life and soul of the party kind of bloke. He was a petty thief, you know turning over warehouses, shops and the like, and used the money to have a good time. Anyway, we were all out one night having a few drinks and he's pulled this right beauty. Ricky I'm talking legs right up to her neck and she is all over him. We all thought it'd be a one night thing but he kept her on firm month in and month out and she loved being around him, us and the good times we were all having. The next thing you know he's announced, in the pub, that he'd got married that morning in a registry office. Her parents didn't like him and she rebelled and did what she thought she wanted. Within just months, and Ricky I mean two or three months, he was down the pub as usual but on his own and he'd say that the bird was getting right short and sarcastic with him because she didn't like the flat they lived in. She would slag all of us off and refused to see his family, calling them peasants. Mate you could see the change in him, one minute he's buzzing about and the next he's quiet and distant. When pushed he said that sex or any kind of physical contact was out the window. He reckons when he walked in the flat, he could almost feel the misery she was creating and she told him that she had made a huge mistake because he would never amount to anything. Ricky it was bloody sad to watch this bloke fade away in front of your eyes and all because of this bird," Bill said.

"I would have binned her," Ricky said.

"Yeah, me too but he didn't. He loved her mate and just stuck it out in some vague hope that it'd go back to what it was when they were first together," Bill said.

"What happened?" Ricky said.

"He got sloppy and left prints and evidence that led the old bill to his door and do you know what?"

"What?" Ricky said.

"She told the gavvers that he was a thief and actually gave evidence against him. The poor bastard got banged up for eighteen months," Bill said as he poured more malt whiskey into both their glasses.

"What a bitch!" Ricky said.

"Yeah, right, and when you see and hear stuff like that it just makes you cautious, you know, I would hate to end up being that unhappy and then dobbed in to the old bill," Bill said.

"Yeah but Kaz ain't like that. I mean she's clearly taken with you mate. That is as obvious as the nose on your face, and besides Kaz is at it herself. You know she's out hoisting most days for Doreen so she's not going to grass for a bit of money lending, maybe handling a bit of stolen gear," Ricky said.

"Don't forget beating the shit out of people," Bill said.

"True, but that's just not Kaz in my opinion. Look mate, in life you just have to take chances because this is it, the only life we're going to get. It's no practice run so get amongst it and take those chances and if it doesn't work out then try to end it amicably," Ricky said.

"But if you're looking for the back door before you've even gone through the front one, you already know what you should do."

"I'm going to ask her," Bill said.

"Good for you," Ricky said as they chinked glasses again.

"Cheers mate, I appreciate you listening," Bill said.

"No problem," Ricky said.

"What do you think you'll do?" Bill said before sitting back in the armchair.

"I don't know yet," Ricky said as he stood up turned the record player off and the radio on. *"I love to Love'* by Tina Charles was playing. Ricky left the volume on low.

"It's not like you to be indecisive. I mean you've singlehandedly built a successful business and pulled the Ted Army together despite the many obstacles," Bill said.

"I've been thinking about the Ted Army, and the thing is, Bill, if you look at the old bill, armed forces, mafia or even gangs like The Firm or The Richardson's from back in the 1960s, they all have or had one thing in common. They are or were tightly structured," Ricky said.

"You're right there, mate. The gavvers are probably the biggest gang in the UK," Bill said.

"Some of these organisations have scores, hundreds and even thousands of members but they work by a uniform code of practice. They all have just the one leader, someone who holds the highest rank," Ricky said as he reached out to the coffee table and poured another malt whiskey into both their glasses,

"Well that would be you Ricky. You're King of the Teds now," Bill said.

"Not just yet, but I will be," Ricky said. "Anyway, underneath the leader you would have a committee of leaders, and for the Ted Army that would be the individual leaders of each gang. With each of those leaders holding a position on the committee they can retain their local identity but be called together under a common cause. It's a bit like we did with those right-wing North London mobs."

"What are you getting at Ricky?" Bill said as he took a large swig from the crystal cut glass.

"Deano had a vision. It was a basic vision, but none the less, with structure, discipline and a clear set of rules, it could be extremely powerful. I want to take the Ted Army to another level. I want Teddy Boys from all over London to fall under a single banner with each member safe and protected from any rival, whether it be a Skinhead gang or some wannabe Bully Boy trying to impress some bird at a party or a nightclub. Teddy Boys in every corner of London will be feared and revered in equal measure."

"Yeah, sounds good, but Ricky, what is the end game?" Bill said, lounging back in the armchair.

"There are probably five or six thousand Teds all over London. Some in large or smaller gangs and there's hundreds more that wear the drape suit, listen to the music and love all things Ted related, but stand alone or with just a few mates. By bringing all these Teds together under a clear organisational structure it will allow the committee, that's the leaders of all the gangs, to shape the Ted Army towards its goals and long-term objectives. Can you imagine, Bill, how powerful it would be to have thousands of soldiers all over London under a single banner?"

Bill sat bolt upright and leant forward.

"Scary, that's what that would be. Maybe too much power for any one man," Bill said.

"Maybe, maybe not," Ricky said as he took a large swig of his drink.

"What's next then, Ricky, Manchester, Birmingham?" Bill said, refilling both their glasses.

"Right now my focus is on uniting London, but there's nothing to say that other cities can't be recruited and brought into the fold in the future. Once the organisational structure is in place and proven, we have a model that could be replicated anywhere. Sure it could be Manchester and Birmingham, but what about Leeds, Newcastle, and Bristol and that's before we even start looking at the Home Counties like Kent, Sussex and Essex," Ricky said. "I know it's not on the same scale but it's what I've done with my tyre business. I set up London Tyre Co with a clear brand with uniform overalls, working times, service and quality standards and then when I bought out N&M Tyres and the three branches I just replicated what I had already created and it worked. Do you know every one of those branches went into profit within a few months? Look Bill, I know it was a much smaller scale but the model is the same."

"I can see what you're saying Ricky but this is strategic stuff, so why are you telling me?" Bill said.

"I want a number two, a second in command, Bill. Just as I was to Deano I want you to be to me. You can handle yourself; you've got bottle and don't run when it kicks off, you're loyal, trustworthy and people like and respect you. Plus, you're Milton Estate, even if you were away for a time. Besides Deano trusted you and chances are had you still lived here it would have been you in Mickey Deacon's spot. So Bill, do you want the position?"

"Mate I'm honoured and touched by what you've just said. What about Terry and Steve, Won't they be put out?" Bill said.

"I have other plans for them which we've already discussed, so you will have their support too. I'm setting up a meeting with the leaders of the largest gangs first and I'd like you to join me, as my second in command, with Terry and Steve as the Milton Road Teds' First Lieutenants," Ricky said putting his empty glass on the coffee table.

"I'm in Ricky. Let's bloody well do this and I will not let you down!" Bill said.

"Good, so fill the glass," Ricky said with a chuckle.

"Love to Love you Baby' by Donna Summer played on the radio.

"Have you heard this record Ricky?" Bill said.

Ricky turned to the radio.

"Yeah," Ricky said with a wry smile. "She's a cracking looking bird."

"Yeah, she certainly is, but all that moaning and groaning... It's like she's simulating sex. Have a listen," said Bill.

The two lads sat back in the chair and listened to Donna Summer sing.

"That's a pretty damn convincing orgasm," Ricky said.

"I wonder what she was thinking about when she was recording it," Bill said.

"Either me or Dave Bartram," Ricky said with a wry smile.

"Get out," Bill said before breaking into an all out belly laugh. "I can't see the Queen of disco music having a thing for either you or Dave Bartram."

"Yeah, but we can dream," Ricky said.

Chapter 21

Ricky had just finished his meeting with Nigel at London Tyre Co. The re-branding plan was coming together on time when Connor made an unexpected call on him. Ricky greeted him as he would any customer or supplier and then led him through to a meeting room he had recently had constructed.

"You don't look your normal self," Ricky said as he pulled out his chair and invited Connor to sit down.

"No, it's Sean. He's only gone and got himself nicked," Connor said.

"You're joking me," Ricky said.

"I wish I was mate, I really do," Connor said.

"What's he nicked for?" Ricky said.

"Sean is a bit of a ladies' man, you know. He flutters those big blue eyes and the panties just fall to the floor. So while we've been scouting around in Kent for possible tyre bays to rob, Sean has met this woman in a newsagents. Well he's just doing all his usual flirting and this married bird has fallen for it hook line and sinker. The next thing you know he's been slipping around there while her old man is at work and giving her a good seeing to," Connor said.

"How does he end up getting nicked for that?" Ricky said.

"Well her old man has come home unexpectedly and Sean's at it in the bedroom. It turns out that her old man is a copper and he's gone berserk and started battering him with his truncheon. The next thing you know he's been nicked, with the copper saying that he came home and found him burgling his house," Connor said.

"Look mate I hate to be mercenary here, but I've just bought three more tyre bays and right now they're being re-branded as London Tyre Co. The next thing I need to do is market them to death with special deals and that's where you and Sean come in. You told me that you had it sorted, tyres already put aside and just waiting. What's changed?" Ricky said firmly.

"Sean's banged up, that's what changed," Connor said.

"Right, but do you have the tyres?" Ricky said.

"Yeah, we've got about four hundred tyres, several boxes of inner-tubes and maybe a dozen or so boxes of wheel balance weights," Connor said.

"Am I missing something? Because other than Sean being out of the frame until his mess is cleared up, I don't see a problem," Ricky said.

"Didn't you hear me Ricky? There are about four hundred tyres. I can't move that lot on my own. Sean and I are a team and we do everything together," Connor whined.

"So your problem is getting them to me, not that you don't have them?" Ricky said.

"Yeah, that and I've never driven a truck before. Sean does that," Connor said.

"So what you need from me is someone to help load a truck and then drive it here?" Ricky said.

"Yeah, kind of, but we need a truck as well. Sean would normally hire one on a bent driving licence or nick one if it's a quick job," Connor said.

"You are bloody useless," Ricky thought. *"Do you need Sean to tell you to put one foot in front of another so you can walk?"*

"I'm getting the impression here, Connor, that you can't call on anyone to help sort this, which is why you're here," Ricky said.

Connor lowered his head and nodded.

"Sean does all the organising," Connor said.

"You don't say," Ricky thought.

"Right this is what you have to do. First and foremost get your brief down that nick and tell him what's really going on. A good brief will have Sean out of there in no time," Ricky said.

"Yeah, but doesn't Sean get a phone call?" Connor said.

"Connor your mate has been banging this copper's missus and he's walked in and found them both at it. Do you really think he's going to work by the book when he's already pulled him in for something he hasn't done?" Ricky said. "So, get on the phone and get your brief down there pronto. The next thing is getting these tyres to me. I have bought and paid for adverts in all the local newspapers so not having the tyres is not an option. I will make some phone calls and see if I can get this sorted. You will owe whoever I manage to get."

"Sean won't like anybody going to our lock up. Only we know where it is," Connor said.

"I'm not asking, Connor, I'm telling you that this will be sorted. If Sean has a problem then he can come and see me when he's out," Ricky said. "Where can I get hold of you?"

"I'll give you my home number," Connor said.

Ricky handed him a sheet from a note pad and a pen.

"I will call you tonight with how we are going to make this work, so Connor," Ricky said.

"Yes," Connor said.

"Make sure that you are home," Ricky said.

"You, mate, are a liability. Sean must have been feeling sorry for you when he brought you in," Ricky thought.

Ricky showed Connor out. He continued to plan the big promotion and then called Justin, the tyre delivery driver. He asked if he could collect and bring the tyres to the depot. Justin said that he would get back to the yard late on Friday so the truck wouldn't be loaded until early Monday morning. He told Ricky that he had a set of keys to the yard and would go in early on Sunday morning and take his truck down to collect the tyres. Ricky promised him a good drink. Later that night he called Connor to confirm that arrangements had been made. Connor said that their brief had got Sean out with all charges dropped and that Sean was on his way back. Ricky reiterated that the arrangement with Justin had been made and they owed him. There were to be no changes. Reluctantly Connor agreed.

Chapter 22

Doreen stood admiring her reflection in the bedroom's full-length mirror. She had bathed using special bath cubes that she'd stolen from a West End shop along with a selection of new lingerie. Doreen had agonised between the black silk stockings, suspender and bra set and the white set. Eventually she settled on the traditional black stockings and suspenders. She had watched herself in the mirror rolling the stockings slowly up her shaven legs like it was a sacred ritual. With each inch of the stocking rolling further up her long, shapely, legs she felt increasingly sexy and desirable. Doreen was becoming progressively wrapped up in the anticipation, confidence and excitement of the magical rendezvous she had planned with Neil. She turned to her left and then to her right before parading back and forth and admiring how the stockings enhanced the natural shape of her legs. Doreen was confident that the rich red satin panties matched perfectly with the terracotta eye shadow and the cherry red lipstick. She glanced down at the flesh at the top of her stocking tops. Experience in life had taught her that the reason men found the thigh gap so sexy and a huge turn on was because that hallowed area is only ever seen behind closed doors and when sex is about to happen. Doreen stopped and looked at herself face on and slowly ran her hands over her supple, curvaceous figure. She understood that most men wanted a sexy woman that could hold her own in any conversation and the importance of a sense of humour. The dumb blonde act would only ever attract the one night stand and she had Neil hooked. She revelled in how he was smitten by the older, experienced, woman and how easily he succumbed to her control.

Knowing that Jackie, Neil's girlfriend, was her best operator, she had given her more orders than could be realistically stolen in one day. Doreen had stressed the importance of completing the orders and offered to pay for her to stay overnight in the West End so she could make an early start and then take a taxi back to Doreen's the following day.

There was a knock at the front door. Doreen looked over at the bedside clock and quickly took one last look in the mirror. She took her dressing gown off the hook on the back of her bedroom door and raced down the hallway. She stopped just a few feet from the front door and took a deep breath and smiled.

"Hello Neil, come in," Doreen said as she closed the front door behind him.

"I'm sorry am I early?" Neil said.

"No, no, you're fine," Doreen said.

Neil handed her a bottle of Gordon's London Dry Gin.

Doreen beamed

"That was very thoughtful. It's my favourite gin, Neil," Doreen said as she opened the drinks cabinet. "What would you like?"

"I know that Ricky has been drinking malt whiskey, and apparently Ronnie has some in the Arms now. I've never tried it. Have you got anything like that?"

Doreen picked up a bottle of Bells whiskey.

"This is all I have on the whiskey front. It's been here a while but you're more than welcome," Doreen said, holding up the bottle.

"That'll be great, thank you," Neil said as he sat back on Doreen's new arm chair. "This is new isn't it?"

"Yes, a couple of lads I know nicked it to order but then their customer went and got nicked so they were stuck with it. I made them an offer and they dropped it round yesterday. Do you like it?"

"It looks the business. I really like it and it matches your curtains," Neil said.

"Yeah, they're new too. I've been having a bit of a change around," Doreen said as she handed Neil a full glass of neat whiskey.

Doreen took a sip of her gin and tonic.

"Have a look through those new records on the sideboard would you, and then stick half a dozen on the record player," Doreen said as she wandered over to the door. "I'll be back in a jiffy."

Neil took a second sip of the whiskey.

"Hmm, not bad," Neil muttered as he flicked through the pile of new chart records. He made his selections and put them on the stereo and then sat back in the armchair.

The first record to play was *'You'll Never Find Another Love Like Mine'* by Lou Rawls.

"Good choice. I love this record," Doreen called out from the bedroom.

Neil took a longer swig from his glass.

"Not bad at all," Neil muttered to himself

"Sorry, what was that?" Doreen called out.

"Oh, nothing, I was just saying that this is a nice drop of whiskey," Neil said before taking another sip.

Neil looked up to see Doreen posing seductively by the door. She leaned against the door frame with her left stocking clad leg protruding through the dressing gown. On her feet she wore black fluffy Mule shoes with kitten heels.

Neil sat bolt upright and placed his drink on the coffee table. His eyes were fixed on Doreen

Doreen took two steps into the room and quickly turned her head to make her long platinum blonde hair twirl. Neil was instantly aroused by the sight of Doreen, the smell of her perfume and the anticipation of what was to come. Doreen took another slow step into the room and then, with her alluring galaxy blue eyes fixed on Neil, she bit the corner of her lower lip. Neil could feel his heart pounding and his manhood constrained by the cut of his trousers. Doreen moved her hands to each side of the dressing gown's collar and slowly pulled the gown down over her shoulders. She stopped when the gown was level with her cleavage. Neil gulped, his mouth had become dry but he couldn't move. Doreen allowed the dressing gown to slide effortlessly to the carpet. She posed, her eyes fixed on Neil's, in her matching black silk stockings, suspenders and bra. Neil could feel his mouth drop but was helpless to stop it. Doreen took several steps forward and held out her hand for Neil to stand.

"Look into my eyes, Neil," Doreen whispered.

Neil put his hand around her body and rested it on the small of her back. Doreen slowly moved her head forward and kissed him gently on the lips. Neil lowered his hand, squeezed her pert bottom and pushed his groin against her. Doreen kissed his neck and then slowly undid his shirt buttons while kissing the part of his chest that she had exposed. She continued right down his torso. Then she unbuttoned his trousers and slowly unzipped him. She gripped the top of his trousers and underwear with both hands and slowly slid them down his legs. She stood back, looked down at his excitement, and then kissed him passionately on the lips while holding his manhood firmly in her hand.

"Do you want me to take you in my mouth," Doreen whispered.

"Oh, my God yes," Neil blurted out.

Doreen got down onto her knees and looked up at him with her glowing galaxy eyes.

KNOCK! KNOCK!

Doreen turned to the door.

"Leave it Doreen," Neil said with a hint of desperation.

KNOCK! KNOCK!

Doreen looked at Neil and then at the door.

KNOCK! KNOCK! KNOCK! KNOCK!

"Who the fuck is that?" Neil hissed.

Doreen got back onto her feet.

"I'll try and get rid of them," Doreen said as she raced out the door and down the hallway.

She opened the front door and peered out. It was Kathy the Candle.

"What are you doing here?" Doreen hissed.

"We need to talk and we need to talk now!" Kathy said as she pushed the door open and barged her way inside.

Doreen closed the door and followed her down the hallway. Kathy stepped into the living room and saw that Neil was tugging at his trousers and trying to do the buttons on his shirt.

"Hmm, caught you both at an inconvenient time," Kathy said.

"No, it's not what it looks like," Doreen said as she tightened the belt around her waist.

"Really, a blind man and his guide dog could see this for what it is," Kathy said with a sneer. "You're going out with that nice Jackie, aren't you?"

"Yeah, and what has it got to do with you?" Neil said.

"Don't go getting brave my lad, because you've just been caught with your trousers around your ankles and I mean literally," Kathy said.

"What do you want?" Doreen said, putting her hands on her hips.

"And you can stop with the attitude too. Look at yourself Doreen, you're old enough to be his mother!" Kathy said.

"You need to leave," Neil said.

"Not until I have my say," Kathy said firmly.

"Well what have you got to say that is so important that you have to come around to my house and just barge your way in?" Doreen said.

"It's simple, and even a vixen like you can get it. I want in Doreen!" Kathy said.

"What do you mean, you want in?" Doreen said.

"I want to be part of your hoisting crew. I've heard that some of these girls are pulling four and five hundred quid a week and I want in!"

Doreen dropped her hands to her sides and began to shake her head.

"That ain't about to happen! You don't have what it takes and you've got ex-con written all over you. My girls work the biggest and best shops and you," Doreen said looking Kathy up and down, "will stick out like a sore thumb."

"I'm not asking Doreen, I'm telling!" Kathy said. "I want in and I want five hundred quid a week!"

"Not happening!" said Doreen.

Kathy looked back down at Neil still struggling to button up his shirt.

"Maybe you should try and talk some sense into your bit on the side. This can get very nasty, believe me," Kathy warned.

"Neil has fuck all to do with my business so take your ugly mug and fuck off out of my home!" Doreen yelled

Kathy quickly reached into her bag and produced a small brass candle stick holder. She took it by the end and made a swipe at Doreen. The weapon missed her face by just a few inches. Doreen yelled, and staggered back. With her teeth clenched and with red blazing eyes, Kathy stormed towards her with the brass candle stick holder. Kathy took another swipe, but Doreen leaned backwards. The attack missed her but she tripped on the coffee table and fell awkwardly to the floor. Kathy shoved the coffee table to one side while Doreen pushed herself along the floor in a bid to get away. Kathy stepped over Doreen's wriggling body and dropped down onto her stomach. She grabbed Doreen by the hair with her left hand and pulled her head up towards her face. Kathy ran the brass weapon slowly over Doreen's cheek."

"Fuck you Doreen and fuck your hoisting crew. From now you're going to pay me five hundred quid every Friday or I'll fucking mark you so bad no one will ever look at you again," Kathy said, putting her face closer to Doreen's.

"Fuck you!" Doreen yelled and spat into Kathy's face.

Kathy paused for a second, tightened her grip on Doreen's hair and then glared down at her victim.

"Now you're dead. You're fucking dead!" Kathy said, raising the brass candle stick holder above her head.

SMACK!

Neil had picked up the thick cut glass ashtray from the table and smashed it on the back of Kathy's head. Her limp body collapsed onto the carpet, face down. Blood was streaming out of the wound. Neil pulled her body off Doreen and helped her to her feet.

"I think I might have killed her," Neil said.

"Good, fucking good, the bitch deserves to die," Doreen said.

Neil looked down at Kathy's still body.

"What do I do, call the old bill?" Neil said.

"And tell them what Neil? That Kathy the Candle wanted in on my shoplifting operation and when I refused you smashed her on the head with an ashtray? For fuck's sake, Neil, wake up and smell the coffee," Doreen said.

"What then?"

"Arghh!"

Neil turned to see that Kathy had clambered onto her feet and while still dazed she ran towards him wildly slashing the brass candle stick holder back and forth. Neil was frozen, he held his hands to his face.

CRACK!

Doreen had grabbed the bottle of Gordon's London Dry Gin and cracked Kathy around the head. She staggered back and shook her head while still holding the brass candle stick holder.

CRACK!

"Have that, bitch!" Doreen yelled.

CRACK! SMASH!

Doreen smacked Kathy across the side of her head. There was a thud as the bottle smashed and gin covered the rug and the sofa.

"I'll fucking kill you!" Kathy screamed, blood streaming down her face.

Doreen held the jagged neck of the bottle in her hand. Before Kathy had even raised her weapon, she lunged forward and sank the jagged glass bottle neck into her neck. She pulled back and then did it again and then again until Kathy slumped onto the rug with blood pumping out through the gaps between her fingers. Neil and Doreen looked down as Kathy gasped desperately for air.

"Help me," Kathy gurgled as blood began to stream from her mouth. "Help me please."

Doreen still held the jagged glass bottle neck. Neil slowly prised it out of her hand while Doreen watched Kathy take her last breath. She was dead.

"Are you alright?" Neil said

"That bitch deserved to die," Doreen said.

"It would have been her or you Doreen," Neil said as he stroked her shoulder. "It's self-defence."

"She started it," Doreen muttered. "The bitch started it!"

"I know, I know and that's what we'll tell the police," Neil said.

"The police, the fucking police Neil? They will take us away and lock us both up for good. This is murder Neil!" Doreen bellowed.

"Yeah, right, okay so what do we do?" Neil said while panic hopping from his left foot to his right.

"I don't know, Neil. You have to help me, please. I do not want to go to prison for the rest of my life," Doreen said as she threw her arms around him.

"I'll call Ricky," Neil said finally.

"Ricky? Ricky Turrell?" Doreen said.

"Yeah, he'll know what to do. If there's anyone that can help us out, it'll be him," Neil said.

"So call him," Doreen said, looking down at Kathy's dead body.

Neil picked up the telephone and dialled Ricky's home number.

Ricky: Hello

Neil: Hello Ricky, mate, it's Neil. I really need your help.

Ricky: What's up Neil, have you been nicked?

Neil: If only it was that simple. No, this is major stuff and I need a mate.

Ricky: What is it, Neil?

Neil: I can't say over the phone.

Ricky: Okay, so how urgent is it? Can it wait until tomorrow?

Neil: Ricky I need your help now, and I mean right now.

Ricky: Where are you?

Neil: I'm at Doreen's place, please hurry mate.

Ricky: I'll be there in fifteen minutes.

Neil: Cheers mate. I owe you.

Ricky hung up the phone.

Doreen and Neil sat on the couch and stared at the door.

Fifteen minutes passed and there was a knock at the door. Neil pounded down the hallway, opened the front door, and ushered Ricky in.

"What's the problem, Neil?" Ricky said as he followed Neil down the hallway and into the lounge.

"What the fuck?" Ricky said as he looked down at Kathy and the blood-soaked carpet around her head.

Doreen and Neil explained what had happened and how the whole thing had been an act of self-defence.

"Can you help us Ricky?" Doreen said with a plea of desperation.

Ricky turned to Doreen in her dressing gown and then to Neil.

"Maybe. I'll need to use your phone. Doreen, you go and get changed and then stick the kettle on. I think we could all do with a cup of coffee," Ricky said.

Doreen pulled the belt to her dressing gown tighter, nodded, and then left the room.

"Right, Neil, I'm going to call on some people to help. It will cost you. I don't want nothing Neil, you're my mate, but to make this go away it's going to cost."

"Yeah, sure Ricky. What kind of money are we talking about?"

"I'm going to try them with five grand, but they might want more. Can you cover that?" Ricky said.

Neil nodded his head.

"I can do that and if it's any more then I'm sure that between me and Doreen we'll get it covered," Neil.

Ricky picked up then the receiver and dialled a number.

Voice: Hello

Ricky: Hello, it's Ricky I need your help with a clean-up job. There's five grand in it but it needs to be done straight away. Can you do it?

Voice: What do we need?

Ricky: A Granada should do it.

Voice: Okay, where are you.

Ricky gave Doreen's address and was told to expect company within half an hour. Doreen returned fully dressed and carrying a tray with three mugs of coffee.

"Can you help us Ricky?"

Ricky nodded.

"There will be some people coming here during the next half hour or so. When that front doorbell goes, I want you both to go to the bedroom and close the door behind you. Neil can fill you in on the details but you are not to see these people and this problem of yours will disappear. These boys will need paying," Ricky said.

"Yeah, it's five grand," Neil said.

"Five grand?" Doreen said.

"Yeah, you're lucky it's not ten," Ricky said firmly.

"No, no that's fine we can do that between us, can't we Neil?" Doreen said.

"I will pay these boys myself, alright? But I want that money back by tomorrow latest. Is that going to be a problem?" Ricky said.

"No, no problem," Doreen said.

Ricky took a coffee mug from the tray and looked down at Kathy's dead body.

"I never liked you," Ricky thought.

The half an hour passed quickly and a there was a knock at the door.

"Right, you two down to the bedroom, chop, chop," Ricky said, motioning them to leave the lounge. He watched them go down the hallway and close the bedroom door behind them.

Ricky opened the front door and let Terry and Steve Parker in. He placed his finger over his lips indicating that they were to keep quiet. Ricky led them into the lounge and closed the door. The three lads looked down on the dead body.

"Things got a bit out of hand here and a friend called for my help. You said that you wanted to make money. We need for that," Ricky said, pointing at the body, "To disappear without a trace. Can you do that?"

Both Terry and Steve were indifferent to what they were looking at.

"Five grand," Terry said.

"Is that alright?" Ricky said.

"Yeah, you'll never hear about her again," Terry said. "Besides, I never liked her."

"Me either, loud, mouthy, trouble maker," Steve said.

"I'll be able to sort your money out tomorrow at my work and then those responsible will pay me back," Ricky said.

"They better do," Terry said, "or they'll be joining this bitch."

Terry, Steve and Ricky rolled Kathy's body in the blood soaked rug along with the broken glass and blood stained ashtray. Once every piece of evidence had been gathered up, Terry and Steve carried the body down to the Ford Granada they had parked up outside. The car had been stolen two days earlier and was due to be turned into a ringer and then sold at auction. They piled the evidence into the boot. Steve followed Terry across town in a second car where they stopped in a secluded area just a couple of hundred yards from a Gypsy campsite.

Steve took a petrol can from the boot of his car and doused the evidence in petrol. He opened all the car's windows and poured the five-gallon Jerry can over the interior and outer body panels. Terry opened the petrol cap and poured fuel around the opening. Steve took out a box of matches, lit one and dropped it through the car window. The car immediately burst into flames. Steve casually closed the lid of the Jerry can and placed it back in the boot of the second car. The two men got into the car and drove away slowly. Steve looked in his rear-view mirror and saw the car was completely engulfed with flames leaping high towards the night sky.

Chapter 23

"Hello mate," Neil said.

Ricky looked up from his pint of Carlsberg lager.

"Alright Neil. Yeah, what's up? You look a bit on edge," Ricky said as he motioned the barman to bring over another pint for Neil.

"I'm alright, well as alright as one can be," Neil said.

"Whoa, now let me stop you there matey. There is never to be any talk about you know what," Ricky said decisively.

"No, no mate I mean I've been black bagged," Neil said.

"Black bagged?"

"Yeah I got home today and Jackie has stuck two black bags full of my stuff outside the front door with a note that just said: "I know about Doreen you bastard!"

"Well mate I suppose it was only a matter of time. I mean you were round there at all times slipping her one and you weren't exactly discreet about it either," Ricky said as he took the pints off the tray. "Cheers."

"What do you mean discreet? I didn't tell anyone except you," Neil said.

"You better back up Neil if you're insinuating that I said something," Ricky said sternly.

"No, no of course not. I just meant that I didn't tell anyone," Neil said.

"Well what about the Beano down to Margate?" Ricky said.

Neil shrugged his shoulders. "So what? It was just two friends hanging out," Neil said.

"Who are you trying to kid Neil? I mean you were all over each other. I couldn't have been the only one that saw you in the 'Jolly Dog' over by the pool table. I mean, come on Neil Doreen works with Jackie, Melanie, Kaz and Donna. Did you not think that sooner or later something was going to give?" Ricky said.

"No mate. I thought I'd get my cake and eat it. I couldn't give up Doreen because frankly the sex is just brilliant and Jackie, well she's just lovely and I always liked her, even as a kid, so I kind of wanted her too," Neil said as he took a sip from his pint.

"So what's the plan now?" Ricky said.

"I think the shit is going to well and truly hit the fan when I tell Doreen. Jackie is her best operator. She can hoist double what the other girls do and she's quick, smart and looks the part so she's unlikely to get caught," Neil said.

"Oh shit, this is going to get nasty," Ricky said with a wry smile.

"What you think this is funny?" Neil said.

"Mate you and Doreen have bolloxed up thousands of pounds a week for what… sex?" Ricky said.

"What you do mean Melanie, Kaz and Donna could fuck off too?" Neil said.

"What do you think? It was Jackie that brought all three of them in and girls can get mighty funny over loyalty or lack of it, Neil. With that in mind, you might want to avoid them too," Ricky.

"Oh Ricky mate, this is far worse than I thought. Doreen will go up the wall. She's expanded her customer base and she needs top quality shoplifters out grafting six days a week," Neil said.

"The sooner she knows then the sooner she can try to make some kind of contingency plan," Ricky said.

"Do you reckon she'll put me up? You know, let me move in with her?" Neil said.

"It's possible, but you and your cock will be at the bottom of her list if she loses a big part of her shoplifting crew," Ricky said.

Neil leaned forward with his elbows on the table and rested his head in his hands.

"This is a bloody nightmare," Neil said. "Ricky?"

"What?"

"Can I move in with you until I get myself sorted?" Neil said.

"No mate," Ricky said as he shook his head slowly.

"No?"

"That's right, Neil, the answer is no and I'll give you my reasons. Number one. You dropped me and our bit of motoring business when Jackie told you to do so. You could have left me high and dry with Frank Allen and mate, you knew that. Number two. Melanie, Kaz and Donna are all my friends and an integral part of the Milton Road Teds and I cannot be seen to be siding with a bloke who was shagging one of their best friend's employers. So Neil, you are my mate but in this you are on your own. Don't try giving me some old sob story about having no money because we both know that would be bollocks. If you want my advice, I'd say that you best go and give Doreen the bad news quick and if she doesn't want you there then you best go and book a hotel until you can get something sorted," Ricky said.

"Mate, will you come with me?"

"What, are you having a laugh? Not a chance Neil. I have my own shit to deal with so you need to crack on with yours. Come with me… Whatever next, tell her for you? What the hell are you on mate?" Ricky said.

"I thought we were mates," Neil said.

"Yeah and so did I, until you dropped me in it. Now think very carefully before you say anything else because you're venturing onto thin ice," Ricky said.

Neil placed his three quarter full pint back on the table.

"I suppose I'd better go see Doreen then and get this over and done with," Neil said, smiling bleakly.

"Alright Ricky, Neil," Bill said as he walked towards the table. "Sorry to hear you got black bagged mate."

"How the hell do you know?" Neil said.

"Kaz told me earlier, and boy has she got the hump with you and Doreen. Still, hopefully it was worth it," Bill said as he shot a sly wink to Ricky.

"Has Kaz said anything to Doreen?" Neil said.

"No she had a coffee in town with Jackie and that's when she found out. It's a bit embarrassing, you know, the whole black bag thing. I have to say though I wouldn't put it past Donna to not just waltz up and give you a slap. Kaz reckons that Donna is a real sucker for taking on other people's problems," Bill said as he shook his head.

"I better get round there," Neil said as he backed away and walked briskly towards the door.

***

"The things people will do for pussy," Bill said.

"Mate, despite whatever you read or hear in the media, we men are definitely the weaker sex. Men, in general, are not strong enough to control their emotions and will have sex with somebody that they don't really want to, too," Ricky.

"True," said Bill. "I've been there, done that, and paid the price for it. I've known mates that have just passively allowed themselves to get trapped into marriages that didn't really work out the way they hoped."

"Bill I have mates who have completely changed their personality just so that they can go out with a bird. Can you imagine that? Waking up every day and trying to be someone else just to get laid," Ricky said.

Bill laughed out loud and held his hands up. "Ricky I've done that too. Not for long mind, because I just couldn't keep it up."

"Was she worth it?" Ricky asked.

"She was a right cracking looking bird Ricky, and I mean she had legs that went all the way up to her armpits, but I knew that she would never fancy a bloke like me unless I could be someone important," said Bill.

"Well go on then, what did you tell her?"

"I told her that I was an undercover police officer working on a big case involving murders, violence and six figure robberies," Bill said.

"How the hell did you keep that one up? I mean you're not exactly the type of bloke who gets into the old bill," Ricky said.

"Ricky you would have been proud of me. I laid it on nice and smooth and believe me I had her eating out of my underpants by the end of the evening. Now I'd like to say that she was the fuck of the century but like most good looking birds she was just lazy. No imagination and just lay back there while I did all the work. The next morning I was tempted to come clean and tell her that actually I duck and dive, buy and sell a few motors but opted to just say that my cover might have been blown and it wouldn't be safe for her to be around me for a while. To be honest she didn't seem too bothered and left without drinking the coffee I'd made her," Bill said.

"Maybe she didn't rate you as the fuck of the century either," Ricky said with a chuckle.

"Damn, I never thought about that. You've done it now, mate, I can feel a complex coming on. I'll have to write in to one of these problem pages. You know the kind you get in bird's magazines that wind up in the doctor's reception area," Bill said.

Chapter 24

Bill drove over to Wimbledon and parked behind the supermarket before taking an underground train to St James Park where he walked the last three minutes to Scotland Yard. He signed in at the main desk and went upstairs to meet with DCI Mike Wilson.

"Bill, good of you to meet me," DCI Wilson said.

"It's good to be here sir," Bill said.

DCI Wilson opened a file on his desk.

"There's quite a picture forming here," DCI Wilson said as he reviewed the telephone conversation he had been sharing while Bill was undercover.

"I'm in deep sir and I'm trusted," Bill said.

"I think that you must have one of the most interesting roles in policing Bill," DCI Wilson said. "It must be exciting living a double life."

"I'm just doing my duty," Bill said.

"All those secrets you must now have by talking directly to the people on the streets. You must be getting so much more than any of the uniform branches," DCI Wilson said.

"It's like I said sir. I am in deep now on the estate. I have a solid cover," Bill said.

"It must be tricky sometimes, you know, remembering that you are one of the good guys sent in to bring them down," DCI Wilson said.

"No, not at all, sir. I'm clear about my role and what is expected of me," Bill said.

"The courts aren't always keen on our undercover operations because by the very nature of your assignment you have to break the law to enforce it," DCI Wilson said.

"Yes, sir," Bill said.

"Hmm, yes. What crimes have you committed to establish yourself so deep undercover?" DCI Wilson asked.

"The bare minimum sir, only what I deemed essential." Bill said.

"Can you be specific please Bill?" DCI Wilson said.

"I have had to engage in violence to secure my position in both the Milton Arms pub and with the Ted Army," Bill said.

"Hmm, violence and the Ted Army. I'll come back to that," DCI Wilson said. "How are you in yourself? You've been undercover quite a while. Are you feeling the stress, are you suffering from anxiety? Are you drinking too much?"

"Sir, I'm fine. This is an operation like the others only there is so much more than what we originally thought. The entire estate is a den of iniquity," Bill said.

"I have to ask you Bill or I wouldn't be doing my job," DCI Wilson said.

"I understand sir," Bill said.

"I'm concerned that you could be putting yourself at risk," DCI Wilson said.

"It's part of the job, sir," Bill said.

"I'm reading through this and we have a shoplifting ring that's probably responsible for over a hundred thousand pounds of stolen property. The theft of high value cars and the landlord regularly engages in serving customers after hours," DCI Wilson said.

"Sir, that's just scratching the surface. With time I'll be able to uncover a great deal more," Bill said.

"Yes, you've mentioned organised violence, which could amount to conspiracy charges," DCI Wilson said.

"It's so much more than that sir. We're talking about an army from every corner of London. These are not just your Friday night tear up boys, sir. This lot will turn up fully armed with the sole intention of causing as much pain and destruction to property as possible. I don't mean ten, twenty or even a hundred battle ready Teddy Boys. I'm due to go to a meeting between all the biggest gangs in London about finalising the Ted Army, sir. We are talking about an Army with over one thousand troops," Bill said.

"One thousand troops you say?" DCI Wilson said with a look of astonishment.

"Yes sir and I will be right there with the leaders of all these gangs," Bill said.

"Who is behind all this, Bill?" DCI Wilson said.

"Ricky Turrell is one of my primary targets sir. Ricky is the leader of the Milton Road Teds. He's acknowledged as a senior figure on the estate and, sir, he is the driving force behind the Ted Army," said

Bill. "The more you dig you more you find Ricky Turrell is somewhere behind it. I believe that he's involved in a great deal more."

DCI Wilson scribbled the name 'Ricky Turrell' in large letters in his file.

"Okay, now what about the murder of Deano Derenzie. Have you made any progress there?" DCI Williams said.

"I don't have any firm evidence yet, sir, but from what I've heard, it was an old school villain known as Fat Pat. You should have his file sir. My understanding is that Clifford Tate, the leader of a gang on the Bedford Estate, was the getaway driver," Bill said.

"Do you know why they did it?" DCI Wilson said.

"I believe that an individual known as Eddy Boyce was responsible for a stabbing incident that involved Deano Derenzie. He has since gone missing, but most people seem to think that he's dead and at the hands of Deano Derenzie and maybe others. Fat Pat, sir, was his uncle and Clifford Tate his best friend," Bill said.

"We seem to have a lot of speculation and circumstantial evidence at best," DCI Wilson said.

"We need more time, sir. Ricky Turrell is connected to Frank Allen. They're friends and they are doing business together," Bill said. "I have seen them together and Ricky is part of the fabric. It's way more than just casual acquaintances, sir."

"Frank Allen. The time for bringing him in is well over due. What do you have, Bill?" DCI Wilson said.

"I don't have anything concrete yet sir, but I am in at the Arms pub which no other undercover detective has ever achieved. I'm right in there tight with the key movers and shakers. In addition I am now a regular at the Cadillac Club with access to the VIP Lounge, again something no one else has ever achieved. Mike, we are making good, solid, progress and it's only time before all the parts of the jigsaw puzzle come together and then sir, with your go ahead, we can bring the whole lot down," Bill said.

"It's very tempting Bill," DCI Wilson said.

"Tempting, sir?" Bill said.

"Yes, tempting to keep the investigation running rather than have one big clear up on what we already have," DCI Wilson said.

"Sir, you can't stop now. I'm pretty certain that something has happened to Kathy the Candle. Someone on the estate has taken her out. I believe she's dead sir," Bill said.

"Kathy the Candle?" DCI Wilson said with a quizzical look.

"Kathy McCrea, sir. She was released from Holloway earlier in the year. She's an aggressive alpha female with a lot of enemies on the estate and in part fell under the protection of the pub's landlord," Bill said.

"Do you have any idea who is responsible, if she has been murdered?" DCI Wilson asked.

"I have my suspicions sir, but the answer will come. It's like I said sir, they talk openly around me. I am considered as one of their own," Bill said.

"These undercover operations are funded by upstairs and they expect to see a return on their investment by way of convictions. With what we could actually prosecute for right now would be considered a success," DCI Wilson.

"Mike, Ricky Turrell is travelling to Spain and I don't think for a single moment, that it's a boys' jolly with a piss up in the sun and a few senoritas. This is business, everything about it says criminal business. Frank Allen is big league and he is working on something with Ricky Turrell who has taken me into his confidence. He trusts me sir. When he gets back I'll push him for a part of whatever he and Frank Allen are up to. Then we'll have them sir. It will be a huge score for you and I'll get the Detective Chief Inspector's role. All we need is patience," Bill said.

"Bill I have a lot to think about. I will be speaking with those upstairs. I'll tell them where you are, and what evidence we actually have, so that a decision can be made. If it doesn't go the way you want then I will give you ample warning and bring you in as a part of a wider investigation and as a contingency it'll keep your cover in place," DCI Wilson said.

"Let's hope that they see the bigger picture here, sir. We're talking about murders and violence on an unprecedented scale and that's in addition to whatever we can get on Frank Allen," said Bill.

"Like I said Bill, I'll keep you posted," DCI Wilson said as he closed the file and placed it back in his filing cabinet.

"Is that it, sir?" Bill said.

"I'll be in touch. Keep up the good work, Bill," DCI Wilson said as he shook Bill's hand.

***

Bill left the building. He found himself feeling conflicted and in turmoil. One part of him wanted to do what his job entailed and bring down those responsible for criminal activities, but another, growing part, felt like for the first time in years that he was where he belonged. The Milton Road Estate were his people. They understood him and he them. He was a respected figure that had proved that he had the right to belong under conditions that would have sent a great many police officers running for cover. Bill was at home at the Arms, he enjoyed the conflict and violence and there was Kaz. He had fallen for Kaz. At first, she was the perfect route to get in with the inner circle, and slowly but surely, she had won him over and he'd fallen for her. Bill had even thought about marriage and kids while still supplying cars that he knew would end up being ringers and sold on. He had only said enough about Ricky's criminal involvement to try and keep DCI Wilson from closing down the operation. He had been baiting him with promises in the future because Bill wasn't ready to give up his life on the estate, his friendship with Ricky and the Milton Road Teds, his growing status with the Ted Army and the woman he loved, Kaz.

Bill stood outside the Feathers pub. It was a Victorian building with windows that spanned from floor to ceiling. He went inside and ordered a pint with a whiskey chaser and then took a seat where he thought through where he was and how he could either prolong the investigation or somehow scupper everything while retaining his position with the police and holding on to the secret life he needed with Kaz, Ricky and the Milton Road Estate.

Chapter 25

"Do you reckon everyone will show?" Bill said as he looked up at the underground train line map at the top of the carriage.

"Some will and some won't. Those that do will have a clear understanding of the Ted Army going forward and those that don't will receive an individual visit," Ricky said.

"I'm curious. Of all the places to meet, why The Elephant & Castle?" Bill said as he sat back on his seat.

"For a couple of reasons," Ricky said. "Firstly, the Elephant & Castle was arguably the birth place of the Teddy Boys back in the 1950s and secondly it's where Deano brought the first Ted Army meeting together."

"I wonder if Suzi still works there," Ricky thought. *"I wonder if she's still picking up game lads for her and her girlfriend, Laurie, to share. It could be awkward if she is."*

Ricky had set up a meeting with the leaders of the largest Teddy Boy gangs from across London. He had purposely chosen the Castle pub at the Elephant & Castle because it was where Deano had proposed the unbreakable alliance between the Teds, and where so many had seen the merits and agreed to the alliance. It was just a short ten stops on the Northern Line from Morden, so Ricky had left his car at a local car park. He asked Bill to stand alongside him during the negotiations and Terry and Steve Parker were there to administer pain should there be any violence. The four Teds left the

Tube station and went into the Castle pub. It was just as Ricky remembered. In the far corner was a large group of Teds.

"Excellent," Ricky thought and then scanned the room looking for Suzi.

"Hello mate, I'll have four pints of Carling and send over whatever my friends are drinking," Ricky said as he placed three ten pound notes on the bar. "Have one yourself."

Ricky strode over to meet the other gang leaders, paying particular attention to those who had turned out for the row with the 'White Boy Nation' while Bill found himself talking with Jock Addie, the leader of the Croydon Teds.

"Hello Bill, how are you mate?" Jock Addie said as he shook his hand.

"Yeah, I'm good. What about you?" Bill said.

"I'm a little apprehensive about today to be honest. I mean, we're signed up, but I know that there are those who are not and, well, you never know," Jock said.

"Ricky's got it all in hand," Bill said.

"Oh, I don't doubt that," Jock said. "Did you see that Bill Grundy show, what was it? Today? At the beginning of the year?"

"No," Bill said taking a long sip of his cold lager. "I don't really watch television that much."

"Mate, you should have seen this. There was this bunch of Punk Rockers, The Sex Pistols, being interviewed."

"Punk Rockers? What's all that then?" Bill said.

"Bill you ain't never seen anything like it. Have you not been down the Kings Road recently?"

"No, not for a while."

What about Ricky, has he been down there?" Jock asked.

"I couldn't speak for him," Bill said.

"Well if he hasn't then he should, because this Punk Rock thing is growing and growing fast. I was there with a half a dozen of my lads and there were these birds with bright green spikey hair and another with purple hair. I mean who the fuck has green or purple hair? This one bird was dressed in a black leather skirt and there must have been a dozen zips on it and she had this black leather dog collar on with studs and stuff on it and was wearing Doc Marten boots. A girl was wearing super high leg Ox-blood Doc Marten Boots, can you believe it? There was a bunch of them with blokes wearing these trousers that had some kind of a line of material that joined the knees, and his hair! You should have seen it Bill! I'm not kidding, it must have pointed eight or nine inches off his head. It looked razor sharp and he had some kind of black make-up around his eyes," Jock said.

"What kind of numbers were there?" Bill said.

"I suppose I probably saw maybe twenty or thirty of them just parading around looking well scary I suppose, because people were literally crossing the road to avoid them. They all seemed to congregate at the Roebuck pub. It was then that the gavvers turned up, as they do, and raided the pub. Mate you never seen so much flying out of a window in your life. There must have been all sorts littered over the pavement and the old bill couldn't do a thing," Jock said.

"So, did they nick anyone?" Bill said.

"No, one by one the old bill came out the pub and buggered off and these Punk Rockers were straight back at it," Jock said. "I have to say that some of them did look a handful and that was just the birds."

"What happened on that Today programme then?" Bill said.

"It was these Punk Rockers, the Sex Pistols, and old Grundy was goading them into saying something shocking and so they were calling him a dirty bastard and it went on. Anyway, I remember thinking that something like that had scope to become big and mate, believe me, the Kings Road is spawning a new cult. This is just the start, you mark my words. I was thinking that me and the lads should take up a bit of Punk bashing on a Saturday," Jock said. "Just wearing a ripped T-shirt and a swastika armband is a good enough reason to get a slap in my book."

"You sure it's not just a bunch of middle class kids playing at being rebels to upset mummy and daddy?" Bill said.

"Maybe to start with Bill, but I can see this growing arms and legs and we need to put on a clear show of force in the Kings Road just to let them know that it's Ted territory and there's consequences for stepping out of line," Jock said.

"Maybe this should be a separate meeting with Ricky once this has been put to bed," Bill said.

"Yeah, I'll come over to the Arms and maybe the three of us can come up with a plan of action," Jock said. "I quite fancy a row with a few of those punks."

Ricky had finished shaking hands with the leaders of all the gangs and took his seat at the end of the table. The barman and a waitress brought over trays of drinks. The Teds went quiet and waited for Ricky to speak.

"I'd like to thank you all for meeting with me here. As you know, this was the venue that initially brought us all together to share in Deano's vision of an alliance between all the Teddy Boys gangs in London. It was the beginning of a unified Ted Army with the power and numbers to respond to any threat by anyone, anywhere. Sadly, as you all know, Deano the Dog was gunned down outside the Cadillac Club by two men. Both have since been dealt with," Ricky said.

"We're with you Ricky," Jock called out.

"So are we," Everard said.

Ricky surveyed the room to see several nods of approval.

"Well I'm not," Carly Thompson, the leader of the Mile End Teds said, "And neither are my lads. The Mile End Teds stand alone."

The Teds became quiet with looks bouncing back and forth from Ricky to Carly.

"I think you might find that it's you that stands alone Carly," Ricky said as he turned and fixed his eyes directly on Carly.

"What do you mean by that?" Carly said as he stood bolt upright, knocking his chair over.

Ricky stood up and smiled.

"Carly Thompson you have no vision and no aspiration to be anything more than the little man that you are, and frankly, in an organisation like the Ted Army you add no value. You would be a liability just as you are to the brave, honourable, lads that make up the Mile End Teds," Ricky said as he stepped away from his chair and faced Carly Thompson.

"Who the hell do you think you are? I told Deano the fucking dog and I'm telling you too. The Mile End Teds follow no one but me. We don't need you or anyone else to fight our battles," Carly said as he produced an eight inch switchblade from his pocket. He pressed the button and the razor sharp blade shot out and locked.

"You got away with that last time Carly but not now," Ricky said.

"I'll fucking do you!" Carly yelled as he lunged forward thrusting the blade aimlessly.

The blade missed as Ricky side stepped him. Terry Peters threw over a rubber covered metal cosh. Ricky caught it with his right hand and brought it down swiftly to the side of Carly's head with a dull thud. Carly's legs crumbled and while dazed he persisted in lashing out with the blade. Ricky put the cosh on the table. Carly was opening and closing his eyes, desperately trying to get focused. Ricky moved forward with both fists clenched. Carly made another clumsy lunge forward.

SMACK! Ricky fired a punch.

SMACK! SMACK! Then two more. Carly dropped the knife and rested on his bended knees. The lads around the table looked on. Ricky reached down and picked up the knife. Terry and Steve Parker now stood on either side of him. Ricky nodded and the two brothers grabbed Carly by the arms. Ricky walked around his crouching body and grabbed a handful of hair from the back of his head. Carly winced and struggled as Ricky took the blade and began to take huge slices of his Teddy Boy hair style away. He threw heaps of his greased hair onto the floor

"Strip him of his drape," Ricky commanded as he looked down on the partially balding former Teddy Boy.

Terry and Steve tore the jacket off him.

"The brothel creepers too," Ricky said firmly.

Ricky walked back around so that he faced Carly face on.

"Now listen and listen very carefully. Under normal circumstances if somebody is silly enough to pull a blade on me, I know exactly what I have to do. By rights Carly, you should be dead now and your body carried off to where no one will ever find it. So, matey, you've had a touch. Now believe me when I say that if I come across you again you will not see that day out. If it's not me that finishes you then it'll be Terry, if not Terry then it'll be Steve, if not Steve then Bill and so it will go on until somebody in the Ted Army puts an end to Carly Thompson. Mack is now number one in the Mile End Road Teds, he runs it. You're out and banished from drinking in the same pub or even talking to the members. Your days as a Ted are over. Now get up and fuck off. We've got Ted Army business to discuss."

Carly clambered awkwardly to his feet. He rubbed his head and felt the savage haircut that Ricky had given him.

"There you go Deano, sorted just the way you would have wanted," Ricky thought.

"Everything okay with you Mack?" Ricky said.

"All is good here," Mack said turning away from his former leader as he left the pub in just his socks, trousers and shirt.

Ricky returned to his chair at the head of the table. He scanned the table slowly as he took a sip from his glass.

"Can I have a show of hands of all those that are now tied into the alliance and the formation of the Ted Army," Ricky said.

One by one the hands raised from around the table until the vote was unanimous.

"Thank you. We are now formally an alliance and as such I should explain how we are to go forward. Each gang will continue to operate under its existing leadership but with a uniform hierarchy. At the bottom are the Ted soldiers and while they have no power within the gang, they form the heart and soul. It will be these Teds that make the gangs tough and fearsome. They will use deadly force as and when required. Another part of their role as soldiers is to feed back to the leadership the police or enemy activity. Only proven soldiers will move up the ranks to leadership."

Ricky stopped to take a breath and to ensure that all his words were being heard.

"A separate unit will be created, within six months, and will consist of the most ruthless, fearless and trusted members of the Ted Army. This unit of Ted soldiers will carry out specific tasks on behalf of the Ted Army as a whole."

"You mean like the SAS, you know, the Special Air Service?" Jock said.

"Something like that," Ricky said.

The lieutenants are the gang's most trusted members and right hands to the leadership. They are responsible and accountable for executing all the actions of the leadership. Each Ted Gang will have a First Lieutenant and he will act on behalf of the leader when specified. They will oversee the soldiers and identify, encourage and nurture the up and coming talent. The leadership of each gang remains as it is with each gang leader becoming a member of the Ted Army's controlling commission. You, as leaders, will have a say in the Ted Army's strategic development and will be expected to drive the changes through your gang. From now on, all new members are to be sponsored by an existing member with a minimum of one year with the gang and any problems created by a new member will be managed by their sponsor."

Ricky stopped to observe the nodding heads from around the table.

"Effective from today the Ted Army will operate strictly by these set of rules," Ricky said as he handed out a photocopied sheet, headed 'Ted Army Rules'.

Once every gang leader had a photocopy of the rules in front of them, Ricky slowly but clearly, talked the commission through each one:

Ted Army Rules:

1. *No member can be a police informer or grass*
2. *No member can be a coward*
3. *No member can fight another member without approval*
4. *No member must disrespect any member's family including having sex with another member's wife or girlfriend.*
5. *A member must not steal from another member.*
6. *A member must not create problems or political issues with other members of the Ted Army.*

7. Retaliation must be carried out if anyone crosses the Ted Army, without exception.
8. Vendetta must be carried out even if it takes months, years or decades.
9. If a member of the Ted Army is harmed or killed by the police, rival gang or an individual, retaliation must be immediate, swift, brutal and deadly.
10. The Ted Army comes before family, religion or God.
11. A member must never interfere with another member's business.
12. A member must always treat another member's family with respect and kindness.
13. A member must always protect another member from harm.
14. A member must always treat another member like a brother.
15. A member must deny the existence of the Ted Army to the police or the authorities.

Ricky paused to watch the lads smiling and nodding their heads in agreement. The Ted Army had been forged.

"With this uniform structure, the Ted Army will become the most powerful force on the streets of London," Ricky said. "Existing and new members will share a common identity, they will feel that they belong and are needed. Being a Ted is a life choice and exciting. We want all members to gain status and respect with not just their gang, but with the Ted Army. All members, under these strict rules, are safe and protected from rival gangs or Bully Boys looking to make a name for themselves. You fuck with just one of us and you fuck with fifteen hundred rock solid Teds. That is power!"

Jock Addie was the first to begin clapping his hands with the other gang leaders quickly following suit.

"Thank you," Ricky said. "The leader of each gang will be asked at some point to do something over and beyond the call of duty to prove their loyalty to the Ted Army."

"How do you mean?" one of the gang leaders asked.

"It could be something as simple as an electrician who is busy and needs an employee. He then gives the work to another member who has the appropriate qualifications who isn't working. Or possibly somebody that works in a builder's merchants with the discretion to provide discount. It could be that a member's day job is a builder. He gives the new business to the guy in the builder's merchants and in return the builder gets preferential rates," Ricky said.

"So, we're to help each other wherever possible?" Jock said.

Ricky nodded.

"I like that Ricky. I like that a lot. There must be a hundred and one things that we can do to help each other get ahead," Jock said.

"It would be a key feature and benefit of belonging to the Ted Army. If a member is without work and another, anywhere in London, can help, then he should. Just as some group of lads think they can have a pop at a smaller Ted Gang, they would have the entire weight of the Army behind them," Ricky said.

Ricky motioned the barman over to the table and ordered another round for everyone.

"Tell me mate, is Suzi still here?" Ricky asked quietly.

"No, she left a few months back. The last time I saw her she had dumped all the Ted gear and was dressed in all this punk stuff," the barman said.

"Punk gear?" Ricky said with a quizzical expression.

"Yeah, she had this leather mini skirt with fishnet tights and a black, ripped, T-shirt with 'Bollocks' scribbled across it. I almost didn't recognise her because she'd dyed her hair this kind of black with long spikey, electric blue, tips. As shocking as she looked, there was something kind of sexy about it too, if you know what I mean," the barman said.

"Where did you see her?" Ricky asked.

"I was in the Kings Road doing a bit of shopping and she was hanging about outside the Roebuck pub. It's like I said, I was in a world of my own and she just called out after me. I have to say that she seemed happy enough and was going on about this band, the Sex Pistols, and how she was matey with the band," the barman said.

"Cheers, I'll keep an eye out for her," Ricky said.

Ricky, Bill, Terry and Steve stayed and drank with the leaders of each gang until closing time. Ricky flagged down a taxi to take them back to Morden.

Chapter 26

Ricky was up early and had his bag packed for Spain. He drove down the M23 Motorway to Gatwick airport and parked up at the Long Term Car park by the South Terminal. He carried his case into the airport and joined Frank at the Dan-Air check in counter. Within half an hour they had checked in, passed through customs and were in the departure lounge. Frank headed towards a bar that served food and the two men found a table and sat down.

"How are you getting along with that nice girl, Michelle?" Frank said.

"I'm not sure Frank. All she wants to do is try and change me into something I'm not," Ricky said. "It's a shame because in the beginning it seemed to be me, the person who I am, that she was attracted to."

"It's almost always like that," Frank said. "But I'm sure you'll do the right thing for you."

"Are you married Frank, if you don't mind me asking?"

"No I'm not married, it's not for me. There was one girl, pretty little angel she was, back in 1963. I thought that she was the one. I met her in Esmeralda's Barn, the nightclub and casino owned by the Twins, Ronnie and Reg. Alfie Kray, who was running the place back then, had organised this big theme night and the place was packed with movie stars, aristocrats, politicians, villains and all the candy you could want, be it a working girl or a rent boy. Ron did have a thing for the young boys. I couldn't take my eyes off this girl. Sandra was her name. You must know what that's like," Frank said.

"Oh yeah," sighed Ricky.

"Well Alfie has called this girl over and introduced us. He could see that we were both looking at each other. Very perceptive man was that Alfie Kray. Anyway Sandra and I chatted for hours and hours. It turns out she'd come down for work from Manchester and got a start in the club as a hostess. I thought everything was going swimmingly. We had gone out several times to fancy restaurants, bars and clubs and I thought we had something more and then I went around to her digs one Saturday only to find that she'd gone. Her neighbour said she was married with a young kiddie and had gone back to Manchester. That was a tough one to swallow," Frank said.

"Sorry to hear that Frank," Ricky said.

"It was a long time ago now Ricky, but I still think about her sometimes and wonder where she is and what she is doing. So after that I decided, having looked around at my mates back then and the grief they were getting from their wives that having my freedom was a priority. While others were stressing out over what time they were expected in or taking grief for not spending enough time with the kids, not earning enough, or staying out too late, I could just do whatever, whenever. I was the sole master of my own time and didn't have to answer to anyone. I would have friends ask if I fancied a trip to New York or Las Vegas and I could just go without any explanations. My married friends had other things to consider if they still wanted to be married when they got back. I watched the pain some of these men went through when they traded their Jaguar XK150 for a family four door saloon," Frank said.

"I can get that," Ricky said. "I can't imagine somebody living in my place and then telling me what I have to do."

"It's the excitement too, Ricky. The sixties were wild, promiscuous times, with beautiful women running around in short little skirts and being out on the town with your friends in your handmade suits from Saville Row attracted a lot of female attention. You just never knew what young lady would want to know you better. Every party was an opportunity to meet someone new. It was a very exciting time. I'm sure it isn't that much different now. The only thing that changes is the people and the music. I think it's a generation thing," Frank said.

"I've got a mate, Kenny, he's a good lad but his absolute downfall is women. Everyone he meets is a conquest just waiting to happen whether he likes them or not," Ricky said.

"If I were honest Ricky, I don't think the lifestyle that I've chosen would really have suited me being a father. I'm not sure that I could have done all the nappy changes, walks in the park and playing at happy families. I was always far more interested in doing deals and making money. So for the last ten years you might say that I've just been in love for honeymoon periods. I meet a beautiful girl, we go out, have fun, get to know each other and the sex during that honeymoon period is just the best, it's adventurous and spontaneous. As soon as that moment passes then I know it's time to move on to the next one. In fact to save time these days I may have the replacement lined up a few months before. I don't feel guilty because I don't give any impression that I'm in the least bit serious. My angle is to have fun and when the flame flickers we both move on with no hard feelings," Frank said.

The waitress approached the table.

"Do you want a drink Frank?" Ricky said.

Frank looked down at his watch.

"No, far too early for me," Frank said.

Ricky chuckled.

"I meant a tea or coffee," Ricky said and beckoned the waitress over.

"Coffee, yeah coffee would be good," Frank said.

Ricky ordered two coffees.

"Frank, I haven't asked why you asked me to come to Spain with you. I'm pretty sure it's not for my company. I think that having the heads up before we get there might be of help," Ricky said.

Frank smiled.

"I like Spain," Frank said as the waitress placed two mugs of coffee on the table. "There's sun, sea and no extradition treaty with the United Kingdom. I'm a business man first and foremost Ricky, so it's important to constantly look ahead for new cash generating opportunities and revenue streams. Our little export business is working well for everyone in it. My partner in Africa is making good money and as a middle man I'm happy with my whack and you're looking increasingly affluent. So everybody's happy. That said Ricky, it will not last. I give this another year and then my African partner will be off to America to source left hand drive cars because there are far more countries in Africa that drive on the left than on the right. I can see that, my partner probably hasn't yet, but he will. That's how business generally works. It peaks and then a new product or service comes in and the old revenue stream dries up. I have a whole range of other interests which includes facilitating armed raids on banks, building societies and security vans carrying wages. Some of those old bill at the top are corrupt, Ricky. I have them on the payroll. They take a drink which they spread around with other officers which keeps the lads pulling the jobs out of prison. It's like an insurance which has served both villains and the corrupt coppers well since the sixties, but just like our export business it will not last. When you run an operation like mine Ricky, you have to step back and constantly evaluate the risks, and in my view it's just a matter of time before those corrupt coppers are taken down by their own. It's not if, only when, so I'm looking ahead and something came to my attention during a conversation with a blagger that I knew from way back. He pulled a job, not with me I would add, and the filth had him bang to rights. His old woman found out he'd been shagging her sister and grasses him up. Anyway, he was weighed off for a ten stretch and came out a few months back. He came into the club asking for me, hoping to get a bit of work. I played it down that I was straight because after Bertie Small turned supergrass I just didn't trust him. For all I know he could have been working with the filth to take me down, so I bought him a drink and engaged him in conversation about his time inside. After all the usual bollocks he told me how he had been talking to this peace and love hippy fella who had been caught with over a million quid's worth of hashish and was only serving eighteen months. I put a few quid in his pocket and sent him on his way and then made some discreet enquiries. You might call it due diligence which led to a meeting I've set up with a man in Marbella."

"So, what, did you want me as muscle to back you up if it goes wrong?" Ricky said.

No, no we're meeting a professional Ricky. I want you here because if it looks as good as it sounds then this could be an opportunity for us both. We'll have the meeting and then talk after," Frank said.

Ricky drank the last of his coffee and their flight was called over the Tannoy. The two men made their way to the departure gate. It was the first time Ricky had flown. He looked out of the window at the aircraft. It was grey with a red stripe that ran from the cockpit and along the side porthole windows. The top of the plane was white with the 'Dan-Air London' sign written on it. Ricky felt a mixture of excitement and nervousness. He followed Frank down the jet bridge, the portable connection hallway from the airport to the plane. Frank handed the air hostess who welcomed him onboard his boarding pass, and turned left to take his seat by the window after placing his briefcase in the overhead compartment. Ricky took his seat beside him and buckled up his safety belt.

"Just sit back and relax," Frank said as he slipped off his black leather shoes and pushed himself back into the seat. Ricky looked around at his immediate fellow passengers. Some were completely relaxed, like Frank, while others looked apprehensive. The plane began to backup and then head down towards the runway. It waited several minutes while other aircraft took to the air. Then the plane edged forward onto the runway and Ricky could feel the plane accelerating. He found himself gripping the arm rests for support as the plane increased its speed and hurtled down the runway. Suddenly there was a final punch of acceleration and the plane lifted and was in the air. Like Frank, most of the passengers were now sitting back and looking calm and collected while the passenger to his right had a facial expression which spelled sheer terror. There was a little bumpiness and then complete smoothness. Ricky found himself a little startled as a distant memory of watching the news on television back in 1970 flashed back. The newsreader had said that a Dan-Air Comet Jet travelling from Manchester to Spain had gone missing. Ricky tried to dismiss the memory and forced himself to relax back in his seat.

The plane landed safely in Malaga Spain. The two men collected their luggage and passed through customs, where Frank spotted a smartly dressed, middle-aged man, in brown slacks and an open neck cream coloured shirt holding up a sign which read: Mr Frank Allen. Frank raised his left hand and the man raced over.

"Welcome to Spain Mr Allen. I am Carlos and I drive for Big Jim. Please, let me take your bags. Carlos led them out to a beige coloured Mercedes 450 SEL which was parked right outside the main doors. He placed both bags in the boot and opened the rear door for Frank to get in. Ricky walked around the car and got in himself. Only a few words were spoken during the twenty-five-mile drive to Marbella. Carlos had tried to engage Frank in conversation. Frank limited his answers to a series of yes and no answers and then looked out of the window. Carlos drove them along the sea front and when the boat marina came into view he spoke.

"This is a very famous marina," Carlos said. "My family and I were at the grand opening in 1970. Everyone was very proud when the Aga Khan, Prince Rainier and Princess Grace of Monaco visited our town," Carlos said.

"Is it much further?" Frank said bluntly as he turned away from the Marina and looked at his watch.

"We are very close Mr Allen," Carlos said.

Carlos drove the car through the entrance of the Marbella Club.

"We are here Mr Allen," Carlos said. "Big Jim has reserved a private table in the restaurant for 7.00pm.

"Thank you," Ricky said as Carlos handed him his bag.

Ricky and Frank booked into the hotel and were shown to their suites that were all booked and paid for by Big Jim. They had arranged to meet in the bar at 6.00pm. Ricky stripped off his clothes and put on a pair of swimming trunks he'd brought with him. He found a quiet spot with a comfortable sun lounger and parasol by the swimming pool. As he lay back he could still see the beautiful blue sea washing majestically onto the golden sand.

"This place is beautiful," Ricky thought. *"A bloke could get used to this for sure."*

Ricky ordered an ice-cold San Miguel from one of the three waiters that circled the poolside ready to provide their wealthy visitors whatever they desired.

"Note to self," Ricky thought. *"Book a holiday here for a couple of weeks next year."*

He pulled the new Ray-Ban sunglasses which he had Doreen acquire for him, down from the top of his head and closed his eyes.

***

It was just before 6.00 when Ricky entered the bar. He was surprised to find that Frank was already there talking with a man dressed in a white suit.

"Jim, this is my friend and a business partner, Ricky," Frank said.

"Nice to meet you Jim," Ricky said as he shook his hand

"Let us take a table, shall we?" Jim said as he extended his arm and pointed to an empty table in the far corner of the bar.

The three men pulled back their chairs and before they sat down the waiter brought over a bottle of malt whiskey with three crystal cut tumblers.

"I hope I have your choice of tipple right," Big Jim said.

"I'm not the only one doing my homework then," Frank said with a smile.

Ricky raised his glass and watched how the two powerful villains postured and sized each other up. Finally, the small talk finished and both Frank and Big Jim placed their glasses on the table and leaned forward.

"I want to thank you Frank, and your business partner Ricky, for reaching out to me. I am aware of your reputation as a serious businessman and am excited by what we could potentially do together. Here in Marbella, Frank, I am the go to man for whatever is needed. I've been building my network of politicians, judges and senior police officers for over five years now. I know who is who and they are all, without exception, on my payroll. This situation allows business to flourish without any major problems. I can have money washed, get planning permission on land that others can't or provide you with as much hashish as you can handle. The authorities here look on it as nothing more than forbidden fruit smoked by spaced out hippies and providing their beaks are continually kept wet, there are no problems with police, customs, nothing," Big Jim said.

"Can you tell me about the product and its origin," Frank said. "I need to understand the sustainability of the supply chain to you."

"My sources were right," Big Jim said as he leant back in his chair grinning. "You are indeed astute, very astute. I'm sure if we can get through the finer details, we will work well together for a long time.

The hashish is grown and produced by farmers in the northern region of the Riff Mountains in Morocco. The government and other authorities turn a blind eye to the poor farmers who are trying to make a living by growing the only thing they can there. I have daily deliveries crossing the strait between here and Morocco which could easily be scaled up providing I have partners to move volumes."

"What about the quality of product, Jim?" Frank said as he refilled his and Jim's glass.

The hashish, I'm told, is better than that from the Middle East and of course being in Europe, it's a lot closer to the UK. It leaves the smoker with a euphoric, wonderful sensation. They feel relaxed and chilled. They're left feeling happy and feel good about themselves and everything around them. It's big with the hippy set but the demand is growing Frank. The only downside is it will make the smoker hungry so they might want to keep a couple of bags of Smith's crisps in the house," Big Jim said with chuckle.

Ricky found himself laughing out loud along with Frank and Big Jim.

"What if I took a hundred kilos to start," Frank said as he watched Big Jim intently to see how he would react.

"I have an on-going agreement with Smudge and Warren from Anfield, Liverpool," Big Jim said. "Out of courtesy and respect to them I would have to ask that the initial orders are placed with them, at least until we can build up the volumes. They have the logistics in place and being that your operation is in London, any sales wouldn't affect any market they already have."

"I've heard of Smudge and Warren," Frank said. "I don't know them but I have heard of them. I can't pretend to happy about dealing through a third party but if it helps to make the opening orders go smoothly, and at least until I have my own logistics in place, I'll agree to it"

"Frank, there is a fortune to be made here and you're in at the right time. This isn't just hundreds of thousands of pounds. We are talking millions and the profits will make you smile more than smoking the product," Big Jim said. "I hope you don't mind, but both Smudge and Warren are here in Marbella so I've asked them to join us for dinner at seven."

Frank hesitated briefly, smiled and then nodded his head in agreement.

***

At 7.00 Big Jim stood up and led Frank and Ricky through to the dining room. A private table had been prepared for his guests and a waiter raced over to show them to their table as soon as Big Jim stepped into the restaurant.

Smudge was the first to stand and greet them. He was of medium height and a little overweight from good living. On each of his fingers he wore a gold ring and a heavy gold necklace around his neck with a mounted half gold sovereign. Ricky couldn't but help but notice that Smudge had been in the sun for too long. His face, neck and the top of his chest looked painfully sore.

"Alright?" Smudge said in a broad Liverpudlian accent.

"It's good to meet you Mr Allen," Warren said.

"Call me Frank," he said, shaking them both by the hand and introducing Ricky.

Big Jim had called for champagne but Frank and Ricky stuck with the malt whiskey. They talked price and about how the operation had worked successfully for them for over two years. Smudge boasted that not a single joint had been rolled that didn't have their hashish in it. Frank made it very clear that he would entertain the first few consignments and pay for that privilege, but that he would, in time, be seeking to import the product himself. Both Smudge and Warren accepted that as part of Frank's terms of doing business. Big Jim was a regular at the restaurant and ordered on behalf of his guests. He asked for a bottle of Rioja to wash down the steak. It was concluded that Big Jim, Smudge and Warren would get their product safely to Dublin where it would then be Frank's responsibility to pick it up and get it back to the UK. Frank shook their hands and concluded the deal. Ricky left shortly after and left Frank drinking with his new business partners.

***

Ricky was up early in the morning. He took a long stroll along the beach before returning for coffee and breakfast. He phoned Frank's room but there was no reply. Feeling a little concerned, Ricky approached the reception and asked if they had seen Mr Allen. The head receptionist said that Mr Allen had left with Big Jim during the early hours. He had overheard them talking about a club that Big Jim had an interest in.

"They must have gone out on the pull," Ricky thought. *"Either that or it's a brothel."*

Ricky took a swim and then relaxed by the pool. He returned to his room to get dressed in the early evening and got an internal phone call from Frank asking him to meet him in his room.

Knock! Knock!

"Come in, the door is open Ricky," Frank said. "Close it behind you."

"Did you have a good night last night Frank?" Ricky said with a wry smile.

"Big Jim has an interesting club. I'm not sure I've ever seen so many good-looking brasses in one place," Frank said with a smile "Have you ever had a brass, Ricky?"

Ricky shook his head. "No, never Frank."

"You're missing out there son, believe me. It saves all that wining and dining and they're just happy to leave in the morning without any expectation," Frank said as he lifted a bottle of malt whiskey and offered to pour him one.

Ricky declined.

"There is another reason why I asked you to join me on this trip, Ricky. I've been putting the word about that I wanted to find 'Fat Pat' ever since the shooting outside the Cadillac Club and Big Jim told me during our first phone call that there was a man of that name and description here in Marbella working as a doorman at the Dolphin Club in town. He confirmed to me yesterday, in the bar before you arrived, that he is still here," Frank said as he produced a photograph from his inside pocket and handed it over to Ricky. It was Fat Pat standing outside the Dolphin Club.

Ricky instantly felt a rage climb up from the pit of his stomach as he looked down on the photo of the man that killed his friend Deano the Dog.

"He's been revelling at the notoriety of being a London Face on the run from the old bill," Frank said.

"The Dolphin Club, you say?" Ricky said.

Frank opened his jacket and took out a hand gun that he had pushed into his trouser belt. He held it up for Ricky to see and then put it on the table.

"Would I be right in thinking that you'd like to visit Fat Pat?"

Ricky looked Frank straight in the eyes without blinking and then looked down at the hand gun.

"Big Jim has said that if something was to happen to Fat Pat for past misdemeanours, then he would use his significant influence to smooth over any fallout with the authorities as a goodwill gesture to our on-going business," Frank said.

Ricky picked up the hand gun.

"Are you sure that you want to do this?" Frank asked, staring intently and scrutinising Ricky's every facial expression.

Ricky nodded.

"Okay. I'm told that he'll be starting his shift tonight at 8.00pm. He lives alone at this address," Frank said, handing him a piece of note paper. "I will need Big Jim's shooter back," Frank said.

Ricky nodded and pushed the gun between his belt and his stomach.

"I'll be in the bar all night where, if needed, a stream of witnesses will swear that you were with me and Big Jim. You might want this jacket," Frank said as he took off his lightweight jacket and handed it to Ricky. "It'll cover the shooter and they're selling them in the local markets so you won't stand out."

"Thank you," Ricky said as he looked down at his watch. "I'll see you later, Frank, for a night cap."

As Ricky left the Marbella Club he could feel the adrenaline race through his veins.

"Fucking Fat Pat giving it the big one are you on how you shot down my unarmed mate?" Ricky thought. *"You are going to pay, my son."*

Ricky took a taxi to the Dolphin Club and then walked to the apartment block where Fat Pat was staying. He looked around him cautiously before unzipping his coat so he'd have quick access to the gun. Ricky checked the address for the fourth time. He opened the communal door and walked gingerly towards flat number two on the ground floor. He noticed that the door was slightly ajar and he could hear *'Afternoon Delight'* by Starland Vocal Band playing on the radio inside. Ricky looked quickly behind him, then took the gun from his belt and held it tight in his right hand. He gently pushed the door open. The room was empty and had just two chairs and a sideboard with several bottles of spirits on it. Ricky crept inside and closed the front door behind him. He heard muffling and every so often a gruff voice would sing out 'Afternoon Delight' at the top of his voice from the bathroom. Ricky stood outside the bathroom door gripping the handgun firmly. His heart pounded against his chest as sweat ran down the sides of his face. He took a deep breath and then pushed the door open. Fat Pat stood in front of his shaving mirror wearing nothing but a towel around his waist. He turned quickly and saw Ricky standing there holding the gun. He hesitated for a few seconds then made a clumsy grab for the cut throat razor on the corner of the sink, knocking the soap brush and dish to the floor.

Ricky lowered the gun.

BANG!

Fat Pat yelled out, grabbed his leg and fell to the bathroom's tiled floor. Ricky reached over to the radio and turned it up.

"Don't shoot me," Fat Pat pleaded. "Whatever you think I did, I didn't. It must be some kind of a mistake!"

Ricky looked down on his overweight body as he grappled to stem the blood gushing from his leg.

"Why are you doing this mate? We can work something out. I have money," Fat Pat muttered in between taking sharp breaths to try and dull the pain from the bullet wound. "I'm bleeding here mate. You've got to help me."

Ricky sneered and raised the gun.

"The Milton Road Teds don't show mercy, you low life piece of shit. This is for Deano the Dog, King of the Teds!"

BANG! BANG! BANG!

Ricky shot him twice in the chest and the final bullet was to the head. He closed his eyes and took a sharp intake of breath before putting the gun back inside his jacket and out of sight. He turned the radio down and took one last look at Fat Pat as he lay dead on the floor in a pool of his own blood before casually leaving the apartment block with his head down and quickly moving out of sight. Ricky walked back up onto the main road and then flagged down a taxi to take him back to the Marbella Club. Once back in his room he hung the jacket up in the wardrobe and hid the handgun in the toilet cistern. He picked up the telephone and requested reception to give him an outside line to make an international telephone call.

Ricky wiped the sweat from his forehead and then dialled the number he had been keeping in his wallet.

Ricky: Hello, is Melanie there.

Melanie: It is Melanie. Who is this?

Ricky: It's me, Ricky. I'm in Spain. This is just a quick call to say that the thing we spoke about has been sorted.

Melanie. You mean…?

Ricky: Yes it's been sorted. I'll see you when I get back.

Melanie: Thank you Ricky.

Ricky hung up the phone. He had remained calm and in control throughout, but his heart had been frantically thumping in a bid to escape the confines of his chest. Ricky looked at his reflection in the mirror.

"I don't feel any guilt, only satisfaction that my friend's killer has paid the ultimate price for his actions. Rot in hell Fat Pat!" Ricky thought.

Ricky showered and then took the lift downstairs to the bar where he found Frank chatting with Big Jim, Smudge and Warren.

"Did you get that bit of business sorted?" Frank asked casually.

"Yeah, all sorted," Ricky said.

"Any problems?" Frank said as he poured Ricky a large malt whiskey from a bottle that had been left on the bar.

"None," Ricky said bluntly.

"Good," Frank said before turning back and facing the other men. "Let's toast to getting this first bit of business concluded.

***

Ricky returned the handgun to Frank later that night. They were collected by Carlos in the morning and taken back to Malaga airport in ample time to get their flight back to Gatwick. They didn't discuss Fat Pat Once. Frank told Ricky that the first consignment would be delivered to Dublin and asked him to give some thought as to how that product could be safely brought back to the UK without attracting any Customs attention.

Chapter 27

Ricky was shocked and surprised, but happy that Michelle had called him at work and suggested they meet up for a meal at a new Italian Restaurant 'Tre Fratelli'. Ricky had driven past it a couple of times and had made a mental note to dine there. Michelle had been brief on the phone saying that she had people at her office door waiting to see her. Ricky had made several calls in recent months with each conversation brought to a swift end. *'The Boys Are Back in Town'* by Thin Lizzy was playing on the radio while he checked out his reflection in the mirror. He had had Deano's drape suits dry cleaned and they had fitted him perfectly. He looked down at his blue suede brothel creepers with the knuckle duster eyelets for the laces. With the music blaring out of the speakers, he stood in front of the mirror with his legs apart in an aggressive stance while he combed back his hair. He adjusted the gold 'Razor Blade' bootlace tie that he had had made for him by a local jeweller.

"Deano had big shoes to fill," Ricky thought. *"He'd be proud of how the Ted Army has been brought together. You can rest in peace now mate. Your legacy is alive and kicking plus that bastard, Fat Pat, has been taken care of. I did that for you, me and Melanie."*

Ricky picked up his wallet and walked over to the window just in time to see the taxi pull up outside. The drive into Streatham went quickly with Ricky thinking about how tonight would play out. It was just before 8.00pm when the taxi came to a halt outside the restaurant. Ricky took a deep breath, paid the driver and got out of the car. He looked at the sign and then walked towards the entrance door. Before he could take hold of the door's handle, it swung open and Ricky was welcomed in by a smartly dressed, smiling, waiter. Ricky looked around at the plush décor and spotted Michelle. She looked up briefly and waved.

"This doesn't look good," Ricky thought. *"Not even a smile."*

As Ricky approached the table Michelle stood up. He leaned forward to kiss her on the lips, but she turned her head so the kiss landed on her cheek. Ricky sat down.

"Can I get you drinks?" the waiter said.

"Yes please. What would you like Michelle?" Ricky said as he tried and failed to make eye contact.

"Can I have a glass of house white, please Bruno?" Michelle said as she handed him the drinks menu.

"Bruno?" Ricky said quizzically. "I'll have a large malt whiskey, no ice and no mixer, thank you."

"Oh yes, I've been here a couple of times with clients from work. The food and the service are excellent," Michelle said.

"How is work?" Ricky asked.

"We are really busy and my father has made me team leader over an important project in the City. I'm so pleased that I went back to University and completed my degree," Michelle said.

"I'm pleased for you too," Ricky said.

The small talk continued through ordering their dishes and until they had both finished the main course. Ricky swallowed the last of his drink and put the glass on the table.

"Where are we, Michelle?" Ricky said, sitting forward.

"What do you mean?"

"We both know what I mean. We've hardly seen each other or spoken in ages and on the rare occasions that we were together it ended miserably," Ricky said.

"Well I put that down to you," Michelle said softly.

"Really?"

"Yes really. I've tried to talk to you about giving up all this Teddy Boy stuff and growing up. You have your own business and yet you still waltz around like something from the 1950s. It doesn't look good Ricky, you look like a joke. Take this evening for example. I picked a beautiful upmarket restaurant and you arrive in, what?

"It's called a drape suit," Ricky said, "And I think it looks smart."

"Well you would!"

"What do you mean by that?" Ricky said.

"Oh, nothing," Michelle said as she turned her head away.

"No come on, we're finally getting somewhere," Ricky said.

Michelle turned sharply, she was wide eyed and angry.

"You look like what you are, a bloody working class hooligan!" Michelle hissed.

"Is that you or your dad talking?" Ricky said.

"I hoped that you would change Ricky, so I could finally take you home to my parents and explain how much you've changed but you haven't, and I doubt you ever will!" Michelle said.

"So I'm supposed to change who and what I am to what, appease you and your family?" Ricky said.

"You didn't even try!" Michelle said as she slammed the serviette down on the table.

"Maybe you should be told some home truths," Ricky said.

"Go ahead, why don't you!"

Ricky paused for a while and then stared back at her from across the table.

"Yes I am working class. I was brought up on one of the roughest council estates in London and I know that. I left school with good qualifications, Michelle, but university was never going to be an option for me so I made the practical decision to get an apprenticeship repairing cars, because people will always need cars and they will always need services or repairing and I would always need to make money to meet the bills that arrive monthly. It made sense to me. I saved, ducked and dived and made enough money to buy a broken down dilapidated business on the brink of bankruptcy and turned it around. I created a brand and drove sales through the roof under a new brand that I created, 'London Tyre Co'. That business grew so rapidly with me at the helm that I was able to buy out a competitor. I'm in my twenties Michelle, and I have four successful tyre depots with plans to build the brand further. I did that on my own Michelle, with what I took from school and understanding that you have to work for what you want. So, my drape suit and Teddy Boy image that bothers you and people like you, including your father, is an extension of who I am. I love the music, the clothes and the people who share my passions. These are good, solid, loyal friends that don't sit on the side-lines judging a person for where they come from or how they dress," Ricky said.

"Have you finished?" Michelle said.

"No Michelle, no I haven't. Unlike you I never had a privileged start in life. The opportunity of university was something you never had to think about it. It was there, handed to you on a plate. You took it so much for granted that you took a year out before completing your degree. I mean who does that? Only a person that has never had to think about what you take for granted. Then when you leave, you waltz straight into a job with your father. There's no endless interviews where you have sell yourself and the value you could bring to an employer's business. It's just a smart set of clothes and stroll straight into daddy's business and reign over people who have years more experience than you. You, Michelle, have been spoilt your entire life and yet you look down on me for getting off my arse and making something of myself while not pretending to be anything other than me. Clothes do not define a person, Michelle. You're nothing more than an empty suit strutting around daddy's empire, barking out orders because it's what you've done your entire life. I can't begin to imagine how you would have turned out if you had been born into my humble beginnings," Ricky said.

"I would rather be dead!" Michelle said.

"Yeah, I doubt that you would have lasted a single school term," Ricky said.

"Well since we're giving home truths, you might as well know that I cannot and will not spend my life with some kind of overgrown yob with a chip on his shoulder," Michelle said before pausing for a few moments. "I've been going out with someone else. He's a trained architect like me, his name is Dylan. We met at one of my father's Masonic ladies' nights. He's the son of a local councillor and I've been holding things back until I was sure about us and now I'm sure, very sure that I hope I never, ever, come across you again in this life or the next!" Michelle said as she pushed her chair back and stood up. "You're dumped Ricky Turrell!"

Michelle stormed across the restaurant and disappeared into the night.

"Well I suppose that didn't go quite as expected," Ricky thought. *"Maybe it did. It needed to be said and well I suppose that's it, we're done. What kind of name is Dylan? A sap with a name like that wouldn't have lasted five minutes in our school. His life would have been made hell from the start. He'd have to be one hell of a fighter or be able to run faster than a gazelle. They deserve each other - both entitled and living on what daddy made possible. I probably make more in a month than the pair of them make in a year and when it all comes off with Frank Allen and this new venture into hashish, I'll make more in a year than the pair of you will in your whole damn entitled lifetimes."*

"Bruno, can I have the bill please?" Ricky said as he pulled his wallet out of his pocket.

"Would you like an after-dinner drink on the house sir? We have brandy, malt whiskey?" The waiter said as he cleared the table.

"Yeah, go on, I'll have a malt whiskey in a crystal cut tumbler if you have one," Ricky said.

"Yes sir," the waiter said.

"Can you call me a taxi?" Ricky asked.

The waiter nodded and hurried over to the bar.

"I've been into exclusive London clubs wearing my drape," Ricky thought. *"No one gave me a second look as long as I had the money*

to pay my way and I do have the money. I suppose being with that bird Suzi helped, plus people did think I was Dave Bartram."

Ricky found himself chuckling to himself.

"Damn that was one hell of a night with Suzi and Lilly. I got dumped there too," Ricky thought, still chuckling to himself.

Ricky left a tip with the bill and left the restaurant. The taxi turned into his road and stopped behind a large bright red jaguar XJS.

"Cheers mate," Ricky said, handing the driver a five-pound note. "Keep the change and have a good evening."

"Cheers Guv," the taxi driver said.

Ricky peeked into the Jaguar as he walked by and instantly recognised Jackie. She turned towards him and smiled. Ricky opened the door for her and she got out.

"Nice motor Jackie, very nice. What are you doing here? I have to warn you that I'm in no mood for arguing," said Ricky.

"Can't an old friend just drop by?"

Jackie followed Ricky through the main doors and up the stairs. He opened the front door and he showed her in.

"Old friend? I thought you hated me," Ricky said.

"I wouldn't have described it as hate," Jackie said with a nervous laugh.

"I fancy a drink; do you want one?" Ricky asked as he opened his drinks cabinet.

"Sure, gin and tonic if you have it," Jackie said as she made herself comfortable in the armchair. "Did you know about Neil and Doreen?"

"I know that you black bagged him. He came home and found all his stuff lobbed into a black plastic rubbish bag," Ricky said.

"So you didn't know?"

"I never gave him, you or Doreen much thought. Doreen gets me knocked off gear when I need it and Neil blew me and our bit of business out on your orders," Ricky said.

"Yeah, I'm sorry about that. I was angry with you," Jackie said.

"You don't say," Ricky said sarcastically as he handed her a large gin and tonic.

"My feelings were hurt," Jackie said.

"No explanations needed," Ricky said bluntly.

"It was Melanie, Kaz and Donna who finally told me that they saw Neil snogging the face off Doreen on that beano down to Margate. I didn't believe it at first. I thought Doreen and I were friends. We did good business together. I was by far her best operator and helped to bring on Melanie, Kaz and Donna," Jackie said as she took a long sip of her drink.

"I didn't see anything," Ricky said.

"I suppose I wouldn't expect you to grass on your mate even if you did know," Jackie said.

"Like I keep saying Jackie, I didn't know anything about it," Ricky said.

"I hate all this lying lark and having to justify keeping my mouth shut," Ricky thought. *"I wonder how she would feel if I told her that they both battered Kathy the Candle to death and I organised the disposal of her body."*

"He didn't even deny it," Jackie said. "What does he see in a woman old enough to be his mum?"

"You have to be fair Jackie. Doreen, for her age, is a good-looking woman. I'm not making excuses for what he did, but it's not like she's some butt ugly moose of a bird," Ricky said.

"What does that make me, then?" Jackie said.

Ricky took a sip of his drink and lounged back into his chair.

"Jackie you are a beautiful woman who, like me, got off her backside and made something of her life. This is Neil's loss and you will move on and in time he'll just be a distant memory," Ricky said.

Ricky could see that Jackie was a little taken aback by his comment and began to blush a little.

"I've dumped Doreen," Jackie said.

"I'm not surprised and I can't say that she would blame you," Ricky said.

"He went straight around to hers, you know, and she just moved him straight in. So I've spoken with Melanie, Kaz and Donna and from here on in they're working with me. I'm going to run my own hoisting operation so I'll be out shoplifting myself and building a solid customer base by offering better prices. That will be just the start because I will build something bigger and better than Doreen ever achieved," Jackie said triumphantly.

"I believe you will," Ricky said. "We have that same determination and drive to make more of ourselves and say fuck it to society's rules."

"I heard that you have been busy at work too," Jackie said.

"I have but it's still very early days. I'm just getting started," Ricky said.

"We are the same in many ways, don't you think?" Jackie said.

Ricky nodded and smiled.

"We certainly are and I have wondered, sometimes, how things could have been if I had not been so smitten with Michelle when you called on me that night," Ricky said.

"I poured my heart out to you Ricky," Jackie said.

"I know Jackie and I am truly sorry that you were so upset," Ricky said.

"How are you and Michelle?" Jackie asked. "Melanie mentioned that she didn't come on the Beano down to Margate with you."

"We're finished, or more to the point, she finished with me because I'm a working-class yob that listens to Rock 'n' Roll, has lots of like-minded friends, dresses like a Teddy Boy and most importantly, her daddy would never approve. Oh, and she's been seeing some geek with a double chin and big ears called Dylan behind my back. But it's okay because his dad is a politician and goes to the same Masonic lodge as her daddy. I'm not sure about the double chin and the big ears but I think you're getting the picture," Ricky said.

"So that's both of us then," Jackie said with a giggle.

"What was that song of Gilbert o' Sullivan's that we used to listen to we were kids?"

"Wait, I remember it. We use to get my mum's records out and play them when they were out. She loved that *'Sweet Talking Guy'* by the Chiffons and it was, wait for it, that's it *'Alone Again Naturally'* by Gilbert 'O' Sullivan," Jackie said with a chuckle.

"I never really liked that record," Ricky said.

"Me either, but it was just so naughty playing mum's records when we were told not to," Jackie said.

"It seems like a lifetime ago now," Ricky said. "We have both come a long way in our own ways."

"Yeah, we have," Jackie sighed. "So what happens next?"

"I don't know, Jackie, because with girls time after time I get it wrong." Ricky said.

Jackie stood up and walked towards him slowly. She stopped by his knees and looked down into his eyes while she gently hitched up her short red dress. She raised one naked knee and placed it on the cushion and then sat astride him. Jackie gazed into his big blue eyes.

"I'm not sure if this is our time, Ricky, but I'm happy to give it a try, if you are, with no expectations, no demands and no judgement either way," Jackie whispered.

The scent from Jackie's expensive perfume was almost overpowering. Ricky felt his heart racing and from how Jackie was sitting, his manhood began to twitch.

"No expectations," Ricky said as he looked deeply into Jackie's eyes.

"None," Jackie said and then slowly moved in and kissed Ricky on the lips.

***

It was just after 5.00am when Ricky was woken by the phone ringing in the front room. He turned to see that Jackie was still deep in sleep. Ricky got out of bed and slipped on his dressing gown and traipsed sleepily to the front room and answered the phone.

Ricky: Hello, who is this?

Bill: It's me mate. The gavvers have been swooping in on everyone. Doreen, Neil, Kenny, Lee, Ronnie the landlord, Melanie, Kaz, Donna and others.

Ricky: Are you sure?

Bill: Yeah I'm sure. I was out early because I couldn't sleep and I saw several old bill motors going off in different directions. When I got down to the newsagents there were people talking about how the old bill were nicking people left right and centre.

Ricky: You better get out of your place for a while.

Bill: I think it's too late mate, there's an old bill motor just pulled up outside.

Ricky could hear several loud bangs and some muffled noises.

Ricky hung up the phone.

"What the fuck do the old bill have to nick so many of us?" Ricky thought.

Ricky paced over to his stereo and turned it on. He flicked calmly through his record collection and placed the 'B' side to

Showaddywaddy's Step Two Album onto the record player. *'Three Stars'* began to play with the band harmonising about the loss of Big Bopper, Richie Valance and Buddy Holly in a plane crash. Ricky picked up the telephone and dialled his solicitor, Gerald Hart, and left a message on his answer-machine.

"Hello Gerald. This is Ricky Turrell. I'm expecting the old bill to come crashing through the door anytime. When you get this message, please get yourself down to the station. Don't worry, I know the rules, I won't say a word until you arrive."

"The second part of the first track played *'Rave On'* when Ricky heard a thundering of footsteps outside his front door.

"THIS IS THE POLICE! OPEN THE DOOR IN THE NAME OF THE LAW!"

Books by Dave Bartram

With Dean Rinaldi

King of the Teds: Inception

King of the Teds II: Unification

King of the Teds III: Infiltration

Coming Soon!

King of the Teds IV: Subversion

King of the Teds V: Misdirection

King of the Teds VI: Retribution

Facebook: Dean Rinaldi Ghostwriter Publisher & Mentor

www.deanrinaldi-ghostwriter.com

Printed in Great Britain
by Amazon